Also by Megan Mayhew Bergman

Birds of a Lesser Paradise

Almost Famous Women

HOW
STRANGE
A SEASON

— *Fiction* —

Megan Mayhew Bergman

SCRIBNER

New York   London   Toronto   Sydney   New Delhi

Scribner
An Imprint of Simon & Schuster, Inc.
1230 Avenue of the Americas
New York, NY 10020

These stories have appeared previously in print: "Wife Days" (*O, The Oprah Magazine*); "Workhorse," "The Heirloom," and "Inheritance" (*The Sewanee Review*); "A Taste for Lionfish" (*Narrative Magazine*); and "Peaches, 1979" (*Shenandoah*).

First Scribner hardcover edition March 2022

SCRIBNER and design are registered trademarks of The Gale Group, Inc., used under license by Simon & Schuster, Inc., the publisher of this work.

For information about special discounts for bulk purchases, please contact Simon & Schuster Special Sales at 1-866-506-1949 or business@simonandschuster.com.

The Simon & Schuster Speakers Bureau can bring authors to your live event. For more information or to book an event, contact the Simon & Schuster Speakers Bureau at 1-866-248-3049 or visit our website at www.simonspeakers.com.

Interior design by Wendy Blum

Manufactured in the United States of America

1 3 5 7 9 10 8 6 4 2

Library of Congress Cataloging-in-Publication Data has been applied for.

ISBN 978-1-4767-1310-6
ISBN 978-1-4767-1312-0 (ebook)

To my North Carolina family

CONTENTS

A *wounded* Deer – leaps highest –

—Emily Dickinson

I don't believe that the meek will inherit the earth. . . . They
decompose in the bloody soil of war, of business, of art, and
they rot into the warm ground under the spring rains.

—Sylvia Plath, *The Unabridged Journals*

HOW STRANGE A SEASON

Workhorse

U pon retirement from his banking job, my father took his wealth and custom shirts and rented the top floor of an ancient, salmon-colored apartment building on the Piazza San Domenico in Cagliari. His younger brother Paolo ran a café on the bottom floor, a business that spilled out from the sidewalk and onto the piazza.

"People talk like they mean it there," he said when he explained his decision to me. "I need things that feel real. I need anchors."

I thought it was natural that Dad should return to Sardinia, the island that made him. He always said he missed the olive groves, strong sun, and loud conversation.

I sensed he was waiting for me to talk him out of it, to beg him to stay in New York. The truth was that I wanted him gone. I was in the process of getting to know myself. But you had to fight smart with my father.

"You'll *love* it," I said, drawing tiny stars on the corner of an envelope. I often found things to do while talking with him on the phone, small acts of self-protection. Weeding the neighbor's garden. Flossing my teeth. Browsing my grandmother's six recipes for gnocchi. The less you listened the less you got hurt.

"So you can't wait for me to leave?" he said. "I *knew* it."

"No, Papa. I'm happy for you," I said, somewhat absently. "Going back home."

"How's business?" he asked.

"Steady," I said, meaning steadily nonexistent. I'd taken the little bit of money my mother left me and invested it in a boutique floral business. I made large-scale plant installations for fashion shows, commercial shoots, corporate launches, high-net-worth engagements. A coverlet of two hundred red roses for the tech entrepreneur caught in an extramarital affair. Pale pink grass for an alt-folk album cover. Business was episodic, even a surprise.

"It's time you did something extraordinary," he said.

"Each installation *is* extraordinary," I said, offended. I thought of the carpet of Bermuda grass and birds-of-paradise I'd installed in a corporate bank lobby a few months before. The bank was advertising a wellness initiative. The brochure model wore three-inch heels and held an apple out toward the camera; she struck me as some sort of supermarket Eve. I had to leave when I saw her standing in the middle of my installation. She cheapened the art.

After that disappointment, I conceptualized a big, signature project, something unusual and iconic. I purchased an enormous, twelve-foot-high terrarium from Austria and had spent the last two weeks cursing as I attempted to assemble it in my shop.

"Let me review your balance sheet," Papa said. "Send me a copy."

"No."

"No? Don't be ridiculous. I'm an expert, and I'm free."

My father loved Jack Welch, barking into the telephone, and making deals. He *told* you what you would do with your life. He told my mother, me, his brother, the woman who cleaned his house. And to reassure myself of my independence, my own strength, I'd spent the last three years steadily defying him. No, I would not take his clothes to the cleaner after Mama died. No, I wouldn't listen to his thoughts about Berlusconi again. I wouldn't grow out my hair to soften my face. And I would not give him my outdated balance sheet or visit Cagliari. Not now, anyway.

"My world doesn't revolve around profit," I insisted.

"Maybe it should, *piccola*. Maybe then you'd feel satisfied."

It was important to my father to win. But I'd come to see that he did not respect people who agreed with him. His love language was war.

=

Zach, my gently estranged husband, lived with his parents and our old cat Zipper on the Upper West Side. We'd planned to divorce, but neither of us liked paperwork.

A few days a week he would visit the shop to see what I was working on. My atelier—I preferred to call it that—was three hundred square feet, a spare corner of the Village with high ceilings that once housed an eyewear shop. I often found contact lenses pressed into the soles of my shoes.

Zach was two months out of a luxury rehab center in Malibu, and had the careful face of someone who'd not quite beaten his addiction. His eyes were wider these days, like he was waiting

3

for his addiction to meet him around the next corner, springing from the darkness like a film noir villain. I suppose it was.

He rested a hot to-go cup of green tea on the counter and pushed it toward me. Every act of kindness felt like a small apology, two years too late.

"What's with the glass cage?" he asked, running his fingers on the iron part of the new structure. "It's pretty. Looks like a Victorian greenhouse."

He took public transportation and carried a skateboard, which he set by the front door. He'd grown his hair out into lush, boyish curls, and I hated how much I liked it.

"A work in progress," I said, wondering how he'd landed on his feet again, looking younger. Sometimes I thought it would've been better if we let him fail completely, to see what bottom felt like in a way that other people had to experience. My therapist said I needed to let go of revenge fantasies.

"Is it, like, a giant terrarium?" he said, tapping on the thick glass.

"It's a personal project."

Our words bounced from the concrete walls to the glass windows. The atelier was dark except for one piercing ray of early sunlight.

"About what?"

"About something personal."

Not everything is about you, I thought, wishing it were true.

I thought I could afford to ignore Zach now; the worst-case scenario had already happened. The man who'd once been the center of my existence had self-destructed and left me wondering who I was and how I would live my life. Today, I told myself, he was like having a fly in the shop, and I always had flies in the shop, or some exotic bug that had come to life as a foreign flower thawed, gasping for sun, blooming wide open.

After renting the atelier a few months before, I set up a small, refrigerated display. I bought exorbitant stems and watched half of them die of pure negligence: canisters of *Gloriosa*, *Stephanotis*, and a few white lotus. I purchased them to see who would come in and value such an object. I was a half-hearted businesswoman, perhaps more of a social scientist.

"I'm just going to observe today," Zach said, settling into the worn chair in the corner, one I'd taken from my dad's office after the move. "If that's all right."

He'd maxed out my patience and affection years earlier, emptying our joint bank account, disappearing for days at a time. But sometimes I felt compassion for him, for what he could have been. When I met him a few years after he graduated from NYU, I thought he had the most agile mind I'd ever encountered. He composed post-modern micro-symphonies, was fluent in the politics of the Arab Spring, and had a good eye for contemporary art. He baked his mother's rugelach on holidays without a recipe. He'd begun coursework for a joint degree in law and international relations when an addiction to Oxycodone jumped in front of it all. A doctor prescribed Oxy after Zach tore his ACL skiing. When his prescription ran out, he bought it on the street. I lived with him for months before really knowing something was wrong. What can I say? He was resourceful and I was in love.

I wasn't supposed to take any of it personally. Addiction was a disease, people told me, as if I were wrong for feeling hurt.

What kind of wife had I been, anyway? I hadn't even realized how hungry Zach was. Starving, my therapist later told me.

"But aren't we all?" I said.

"Were your parents particularly empathetic?" she asked, suspicious.

$$=$$

My father called me a week after the big move to Cagliari. "Marianna," he said, coughing and clearing his throat. "No one talks to me here."

"Papa," I said. "Are you smoking again? I hear it in your voice."

I couldn't bring myself to feel pity for him. Some people had fathers who'd earned that kind of devotion, who sat through years of dance recitals and graduations. Papa paid the bills while Mom reluctantly doled out love. He and his job were the anchor of all things. We set our clocks to his needs. We toured the new power plants his company financed, donning gray hard hats, pretending to be impressed, fishing warm sticks of gum out of our pockets to stay awake while walking through cement corridors. I can still recall the sound of my footsteps in those empty places.

"Nato's daughter visits him every two months," he said.

"Nato's daughter married an investment banker," I clarified.

"Is that such a hard thing to do?" he asked.

"There aren't many investment bankers coming through the shop," I said.

"A film director, then." He cleared his throat again.

"Of course, Papa. No problem."

"I could set you up with someone here. Someone who knows the value of family and commitment."

"Paolo called," I said, changing the subject. "He says you're smoking again."

"Paolo doesn't know how to run a business. I have to look

over his shoulder, or he gives away his money. He just hands it out—fistfuls of cash. Francesca needs cigarettes. Marco must buy fresh cheese. You wouldn't believe it!"

"We're talking about *you*."

"If no one talks to me, I smoke," he said, pouting.

I pictured him at one of the small bistro tables at Café Paolo, too much man for the little chair, sweating in his navy blazer, looking furious and unapproachable. He'd watch the women watering the bougainvillea and tomatoes that grew on their balconies, the dogs wandering the piazza. I hadn't seen him smoke since I was a child, but I remembered the way he spun the pack of cigarettes on the table when the conversation grew idle.

"Bring a novel to the café, Papa. Then you won't be lonely." I could feel myself softening, and I hated it. I could only hold off for so long.

"I'll book a hotel room for you. You like Cagliari. You always have. What about next week?"

"I'm working on a special project."

"Why be addicted to work if it doesn't make you rich?"

"You're impossible."

"Next month, then," he shouted into the receiver as I was hanging up on him.

Before moving to Cagliari, Papa lived a sad bachelor's life in New York. TV dinners, instant coffee, a mostly empty refrigerator with expired milk and a half-empty jar of capers, which he spooned on top of the TV dinners. He said he was watching a lot of *Matlock*. I said he was overly familiar with the waitresses at the diner down the street from his apartment. I worried he would marry one, because like most of us, he was still in search

7

of a mother, someone who would fold his shirts and love him best of all.

"I just want to feel like I'm thriving," he told me one day in the diner, pounding his fist on the Formica table, sticky with old syrup. "Like I'm at the top of my game again."

He talked about "the top" as if it were a place in New Jersey he might visit if only the conditions were right, if only he could get his car pointed in the right direction.

But what did I know? I'd never been there.

====

What I was making inside my terrarium wasn't from nature. It was a fever dream.

I wanted to let my ego drive, to create something superfluous and ambitious. I wanted to be the one out of control for once. I spent a lot of time researching plants and earmarking old botanical prints.

We hadn't spent much time in nature when I was a child. Just dirty city parks with cigarette butts in the sandbox, and a few obligatory ski trips to Vermont where we put on expensive ski bibs and spent most of our time in the lodge. Mom got her nails done in the spa and Dad took phone calls in the lobby while I suffered through ski school, looking for the other only children abandoned by their parents.

I placed a big order on my credit card. I wanted the good stuff. The endangered plants. The ancient jade, as big as a mannequin. A black market ghost orchid. Something truly obscene.

I called my agent, who booked commercial shoots for my work, and told him I could host half-price shoots for anyone who needed a lush, otherworldly setting in a human-size terrarium.

"I made something radical and I want to use it," I said.

My agent wasn't surprised. He tried an organic tea company, a Montessori school, and a luxury shoe brand, but only a nonprofit called back. They wanted to shoot an anti-fur campaign.

"Fine," I said. "They can come in next week. Monday."

I hung up when a noise outside caught my attention. I recognized the sound of Zach's skateboard on the sidewalk, the way it scraped the pavement.

Or maybe I knew when he was bound to approach the shop. In good times, we operated on synchronicity. We could find each other on a busy street, raise an eyebrow at the overeducated housewife complaining about the strain of six-figure home renovations.

"Hey, Mari," he said, tucking his skateboard behind the chair. "That terrarium is starting to look good." He handed me the habitual to-go cup of tea and I took a sip, even though it was too hot.

"Who told you it was a terrarium?"

"Can I get inside for a closer look?" He headed toward the door.

What would happen if I told him to get lost, said that he'd caused me enough grief? Why did I still feel like I had to watch out for his healing?

"No," I said, riffling through unpaid invoices behind the counter. "That would be an invasion of privacy. It's a work in progress. There are sensitive plants inside."

"But I was thinking about it last night." Zach looked hurt. I used to hate when he looked hurt. Now I relished the fact that I could make him feel anything.

"Well, I was thinking about it, and it needs dissonance. It needs a discordant note. It can't be too beautiful, or it's not real."

It's amazing how broken lovers can conjure years of hurt and let it hang there, invisible, in a room between them. How two people who are supposed to love each other best destroy one another, day after day, and with such skill.

"Do you know what I mean? How things can be too perfect sometimes?" Zach started to walk toward me.

"I'm going to lunch now."

"At ten?"

The door of the atelier chimed behind me. Maybe I was hungry; maybe I was running away, but I couldn't look at his curls much longer without wanting to touch them.

==

Papa once said I had a sixth sense, that it was the Italian in me. It was one of the nicer, more personal things he said, so I held on to it. He called the intuition my Big Feeling.

I felt like something was wrong, so I called Papa collect from the shop later that afternoon, like I used to do when I was on field trips in high school. It amazed me that it was still possible. I imagined his telephone ringing in the apartment above Café Paolo. You could probably hear the ring through the open window and into the piazza.

"Only drunk teenagers call collect," Papa said, answering. "It's almost dinnertime."

"I don't know why I called you at all," I said, exasperated. "You make me feel horrible."

"I smoked an entire pack today!" he said.

"Don't say that," I said, watering my refrigerated canisters of white hydrangeas. "You just want attention." I set down the watering can.

"What's wrong with wanting attention?" he asked. "You used to dance naked in the living room to Olivia Newton-John."

"When I was four!"

It wasn't unusual for us to go on this way, but it seemed to be getting worse the longer he was in Cagliari.

"Is there something going on? I had one of my Big Feelings."

"Nato has all these beautiful grandchildren. They sit in his lap and run around the piazza with balloons. It's like a movie."

"I'm sorry you don't have grandchildren," I said.

"You aren't sorry," he said accusingly. "You're *glad*. You're a modern woman, and you delight in thumbing your nose at your upbringing."

"I'm not thumbing my nose at anything," I said. "No one does that anymore."

He coughed.

"Is this all you need right now? To complain about your lack of grandchildren?"

"My heart feels funny. I walked on the beach today, and it beat too quickly."

"Have you tried breathing exercises?" I asked. "Or going to the doctor?"

"I don't care enough to take the trouble."

"You're too much," I said. I was thinking about something Mom had said, when her cancer returned and she began preparing us for life without her. "You can't let him become even more of a tyrant when I'm gone," she said. "Best-case scenario, it will be one long, beautiful fight, the two of you."

"You'd be easier to love if you were nicer," I told my father. I was sort of joking, but there was enough reality in what I'd said to make us both uncomfortable.

"Why fake it?" Papa said. "The problem, *mia cara*, is I don't belong to anyone anymore."

There was something in his tone that made me pause. Or was it his words?

"Papa, please."

"I'm asking for help. Come visit."

"I can't," I said. "Not now."

I looked up ticket prices. I imagined the sun on my face, the bitter morning coffee, the sound of the piazza waking to a new day.

＝

The atelier windows fogged when it rained. I drew a heart with my finger on one of the large panes. Something I hate about myself: my needful heart. I've tried a hundred ways to disguise and disfigure it: wearing all black, cutting my bangs crooked like the truly artistic women do, feigning disinterest in the world around me. But it beats on its own program.

The endangered plants arrived at the atelier early Monday morning, and I finished the terrarium, fastening the grass to a thin layer of soil in the bottom, using clear fishing line to animate the fig vines, attaching blooms in places where they didn't belong. I misted everything twice an hour and turned the thermostat up to keep them warm.

I liked being inside. It made me feel small, as if I were some idyllic child inside an eerie, overheated snow globe. A paradise strangely altered.

The terrarium was fragile and temporary. I liked it too much, and the minute it was finished I was sad that it would brown and fade and have to be disassembled. I knew without telling anyone that it was my masterpiece, and likely my last installation. I was out of money, at least until Zach and I moved forward with the divorce.

I misted the plants continuously before the nonprofit team and photographer arrived for the shoot.

The anti-fur models came in, thin limbed and hollow cheeked. One of them smoked inside the shop while the photographer set up bright lights and worried over the reflective properties of the terrarium glass.

The creative director, an impatient man with stiff white hair like a movie villain, closed two models inside the terrarium. They were tall and had to crouch. "Will the door open again?" one asked. "I don't want to be locked in here. The air isn't good."

"This isn't helping my anxiety," the other said.

The man with stiff hair rolled his eyes. "You're professionals," he said. "Get on with it."

"Rewild—Without Fur" the models' T-shirts said. They peeled them off and revealed their breasts. The creative director stepped in to apply rouge to their nipples, which I swore to remember if I ever dated again.

The naked models pressed their mouths to the glass like fish while the photographer snapped away. They looked hungry and trapped.

I felt like I had created a world I was master of, at least for two hours.

I took my own pictures when nobody was looking. I was almost satisfied.

==

I was cleaning out the terrarium with Windex the following day when Dad called again. "I'm moving out of the city and up into the hills," he said.

"What hills?" I said, phone tucked into the crook of my neck. "I worry that you'll feel even more isolated."

I scrubbed a pane. I was going to resell the giant terrarium online.

"It's the place I like," he said. "It's quiet. I've decided. A little cluster of homes near the cliffs. You can see the water through the olive trees. It reminds me of my childhood."

"Just wait a month or two," I said, standing up straight to stretch. "Give Paolo's place time."

"We aren't getting along," he said. "And I've already put down the deposit."

I could hear so much in his silence.

"I'll think about it," I said, softening. "Let me talk it over with Zach."

"Is he at some halfway house now?"

"A very nice one, where his mother makes him breakfast."

"Why do you have to talk with him?"

"We share a cat."

"That doesn't count—"

I hung up. I wanted to arrive on my terms, not his.

==

My childhood home—an apartment on the West Side of Manhattan, near Zach's parents—felt generic to me when I was young, except for the interesting flowers my mother set out. Anyone could have lived there, I thought. Any executive, any wife, any daughter. We had thick Persian rugs with the burgundy and navy designs that our friends had, too. Our furniture was dark, polished, and expensive.

I lived for our annual visits to Italy and kept a poster above my bed of a Sardinian sunset over the water. I washed the glass olive oil containers that we brought home to New York and used them for Mom's cut lilies in the spring.

I think Mom and I were both jealous of my father's strong sense of home, the way he revered Sardinia, even if it had become too small for him as a young man. There was no room in Sardinia for the next Jack Welch, he said.

"A man is made by forging himself against his father and homeland," Papa liked to say when I was growing up.

"And what of a woman?" my mother would interject.

"And what of her?" he'd say in response, daring her to answer.

She'd trained to be a psychoanalyst, but never practiced because my father advised against it, claiming it was an insult to his ability to provide. Their relationship was adversarial; if they were soft with each other, I never saw it. When they met, she was working in her father's flower shop outside the subway station, selling clusters of tulips and lilies as a summer job between classes. For years she kept calla lilies all over the house, on the kitchen table, her bedside table, and the shelf over the bathroom sink. She liked the maroon ones, and blackened purple. "Extravagant darkness," she said.

I wanted to know her better now that she was gone. I wanted to understand her. But there was always a part of her that seemed walled off, a part she kept for herself. Maybe that was the part you resurrected when you inevitably lost the rest.

It must have hurt her when I begged to move to Italy halfway through college, as if I was choosing my father's side.

But I loved the contrast of Uncle Paolo's apartment building in Cagliari, its shameless pink facade, crumbling steps, bright mismatched tiles. Cousins, aunts, and uncles coming and going. Every morning, my younger cousin Alfonso would burst onto the balcony in his sagging diaper, clutch the iron bars of the railing, and yell out into the piazza: *Voglio tutto!*

It was something he'd heard on a cartoon. He'd gotten laughs the first time, months before, and it had quickly become entrenched in his routine.

The last time I'd seen him, Alfonso was a teenager in tight black jeans, smoking a cigarette with one leg over the seat of his scooter. Did you get it? I wanted to ask. Everything you wanted?

Even then I knew he, like my father, had a better chance than I did.

===

My last day in town, Zach burst into the atelier, blinking as his eyes adjusted to the dim lighting of the store. "I wrote a new piece of music," he said triumphantly. "Inspired by the terrarium. Listen."

I was holding a broom, and for a second I thought about sweeping him out like an empty wrapper, a cut stem. I'd given my landlord notice that morning that I would be vacating the atelier and quitting my lease.

"It's got some really cool reverb happening," he said, playing the song from his phone. The discordant notes bounced around the bare room, hitting the concrete floor and glass windows.

I hated to tell him that his old genius had gone. He'd used it up, or I could no longer bear to hear it. Or maybe I was tired of being a human buttress, holding up someone else's life, witnessing it.

He looked around. "Where's the terrarium?"

"I cleaned it out."

"But I didn't get to see it finished!"

The minor key of the song reminded me of the time he'd gone missing for three days and I thought he was dead. I still didn't know where he'd been. Kentucky? An unfurnished apartment in Queens? A bus station in the Midwest, maybe.

"You know what?" I said, my voice rising. "You deserve some disappointments."

I was running for the door before the words left my mouth, and he was running for me. His fingertips grazed my back, that's all. It was a half-hearted action, which is all you need to know.

=

My uncle Paolo called. "I have an emergency notification for you," he said. "The recent move has not gone well."

"What do you mean?" I was used to the drama. My father and Paolo were in a fight as often as they were not.

"Your father has taken up with a mule," he said.

I figured we were having a miscommunication. Paolo's English wasn't great. "Why perfect *their* language? Why cater to *them*?" he said. I got a bad feeling when he talked like that about

Them. I was Them. The Italian American, more American than Italian.

"Americans have no soul, no nuance," my father agreed with Paolo. "But that makes them exemplary at business."

"*Scusi?*" I said to Paolo.

"He has taken a mule into the home, Mari."

"Into his *house*?"

"He found it on the side of the road and walked it home. It sleeps by the fireplace and shits in the kitchen. It is a small one, but we are still concerned."

"What do you need me to do?"

"He has to go to the doctor," Paolo said. "Oh my God. He is *crazy* now. I am helpless. You must come at once."

==

The man sitting next to me on the plane to Naples told me that he was going to Pompeii.

My father had taken my mother and me there when I was in sixth grade. The truth is that it horrified us. That people could be taken like that, unaware, just living their lives, claimed by molten lava while in a lover's embrace, walking home from work, fixing tea.

The truth about Zach is that I didn't see it coming; that's why it hurt. I was proud of us. I thought we looked good together, had imaginative sex, and were fun at dinner parties. Why hadn't it been enough? I remember a night when I found him asleep in the bathroom, a small stream of drool connecting the corner of his mouth to the tiled floor. I put his head in my lap. I touched his curls like his mother must have done decades before. I told myself to let go, to stop caring, but the heart doesn't work like that.

I closed my eyes on the plane.

I could remember my father pacing the ruins of Pompeii.

Just like that, he kept saying.

=

"Did you know," Papa said without turning around to face me when I arrived, "that there are twelve types of wind here?"

"You used to tell me when I was younger," I said. "One night when I had a stomach flu, you told me."

Mom had been out of town that weekend. Papa had to tend to me, and he'd done it bitterly. He sat at the foot of my bed with a faraway look in his eyes, talking about wind. I was hurt that he wouldn't touch me. And I was jealous of the way he loved his childhood. I hadn't had the one I wanted, one that suited me. I had wanted more love. More sunshine. I wanted more everything.

It was the mistral that he missed, he told me that night when I was sick. The wild, warm wind that shaped him. It could bend a sturdy oak like an old man, making an arc of his body, pointing him south.

Papa was wearing a beautiful cream-colored linen suit. He opened his arms for a hug, and I ran to him. When I looked over his shoulder, my eyes landed on the mule in the living room. She was white with liver-colored spots and a salty look in her big brown eyes.

"Sophia is a miniature donkey," Papa clarified, his voice

matter-of-fact. "She has a broken leg, and they're going to kill her, Mari."

"What happened to you?" I asked, pulling away from the embrace and looking him deeply in the eyes. I pressed the back of my hand to his forehead. His skin was always warm, even when he was well. "Are you sick?"

He jerked away from me. "I'm as sane as I've ever been! Why does everyone question my sanity?"

"Because this is unlike you. *Extremely* unlike you."

He snorted and walked toward the mule. "They're going to kill her!"

"Who's *they*?"

I examined his new apartment. There was a single expensive couch, three bookshelves, a bowl full of fresh lemons, an antique Turkish rug, and a mule on the hearth.

"You can't come into my house and tell me how to live, *piccola*. No one can."

"I brought you flowers," I said. I knew it was a sentimental gesture. It put Mom in the room, and that was hard on both of us. And maybe necessary.

He didn't say anything, so I found a water glass, trimmed the bruised and weary calla lilies, and let them loll to one side in the makeshift vase on the wooden table.

———

That night Paolo came by with a huge container of fresh ricotta, rustic bread, and olive oil. We ate on the patio surrounded by three stone walls. "*Eccoci,*" Paolo kept saying. Here we are. As if it was inevitable, a relief.

Paolo was only a few years past his prime, his beard going gray, his skin yellowing from cigarettes and sun. He lit two wide candles and took a moment to breathe in the air. "As you know, I do not agree with you moving here, but it smells divine."

"I always said his favorite things are to kiss," Papa said, nodding toward his brother, "and to argue." Paolo, wearing his years of restaurant ownership, topped off everyone's wine and sat down at the opposite end of the long, wooden table.

"I always thought he would write a strange and tragic novel," Paolo said, as if my father wasn't sitting across the table from him. "Before he became a businessman. But he *is* the novel. He is living it."

My father, for once, didn't respond. He smeared a large amount of ricotta on a slice of bread and drizzled it in olive oil. He took ferocious bites and washed them down with his glass of Barbera d'Alba.

"Did she tell you about the giant terrarium she made for naked women?" my father said, too casually.

Paolo turned to me. "Oh my God," he said, shaking his head, as if he'd finally been given explicit evidence of my American depravity. "Is it true?"

"She hates attention, you know."

I laughed and glared at Papa. Honestly, it was a relief to give in. To dine with my father, to bring him water before bed, to ask after his medication, to listen to him snore. He was always so gloriously and insistently alive.

I washed the dishes with the moonlight coming in through an open window.

Sophia brayed at night, and when she did, I could hear my father's snoring stop abruptly. He would rise from his bed, walk down the hall, and go to her. He'd made a sling out of a twin bedsheet and he used it to help her get up and walk outside to use the bathroom.

The man who couldn't touch my vomit or change my diapers spent a significant portion of his day shoveling tiny donkey shits and spreading them in his yard.

Paolo brought us coffee and pastries in the morning. My father was walking Sophia out of earshot.

"I think," Paolo said, exhaling smoke and staring at the back end of the mule, "that this is a very strange way to atone for his life of greed. He has always been a creative man."

The thing about the men in my life—even their fuckups were brilliant.

=

I wanted Dad to get more sleep. I thought it might help him. Maybe he was dehydrated or had some kind of infection, and a round of antibiotics might knock sense into him. He'd be horrified when he realized what he'd done, I thought.

So when Sophia brayed at 3:00 a.m., I was the one to rise. "Let me get it, Papa," I said. "I can handle it."

"Be patient with her."

"Sure."

I walked into the dark living room and found Sophia standing on three legs, the fourth one cocked and limp. I put a hand on her neck and patted her wiry mane. "Okay, girl," I said. "Let's give this a try."

I slipped the sling underneath her warm body. She flared her nostrils at me and stared at me wild-eyed while I tried to get her out of the house. She was clearly in pain.

As we stumbled through the door frame and into the side yard, I knew Papa was watching from the window. It smelled of eucalyptus outside.

The next morning I started to make a nest for her, using a pink bedsheet I fished from the linen closet. I cleaned her small hooves and braided a crown of long grasses and pale flowers, which I placed on her head, secured by her large ears. She looked like an object of worship, a *tableau vivant*.

Paolo took a picture. "You are both crazy now," he said. "And I may need proof one day."

"I'm indulging Papa," I said, though I was growing attached to Sophia, too.

Paolo passed the picture around, and people started knocking on the door. They, too, wanted pictures, and proof. They wanted to pose alongside the holy miniature donkey, rescued from certain death by a businessman. The newspaper came. A church group. All of the neighbors.

"It is the installation you needed," Papa said, somewhat gleeful as another photograph was taken. "The big one."

When Papa was busy posing for photos, I pulled Paolo aside. "You have to get the veterinarian over here when I take Papa out for dinner tomorrow night. Leave her on the hearth. Make him think it was a natural death."

He looked at me. "That is a betrayal," he said slowly.

"It is merciful," I said.

=

The last time I'd been in Sardinia was my honeymoon, four years earlier. Zach and I had rented a small house on a cliff overlooking a private beach. Each morning we brought wine, bread, and cheese in a basket and read books on a blanket he spread across the sand. If I could return to a moment in my life, it would be this one, beautiful and boring, the scent of eucalyptus and sea air overhead, our legs touching, our lives ahead of us.

Our last day in town, a mistral had blown in and taken a boy on a raft out to sea. There were helicopters and spotlights out on the water. We watched for the little boy, scouring the waves for his red raft, but also we kept drinking, until when it came time to stand, my legs buckled, and Zach carried me to the bedroom in the dark, kissing my neck, lifting my dress over my head. We felt fortunate, perhaps, that it wasn't our bad luck that day, that we could abandon our watch and go to bed.

I second-guessed all memories now, about how Zach was feeling at any given time.

I thought coming to Sardinia would show him more about who I was. But the thing that came through the loudest was my father, who sat at the head of every table, whose childhood stories lived in every piazza, in every red raft, in every scent on the warm wind.

===

Papa was smoking inside and feeding the mule organic lettuce leaves by hand.

"I have so much guilt, Mari," he said, exhaling. "When I think of the business. When I think of your mother. Like a pile of rocks on my soul. It has accumulated to the point where I can't breathe."

"I guess you have to take them off," I said, kneeling beside him. "One by one."

He couldn't answer. He stroked Sophia's white fur. She was

breathing harder than usual. I watched her belly rise up and down.

"Can I take you out for dinner tonight?" I asked, putting a hand on Papa's shoulder. "The trattoria up the hill?"

He nodded and went to get his jacket. He kissed Sophia on the head before following me out the door into the blue light of early evening.

We make it easy for the people we love. We say it is okay when it isn't. In the end, we want them to carry a lighter burden.

Or is it that *we* want to carry a lighter burden?

We ate fresh pasta and peas and talked about Mom's spending habits, my cousin Alfonso, who'd professed to want everything and now sold cellular phones. Papa gave me a cigarette.

"It was a bad year for you," he said, offering me a light.

"Yes," I said. "It was."

"And you still love him, don't you, *piccola*?"

I nodded. I sent smoke rising into the air above the piazza. The cathedral bells tolled nine. The boy ran in a circle with his balloon across the cobblestone, like it was a movie. We were all just in a movie.

I ushered him into the apartment and to bed. "I should walk Sophia," he said, but I told him I would handle it. She was still on the hearth.

In the morning there were dead lilies on the table, their petals dried and splayed open like fireworks, the bright yellow stamen thrust into the air. The flowers were inside out, revealing everything.

Wife Days

1988

F arrah walked into her grandmother's closet. She loved the shadowy space, as if it were the secret heart of her grandparents' lakeside mansion in the Adirondacks. The closet was where transformative magic happened. What affairs, promises, and deals had been made here among the fur coats, cashmere sweaters, and Italian loafers?

Farrah was drawn to the gowns sheathed in clear plastic, events and dates scrawled neatly on paper tags, a catalog of her grandmother's feminine triumphs: *Miss Lake George, 1932. Coca-Cola Advertisement Campaign Portrait, 1935. Country Club Dance, 1942.* There were shoes dyed to match: *Children's Hospital Board Gala, 1963.* The carpet smelled like Guerlain, the shelves like cedar.

Farrah knew the dress she wanted, a Lanvin, 1934, with capped sleeves, a natural waist, and a full pleated skirt. It rustled as she loosened it from the hanger and slipped it over her head.

Her grandmother had worn this dress when she watched her first love die, or so her mother had whispered once, and the peach-colored dress spoke to a darkness Farrah could sense in the adult world but not yet name. She could feel it growing in herself.

She reached for the pack of cigarettes and a lighter she knew her grandmother kept hidden inside a glass jar of cotton balls. She locked the door, cracked the bathroom window, lit the cigarette, then climbed into the claw-foot tub and smoked the way she'd seen the musicians on the Lovell Boys of Dixie tour bus do, dramatic exhales over one shoulder. Precocious, her mother had said of her. *Ferocious*, lead singer Johnny Lovell countered.

Downstairs her mother and grandmother were yelling at each other. Farrah reclined in the dry tub, admired the salmon-pink fabric of the dress, exhaled a blue stream of smoke, and looked out at the lake.

She wouldn't hate it if a man died for her.

"You can't expose her to these lowlife men and expect her to come out of this a lady," her grandmother snapped. "She's nearly sixteen!"

"A lady is the *last* thing I want her to be!" her mother yelled back. "What good did it do for me?"

"She needs structure and direction."

"She needs *me*."

"*You* can't provide for her."

"We've made it this far."

"But her swimming—"

"She can swim laps in the motel pools."

"What's she going to do while you're traveling with that band of junkies? Fix her own dinners?"

Farrah snorted. Her grandmother had no clue how bad

it was. Farrah had already been alone for weeks at a time and driven herself to a swim meet when she was fifteen. But at least her grandmother *asked* about the swimming.

The water had always called to her. It was the place Farrah was most at home.

When the cigarette was finished, she flushed it down the toilet, sprayed the Guerlain, and rehung the dress. She crossed her arms and leaned forward out the open, second-story window, looking at the water's edge, the place where her mother had taught her to swim, perhaps not realizing it was Farrah's way out, her ticket away from one life and into her next.

She knew the history of this lake; any local did. Across the bay was the place where the grand hotel once stood and burned. To the south, the place where the steamer sank. Due north was where Stieglitz photographed Rebecca Strand and Georgia O'Keeffe, black suits clinging to their skin, full breasts rising from the clear lake water. And directly in front of the house, past the small rock jetty, was the place where Farrah's grandmother liked to swim, the place her grandfather bathed her in summer as an infant.

But underneath it all was where she liked to be. The water filled her ears, and you could see many things in the lake light: a submerged boulder, a birch, and the reach of your own hand as you swam away from everything that troubled you.

=

2010

It's 8:00 a.m. on a Monday, and Farrah makes her husband, Blake, a deal. He's the kind of man with whom you cut a deal, after all.

He's just gotten dressed after a fast shower and is standing in the doorway, trying to say goodbye and get to the office. Blake leaves a trail of cologne that reminds Farrah of a walk in the woods, but also the way gasoline smells on your hands at the pump.

Farrah is lounging naked in their bed, which she does nearly every morning. Her body is lean and muscular. Soon her trainer will come to the house to lead her through a series of isometric movements to tone her muscles. She props herself up on pillows. The bedroom is spare and posh; Farrah likes nice linens—Farrah likes nice *everything*—and Blake can't sleep with visible clutter, because his mother couldn't. It is, Farrah thinks, one of those things people tell themselves and then believe dogmatically for no good reason. But, if anything, she can understand obsessive behavior.

"I'll give you four good Wife Days a week if you leave me alone the other three and let me do whatever I want," she says, her voice plain, almost as if she's discussing a grocery list or necessary car repair. She stares at him, curious as to how he'll react. She watches his mouth, which she has always found to be perfect, almost *too* perfect, precisely drawn. An actual Cupid's bow.

"What the hell is a Wife Day?" Blake asks.

"A day when I act like your wife. We can have sex and go out to dinner, drink coffee on the porch, see friends. But I can't do that every day. I need some days for myself. I need days without rules."

She means what she is saying. She also knows that it is one of the laws of seduction, to take away privileges, to make a man work for access when he begins taking it for granted.

"I don't make rules for you." Blake furrows his brow and

walks closer to the bed. He wears pressed khakis and a crisp blue Brooks Brothers shirt. He has a thermos of coffee in hand. She notes the glint of his cuff links, the small glob of hair gel just above his ear, which would embarrass him if he found it after going out in public. He's a stickler for cleanliness, which Farrah chalks up to his mother and his Scandinavian roots. She finds her husband to be a very fresh person, but very controlled, and she's always looking for the little openings, the places where she can get inside his feelings, get reactions, get messy. How else can you truly know a person? Or truly love them, for that matter?

He didn't used to be as frigid, not when he was younger. When he was younger, he wanted to be a poet, or maybe a rock star, and those were dreams that Farrah knew humiliated him now.

"There are unsaid rules," she said. "Admit it."

Farrah has always been a strong believer in supply and demand. Too much supply and the demand goes away. Novelty is important. Give your husband too much sex and he'll get bored. Keep him thinking about you. Keep him wondering.

"That's absurd," Blake says. He is so close now his thighs are pressed against the side of the bed. She enjoys the way he is towering over her.

"It's my best and final offer." She smiles. She feels dangerous and sensual.

"As far as I know, it's your *only* offer." He turns on his corporate voice, which indicates he has the upper hand. He's hired coaches in the past to help him project authority and close big real estate deals. At his core, Farrah thinks he's probably too kind and too coddled to be a corporate success. They tell him to open up his chest, stand with his feet firmly planted on the ground, one just ahead of the other—power poses. They tell him to shake with a not firm but painful grip, then keep his hands still. He should speak in a low voice. Anger is okay; excitability is not.

"Exactly."

"Well, I refuse. I'm not going to let my wife waste away in bed three days a week watching a weird video of a Frenchwoman washing her face."

"You don't have a choice." Farrah is calm. She likes this about herself, her inherent coolness that comes from a lifetime of protecting herself. She's annoyed that he's brought up the face-washing video, but she won't show it.

"Oh yeah? Try me." Blake takes a sip of coffee and stares at his wife over the thermos.

Farrah sits up in bed, gathers the luxurious off-white sheet to her chest. She realizes that they aren't quite mad at each other yet, and that whatever she says next could turn the conversation.

"I could mention your grandfather's serial arson streak to the press," she says slyly. Everyone knew Blake's grandfather had torched some of the old hotels in order to buy the land cheaply and rebuild.

"You're crazy! There's no truth to that."

"Don't use the c-word. You know that's not allowed." She folds her arms.

"I'm sorry." Blake's voice is sincere; the c-word is out of bounds and always has been. "I know better."

Farrah looks down at the sheets; the air of playful menace has fallen away, replaced by awkward silence. Her blond hair is loose around her shoulders. The light freckles that appear on her face in summer are spread attractively across her nose and cheeks.

"I know. I'm sorry." Blake eases his way onto the bed and wraps his arms around Farrah.

"Your shirt's going to get wrinkled."

"I don't care."

"I *know* you care." She presses her forehead to his chest lovingly. The tone has changed, as she knew it would. This is all part of the narrative of sex and love, hers anyway.

"Not today." He starts kissing her neck. She loves him in the mornings, freshly showered after his bike ride. Getting him out of his work clothes is a victory; it's like having the best of him before he gets to the office.

"We were negotiating," she says, running her fingers through his pale hair. "We were talking about the fires your grandfather started, the very root of your real estate empire."

"It's fucked-up, the way we do this," he says, pulling the sheet away from her body, pushing her into the mattress gently with his fingertips.

Farrah agrees; it *is* fucked-up. She doesn't know if it's the c-word or the absence of kids or the enormous house, but they have ceased to communicate like normal human beings. Lately she has been testing the boundaries of her husband's affection even more than usual. It's equal parts recreation and research. How far can she push him?

As he moves his lips down her stomach she says, "You know this is one of your four Wife Days this week."

"Mm-hmm," he says, face pressed into her body. "Whatever you say," he mumbles, tongue sliding across the inside of her thigh.

When he leaves to wash up again, she stays naked in the bed. The sun is coming in strong through the window, heating up the room. Her heart rate is up, and not just from the sex. She's been getting anxious after sex lately because Blake has been explicit about his desire to have a child, and she's not ready. We're running out of time, he's said, which makes her feel old. But in addition to aging, she's worried about the c-word. She'd heard her own mother say that the real instability—the craziness—would come when the currency of beauty faded.

Plus Farrah didn't get off, and when she doesn't get off, she walks around all day feeling like a loaded gun, looking at other men, even the ones who cut the grass. She looks at men who could never give her what she wants in life. She masturbates while Blake's in the shower because her desire is a problem and she's solving it. There, she thinks, hiding her fancy chrome vibrator in the bedside drawer. Box checked.

In the past when she has hit lows, she has chipped away at her depression the best way she knows how: chemically. Drugs, endorphins from long swims, and orgasms. She'll take ecstasy any way she can find it.

What if I really am crazy? she wonders, stretching her arms, making an arc over her head with one and then the other, leaning over until something in her body says stop. Some days "crazy" feels like a textbook malady that one has or does not have, some dormant condition that's going to rear its head again and fuck up her life.

"We choose our words carefully when talking about mental illness," her counselor had said, eighteen years ago, after she had suffered her first and only breakdown in the wake of a trip abroad and was institutionalized for a month. "You're not crazy. You're traumatized."

"Bye, honey," Blake says, dashing in from the bathroom to

kiss her goodbye again before leaving. "I'm late for a meeting with Dave. We're talking about the Hicks property." Dave is his partner, a lifelong WASP-y friend whom Farrah all but ignores.

"Dave is vanilla," she tells Blake, "and unimaginative."

"He's rich," Blake says, shrugging. "We can do more together than apart."

Blake closed on the Hicks farm months ago but doesn't have the money to complete his project, a high-density, upscale community. "We'll probably do a groundbreaking ceremony to drum up some publicity," he says, refastening his cuff links. "Maybe on the Fourth of July?"

"But that's the day of my open water race," Farrah says, suddenly angry.

"We can be in two places at once, can't we?" Blake smiles. "It's nearby. I need the symbolic effect. I'm going to call it Triumph Point Estates or something. No, Heritage Point."

"I like it when you watch me swim." She crosses her arms.

"We'll figure something out." He blows her a kiss and walks downstairs.

Minutes later she hears the rumble of the garage door going up and then down. Blake is gone.

Sometimes he talks about "the first baby," referring to the miscarriage that Farrah had when she was younger. "We should try again," he says, massaging her shoulders.

"Don't talk about it that way," she tells him when he gets sentimental. It isn't just that it's a sensitive topic; it's that he doesn't know all the details, and she'd like to keep it that way.

Those early years were messy. She's been with Blake for over half her life now. It's not that there weren't other guys; he used to drive through the night from Princeton to see her at UMass, and she'd have to send whatever boy was in her bed out the back window of her dorm room, crashing into the boxwoods.

She hated the way men factored into her self-esteem. Sure, she had a talent for swimming, but she'd never turned it into a career, and now in her thirties, self-worth was getting trickier to manage. Some days she felt desperate for positive feedback. A cat whistle in a parking lot, a compliment in the grocery store, a come-on from one of her husband's friends she could refuse. It all felt better than she wanted to admit.

In college, those nights when he was compelled to drive four hours north, Blake would stagger into her dorm room, cashmere sweater hugging his trim body, and cup her face in his hands, kissing her savagely. That was what she'd always liked about him, the animalistic way he was attracted to her. Or had been. She might still have the sweat of another boy on her skin, but he didn't know, and those moments had electrified her. Never before had she felt so exalted and desired. And never since.

He's the only person in the world who truly loves me, she thinks.

Not the girls she drinks wine with at the Sagamore, or the estranged mother dying of cancer in Albany, or the distant cousins. Blake may not be everything she wants, but he is everything she has.

Farrah reaches for her laptop on the bedside table, brings it to her knees, and opens it. She starts the video Blake hates, the one she can't stop watching, and the sound of water running from a faucet instantly begins to soothe her. There, on the screen, is the Frenchwoman in her white silk pajama shirt, her blond hair pulled away from her dewy, perfect face. She stands at a sink in her chic, minimalist bathroom with white tiles and chrome fixtures. The lighting is dim. She cups her hands and brings the water to her skin, as if offering it something to drink.

I'm going to explain you the difference of French skin care, how to emoliate your face . . . your skin is delicate.

Her voice is elegant and soothing, her syntax strange and charming. She sprays her face with thermal water, then toner, so that the skin can "receive the product."

You dab, you don't rub; your skin is like the silk.

Farrah begins breathing deeply. When the video is done, she goes to her large, state-of-the-art bathroom and plugs the sink. She runs the water, cups her hands, and brings it to her face. She mists her skin with thermal water, dabs it with a high-thread-count washcloth, then smears serum made from neonatal fibroblast—tissue grown from human infant foreskins—underneath her eyes. She looks at her face and asks herself two of the three questions that rule her life:

Do I look old?

Am I insane?

Then she pulls on one of her expensive, silver no-drag swimsuits, and heads downstairs to wait for the trainer. She pours herself a cup of coffee, black, because a tablespoon of half-and-half is twenty extra calories.

I have dick serum underneath my eyes, she thinks. I could feel bad about myself for this but I'm not going to.

Farrah still feels like an impostor in the house. It's a McMansion covered in faux stone, full of overstuffed furniture with gold-flecked upholstery, and built on the lot where her grandmother's home, Five Stones, used to stand. Blake had talked her grandmother into selling it to them on the cheap, never telling her that he'd take a wrecking ball to it a month after she died.

Blake can't stand old things. "I'm dedicated to progress," he tells clients. He hates antiques and mold-infested historic homes, or hokey diners with sports or lake memorabilia. The only old thing he loves is his father's boat, which he's had refurbished to the point where there's hardly an original component. He's impressed with what he calls prestigious locations, huge swaths of lakefront property, of which he has a map in his office, a map his grandfather once owned and used to plot his own real estate holdings. There are a handful of parcels left with large acreage, two that stand out to Farrah: the White Pine Camp for Girls and the Hicks family farm. He circles his ideal conquests in red marker. Farrah finds herself secretly rooting against his real estate deals. Just be satisfied, she thinks. You have enough.

At first her privileged life had felt like its own sort of rebellion, a way of pushing back at the childhood her mother had given her. Now Farrah thinks she can see what her mother had tried to avoid.

The doorbell rings, and Justin, a recent graduate student in exercise science who wears an exclusive wardrobe of spandex and sleeveless shirts, raps on the door. Farrah opens it.

"Are you ready for me to kick your ass?" he asks, grinning with bleached teeth. She's pretty sure he goes to the tanning bed. His eyelids are strangely white.

Farrah nods and walks over to the yoga mat spread across the living room floor, made of imported Macassar Ebony, the planks streaked with chocolate-colored graining. She lies on her back, submissive for the second time this morning. Justin kneels beside her and grips her knee, pressing it first to her chest, then using it to guide her leg in circles.

"Let's open up your hips," he says, brown eyes flashing.

"Yes," she says, holding eye contact with him. "Let's."

She allows the sessions to carry a sexual weight because it's one way of entertaining herself, of seeing if she still has an effect on men. She isn't actually attracted to Justin—he's too one-dimensional, too single-minded about fitness—and she finds traditional masculinity boring. She likes complexity. She likes knowing that people are as fucked-up as she is.

Justin, with his fingers on her knee, begins opening her other hip, exploring her body, pondering what it can do, how it can be perfected. She lets a groan escape her lips as Justin applies more pressure.

She and Blake belong together. They don't need children. They just need each other. How can she help him see that?

====

At the end of each session with Justin, Farrah begins to feel like an elementary school student, bored out of her mind, watching the clock, tuning him out, going through the motions, distracted by the blue sky and bright sun. He has her doing lunges across the backyard with a giant red yoga ball in her arms.

"I-like-my-butt-and-thighs," he says, timing his words with the rise and fall of her ass as she stalks across the grass. "I'm-tight-and-tough-and-hot-and-fast."

"I get it," she says, wiping her sweaty forehead onto her shoulder. "Tight and tough."

"You know your competition is out there today," he says, pointing at the lake, "getting a long swim in."

"Of course," Farrah says. She puts down the yoga ball, walks over to the picnic table, and grabs her pre-swim protein bar. She looks out at the water while she nibbles it, washing the glue-like chunks down with water.

"Thanks for opening my hips today," she tells Justin, reaching for her neon-green swim cap. There is the familiar pressure on her head, the slap and sucking sound over her ears.

"Find the pain," he says as she walks him to the door before her swim. "Make it hurt."

She smiles but only half listens as she warms up her muscles and stretches, rolling her neck in one direction, then the other.

Finally, Justin pulls out of the driveway and her feet are on the wet stone, the one she remembers jumping from as a child, when her grandmother's quiet mansion stood on the lawn behind her, ivy climbing the twin chimneys. Her blazer-clad grandfather would have been smoking a cigar on the back porch, reading the *Boston Globe*. Her grandmother would hover over the gardener's shoulder, telling him where to prune the roses in her quiet, needling way. They were strangers to her. She spent more time at camp than their actual house. They hated her mother, and she always assumed the disdain trickled down to her, and that her visits were some sort of charity act.

She starts her GPS watch so she can track her pace and dives into the clear, cool water, on its surface more black than blue as the clouds crowd the sun. She angles her head just north of her home and across the bay toward state land. The first part of her swim is her least favorite, as she glides past the other mansions and their docks, Chris-Crafts bobbing in the boathouses, Adirondack chairs positioned at the water's edge just so. In the shallower parts she has the sensation of drinking gasoline. But she finds her stroke and forgets about the danger of boats.

"Can we pay someone to kayak alongside of you with a flag

or something?" Blake asks, but Farrah hates feeling tethered to anything. She covets freedom.

Farrah's always been amazed at her ability to swim. At first it was an accident, a realization that she was built for the sport, popping up lengths ahead of other swimmers in relays at the Newburgh rec center. Now swimming serves one purpose only: it holds the crazy at bay. She's convinced that swimming beats back the insanity, that exhaustion brings her clarity, and the only way to keep this clarity is to swim harder and longer. Years ago this took her out of the pool and into the lake.

Smooth it out, she thinks. Find your pace.

Farrah passes through the different temperature zones in the water. She looks up with practiced rhythm, keeping her eyes trained on a gnarled pine tree that juts out from a rocky cliff. In open water swimming, precision is critical. Today there is a headwind.

Pull harder, she thinks. Work smarter.

She can feel the wind moving over her back. Her polarized goggles cast the shore and sky in amber light.

At first she keeps her mind on her form as she fights through the first half mile, where inevitably she debates turning around. But the lazy self is the crazy self, she thinks, and she pushes through, heart pounding, ears ringing a little. Ten minutes into her swim she settles down. The mechanics of swimming become rhythmic and serene, the breathing less panicked. Her mind drifts. *Pull, glide. Pull, glide, breathe.*

If the lake is an ecosystem, then first she is an alien species, invasive, thrashing. Now she is part of it, something subterranean and mythical, gilled and beautiful, at home.

Home. She has always had some ambivalence about home.

Perhaps that's because of the years she spent on the road with her mother, a band groupie, a child of the sixties even when it was the eighties. When her second-grade teacher asked the class to draw a picture of home, she drew the inside of the Lovell Boys of Dixie tour bus, and a picture of a girl sitting on a bed surrounded by blue smoke.

"What is this?" her teacher had asked about the smoke, chin falling onto the neck of her floral turtleneck.

Farrah can still remember the taste of it in her mouth, the rich, aromatic mix of tobacco and pot. She can picture her mother rolling out of the lead singer's bed, Johnny sitting up to smooth his ponytail. Her mother would stumble for a moment in the aisle, then climb up to Farrah's bed, embracing her, both of them lulled to sleep in the fetal position, jolted awake by the bus's brakes or shouting. The memory, she thinks, is rooted on a particular tour in 1987, en route to a Southern rock festival in Texas. The bus was hot. Her mother never wore a bra and pinned her hair up during the day only to let it fall loose at night, because she said it was better for dancing. Always wear your hair down for dancing, she said.

Farrah filed that away as one of the few useful pieces of motherly advice she'd been given.

The men in the band were never bad to her; they gave her rhythm eggs to shake as they practiced songs, and once even recorded her laughter and put it at the start of a hidden track. But they didn't censor their behavior, and she'd seen her temporary father figures on the receiving end of hasty blow jobs. She'd cried as the medics hunched over the drummer after a heroin overdose. Though she knows it might be best if she suppressed those years, they contain some of her most vivid memories, and in those memories it is always dark, loud, and anything is possible. It was a lesson in how to watch and not participate, how to build an invisible wall between the world and yourself. Maybe that world is reading the same *Anne of Green Gables* book while the bus driver smokes cigarette after cigarette and watches over you until 2:00 a.m. Maybe that world is a thirty-two-mile lake.

She hits a cold spot, which must mean the depth has changed. The process of conduction and convection fascinates her, the idea that her molecules are mingling with the water molecules, and there is an exchange of temperature. When she trained as a teenager, her coach had required a regimen of cold baths.

"The Korean divers," she'd said in her thick German accent, enunciating each syllable, "they will be diving twenty meters down in fifty-degree water. The Haenyo divers are swimming in vinter. You can, too."

Sometimes when she hits a cold spot, Farrah thinks of these Korean women, plunging to the bottom of the sea for abalone. If only winning a race were as necessary as making a living, or feeding oneself. Then she might subscribe to cold baths and swimming before the ice sets in across the lake.

Farrah has always had an immediate dislike of authority figures, people like her coach. When she was younger, she had longed for her mother to make rules, but after so many years of premature freedom she couldn't take dormitory monitors, swim coaches, counselors of any kind. She didn't crave their approval the way most girls her age did.

Her grandmother used to swim in front of Five Stones, but never great distances, only painfully slow laps early in the morning. There was something self-righteous about her figure in the water, her gaping mouth, the way she toweled herself off. She had been a great beauty in the forties and fifties, once appearing in an advertisement for Coca-Cola. Someone once told Farrah that her grandmother had been in love with a Cuban race boat driver who was killed in a fiery crash on the lake; this idea intrigued Farrah because it made her grandmother seem more human. But only a little.

This was a woman who kicked Farrah's mother out of the house at eighteen because she refused to wear a bra and wanted to form a band. "Whatever your grandmother thought she was fixing by booting me out of the house," her mother had once said, dragging on a cigarette, "she made much worse." She'd laughed as she said it, but it was a sad laugh.

Over the years, her grandmother had made gestures: money for Farrah's college fund. Money for private swim lessons. And when she was fifteen, a trip to Europe.

Pull, glide. Pull, glide, breathe.

It's hard for Farrah to think of her grandmother without seeing her on her deathbed, which is what she thinks of now, that tiny woman scraping together all the dignity she could find. Her silver hair was done, swept up by the nurse in a chignon. She wore a pale rose-colored, quilted robe and sat propped on her pillows. The nurse had called Farrah in to see her; she and Blake were twenty-five years old and living at his parents' house, which meant interacting with her grandparents more regularly. This awkward proximity only underscored their estrangement. There had been quiet family suppers with steamed mussels and linguine, the formality of the dining room saving them all from meaningful conversation. Always so fucking mannered and quiet, scooping asparagus off floral china underneath oil portraits. Farrah had the urge to scream profanity at her grandmother's dinner table, but never did.

When she'd entered her grandmother's bedroom for the last time, Farrah sat in a stiff, chintz-covered chair next to the bed.

"I plan to leave a portion of my estate to the Garden Society," her grandmother said. "And though your mother will get nothing, I have set aside a small amount for you."

Farrah was still and silent, taking it in. As usual, when faced with an emotional situation, she shut down. She became aware that she gave little in these moments, certainly no comfort. But she was aware of the anger inside her, and the fact that it wanted to get out. She was aware that her grandmother was expecting gratitude.

"Why do you sit there so quietly? Have you nothing to say? Not even a thank-you?" her grandmother said. She was the kind of woman who was easily appalled.

"Do you know what it's been like for me?" Farrah had asked quietly, removing her large designer sunglasses. "Do you know what my childhood was like?"

"I knew you weren't living traditionally. That's why I sent you to Europe. To give you experiences."

"Do you know what happened to me in Europe?"

Her grandmother turned her face toward the opposite side of the room. Her narrowed eyes focused on a window, where the wind gently moved the branches of the large balsam fir. She did not respond as Farrah detailed the trip in a matter-of-fact tone. What it was like to reach a foreign country with only her older cousin Rebecca for a chaperone. What it was like to be in Europe with hardly any spending money, how she ate her cousin's leftovers most meals and hoarded bread sticks and airplane food.

"We went out every night," she said. "I was fourteen but I looked older, you remember. I didn't want to be in the hotel room alone, so

I followed Rebecca out to the disco in Capri. She said, 'Dance with me!' and I did. She gave me wine, and I drank it. Then she went off with a man we didn't know, and I was all alone. A guy approached me and asked me if I wanted to ride on the back of his motorcycle. He spoke good English. I wasn't thinking clearly. I said yes."

"I don't want to hear any more," her grandmother said.

"It was a clear night, and we drove up a winding road where you could look down and see the lights of the yachts in the water."

"Stop."

"He gave me a helmet to wear. And I wasn't some idiot fourteen-year-old. I had been around drinking and drugs and men, and I thought I could handle myself."

"Stop. Please stop."

And so she did. Her grandmother was dying. She knew the end of the story. She could feel it coming; any woman could.

"Thank you for the money."

Farrah kissed her grandmother's cheek and walked out of the room, then to the pale pink bedroom she'd used as a child before and after camp. She flopped across the firm mattress. She was not the kind of woman who cried. She'd dug out a pack of cigarettes from her black leather purse and lit one and smoked it there on the bed, stomach-down, savoring the first inhalation, absorbing the pain, embracing the feeling of almost drowning, filling her lungs with something other than air.

Conveniently, Blake followed up her visit with her grandmother that afternoon with his own, and a proposal to buy Five Stones.

"You said your grandmother would be a hard sell," he said, winking at her afterward over a glass of wine, licking his lips after the first sip went down. "That was *not* a hard sell."

Pull, glide. Farrah reaches the shore, sliding carefully over the rocks in the shallow water, cautious not to nick her knee or foot. The water is warmer here, and the moss on the rocks is soft.

She always feels beautiful coming out of the water, the lake streaming off her skin. Perhaps it's because of the movies, all those scenes of sirens emerging in slow motion, or perhaps it's the truth. Maybe it's because she associates the motion with winning a race, which she plans to do in July. Winning is a product of and declaration of fitness, and Farrah believes in the biology of mate selection, and so she rouges her cheeks and wears red dresses and keeps her body taut. That's where her interest in mate selection stops. She wants men to love her and look at her, but she does not want to bear their children.

She sits on a big gray rock, smooths her hair with one hand. It's cold out of the water, and she'll have to get back in quickly, or her body will cramp up. But she needs this moment alone, thinking of her mother, and what real love felt like washing over her in the berth of a bus traveling a lonesome highway.

They haven't spoken in years, but Farrah is grateful that her mother taught her a few things about life, namely that love changes form. It moves from a balm to something suffocating, and back again. You can't trust it. You just endure it.

After the assault in Capri, Farrah had stumbled back to her hostel room and locked herself in the bathroom. When she rose, she saw her face in the mirror—streaked with tears and engine grease. She splashed water on her face. She scrubbed. But the grease remained. She spent an hour raking a washcloth over her cheeks until they were red and clean. She believed from then on that washing one's face was a reset.

The old trees loom over her. The rock is uncomfortable. Light sticks to her wet skin. She slips underneath the water line and screams. The imaginary gill slits open behind her ears and close. Her body exchanges molecules with the lake. She rises to the air, reborn. Again and again.

The Heirloom

Keenan pushed open the door to the underground bunker, a cloud of sickeningly hot Arizona air following him. His white T-shirt was streaked with red dust, and grease coated his fingers. He'd been fixing the excavator before the next round of guests arrived at the ranch.

"Close the door," Regan said, grimacing from where she was sitting cross-legged on the bed, enjoying the subterranean cool. It was dark inside and simply furnished with a bed, desk, kitchenette, a table and chairs. Her mother's art—made of stark-white bones—was the only decoration. White walls brought light to an underground space. There were a few rooms in the above-ground portion of the Earth House, but they were hot, and better in winter.

"They're ready for you," Keenan said. "A van full of hedge fund guys."

Regan nodded. In truth, the Hedge Funders were her favorite customers. They were clueless about how to operate a bucket loader, and her authority became absolute in minutes. It was delicious to feel the power dynamics turn when she buckled men into the bright orange heavy machinery and turned them loose on their childhood fantasies.

Keenan cleaned his glasses with the bottom of his T-shirt. He came closer to the bed, his tall, wiry form standing over her.

"Are you heading into town?" she asked, closing her computer. She'd been fumbling through the quarter's accounting, wondering if she'd been withholding enough to account for taxes. She hadn't.

"Thought I'd close my eyes for a few," he said. He kicked off his boots and flopped onto the bed next to her.

She cringed, thinking of how dirty he was. She wanted him to shower, but they had to watch their water usage. The only water on-site was trucked onto the ranch once a week. Regan had a solar shower installed behind the barn, a small sack of spare water you could use to rinse yourself clean.

"As long as you get the new cars by tonight."

"I'll get the cars." Keenan was already fading. In a final act, he pulled his visor free from his curly auburn hair and threw it to the floor. His breathing slowed.

Must be nice, she thought. To sleep so easily, so soundly.

Every week Keenan was in charge of selecting eight cars from the DUI crash lot and getting them back to the ranch. Regan didn't like fooling with the men at the lot, so she sent Keenan, who was getting better at picking out cars that still had some life left. Cars that felt satisfying to crunch with an excavator.

She patted Keenan's leg—a year before she might have kissed him or rolled on top of him momentarily—pulled her hair up into a quick bun, ran a sunscreen stick over her cheeks and nose, and left the bunker.

The heat bore down on her as soon as she stepped outside. She'd installed a shade system—a network of triangular cuts of sailcloth artfully pulled over the path between the Earth House and the Big Dig Arena—but sailcloth was no match for the 110-degree day.

She waved to the hedge fund team, four men in crisp shorts (who ironed shorts?) with their arms folded over their chests, expectant in their power poses. She liked when they started this way, confident and put out. It gave her something to work with. Something to break down.

The men stood in a line, gazing in awe at the circular, fenced-in arena where five large machines were parked in various stations. There were piles of dirt, stacks of giant tires, and obstacle courses set up.

"Grab a Gatorade from the cooler," Regan barked. "Trust me, water won't cut it out here in the sun."

The men turned and crouched to fish for Gatorade in the tin cooler.

When Regan had first started the business on the ranch, she realized she was too nice. She felt as though the men didn't listen to her, and everyone was at risk using heavy equipment when they didn't listen. She'd finally taken an online power dynamics course with a dominatrix and learned how to wield her power. Weird, maybe, but it worked.

Everyone is still caught up in their mommy and daddy issues, the dominatrix said. You have to play one or the other.

Regan now knew to take up space with a wide stance. To keep her words slow and minimal. She never started out with warmth, or provided personal information about herself.

"There are four stations," she said, beginning her talk, pointing to each station as she went. "You can stack tires with the skid steer. You can dig a hole with the mini-excavator, or you can choose the bulldozer course. If that's not enough, for eight hundred dollars you can crush a car with the big excavator."

The men looked at one another. Eight hundred dollars was nothing to them. It was a lot to her. It meant fuel for the machines, salaries for three staff, Gatorade in the cooler, food in the cupboard.

"What's crushing a car like, you ask?" she said, putting a hand on her hip. "It's better than therapy. Some say it's better than sex, but I think that depends on your level of skill."

She let the ambiguity hang in the dry air. The men shifted, and she wondered what their eyes looked like behind their expensive sunglasses. She could hear the cactus wren calling from the brush; it sounded like an engine trying to turn over.

"Now I want to talk to you about safety." Regan walked over to the big bucket loader and climbed in. She flipped the ignition, and the machine came to life. She swung the big yellow arm around in a dramatic arc, flipped up a beach ball from the ground, and landed it in the center of a tire.

She slid out of the driver's seat and walked back toward the men, whose faces had slackened a little. She had their attention. One man—the tallest—clapped.

"This is a place where you can work out your feelings. You can break things. You can feel the primal power of a big machine at your fingertips. But you must be *precise*, and you must be safe. Otherwise you're out. Understand?"

The men nodded.

"I will pull you from the machine if I think you're a danger to yourself or others."

She was playing Mommy now.

They clapped one another on the back. "Let's do this!" the tallest man said.

"You'll watch a ten-minute safety video inside the gift shop," Regan said slowly and in a low voice. "Sam will get you started."

Sam was a 250-pound former tight end who drank a lot of tequila and was uncanny with machines. He wore gas station aviators, and his sweaty, muscular arms shone when he worked outside in the sun. He kept his blond hair shaved.

He was deferential to her, sweeter than he looked. Sam played piano—mostly Elton John covers—and had a small fawn-colored Chihuahua named Lucy Diamonds who rode shotgun in his turquoise pickup.

"Let me establish power first in the introductions," she'd told him early on.

"Got it, boss," he'd said, and he had. Regan knew if she didn't talk first, the men naturally turned their attention to Sam. Somehow, despite her initial suspicions, Sam was one of the few men who really seemed to understand her need for authority. He stayed out of the picture until the safety video, and she silently thanked him for it.

The "gift shop" was a bright orange shipping container with spotty air-conditioning and a composting toilet, and one rack of T-shirts that said "Ask Me About My Big Dig." Regan wasn't proud of those, but they sold well and she needed the money. Lucy Diamonds slept in a small, fleece bed underneath the counter, the tip of her pink tongue hanging out. As long as she was asleep under the counter, she wouldn't bark. She had faith that Sam would come for her at the end of each day, scooping her up in the safety of his big arms.

While the men sat on the wooden bench watching the video,

Regan took them in. Always better to watch than be watched, especially when you were a five-foot-two, twenty-nine-year-old woman trying to launch a business geared toward the thwarted little boy inside men with disposable income.

Regan worked to identify her victim, the one which she'd force the family heirloom ploy on. Either she or Keenan would toss a faded bronze war medal into one of the holes-in-progress and stop everything, only to pretend that the customer had found a family heirloom.

The family heirloom was an old war medal she'd purchased on eBay.

She didn't feel that bad about the deception. Her clients were Basic Rich Men. Golfers, just short of six feet tall, Brooks Brothers shorts, same clean-cut hair and expensive watch. She liked the look of the tall one who'd applauded her party trick with the bucket loader, the one whose knee was bouncing as he watched the video. He seemed vulnerable, responsive, *almost* emotionally available. He probably had daughters at home, or had done some therapy.

"What's your name?" one of the Basic Rich Men turned to ask her.

The dominatrix taught Regan one essential rule of power: always answer a question with a question.

"Why do you need to know?"

He shrugged.

"Regan," she said, offering her hand. "Regan Love." She squeezed his hand as hard as she could, and he let go first. Just right.

"Regan Love?" he asked, incredulous. He was clearly too stupid or lazy to think about all the times she'd endured the joke. "Was your mom a die-hard Republican?"

She didn't answer him. That was another trick she'd learned from the dominatrix. You simply stop responding to a conversation you no longer want to have.

Plus, her mother had been *far* from a die-hard Republican. She was a first-wave feminist, the Betty Friedan kind, with a lot of purple sweat suits and no bra on the weekends, suspicious of men but nervous about extremism of any kind. "Can't we just all get along and drink a glass of zinfandel?" Regan remembered watching her mom write in looping script in a birthday card to a friend.

When the video finished, Regan had the finance guys sign their waivers, listened to their clichéd jokes about needing their lawyers to read it over first, and let Sam lead the men to their different stations.

She waved to Keenan in the distance. He was walking to the Jeep, en route to select the impounded cars. He waved back, the dry hills and low, scrubby brush behind him. His hands were shoved into his pockets, and his gait was long and goofy. He always seemed so young compared to Basic Rich Men.

What she needed in a man right now was different from what she wanted. Or did everyone go to bed feeling that way?

Everything was so stilted now, so heavy with work and the world.

==

Her mother, Molly Love, had willed Regan the ranch with beautiful intentions. A single mother, Molly had found her best self out here, building an Earth Home in a community of environmentally minded ranches owned by single women, who gathered to drink mescal on the flagstone patio on the weekends.

The women used to laugh loudly together. They called Molly's place "The House of Fallen Women" because it had become a haven for divorcées and women who'd baled on a prescribed life and ended up in the desert in search of real freedom.

Molly paid for the Earth House by picking up freelance copyediting while she continued her artwork, drilling lacelike designs into bleached cattle skulls. She was living the life she'd always wanted, until one summer morning she'd fallen from her horse while out trail riding alone. She died from the head injury the next day, while Regan was midair on a flight home.

Regan had immediately left her conservation job in the Hudson Valley, flown to Tucson, rented a car, and never returned east. Still numb with grief, she'd met Keenan free-climbing a boulder near her property a few weeks after her mother passed away. He was conveniently aimless and moved in, saying he'd do odd jobs and pay rent. A few months after that, the ranch's well ran dry, and the whole place became worthless, unless Regan came up with forty thousand dollars for a deeper well. She conjured up a business plan for the Big Dig instead.

Apparently, the cattle ranchers, corn farmers, and pistachio groves had sucked the region dry. "The only thing this place is good for is dirt," she heard someone say, and she knew, suddenly, how she could use the ranch.

The weird part was that her mother's horse, Jillian, was still alive. Jillian paced the fence line of the pen near the Earth House bunker.

"I mean—you feed the horse that killed your mother?" Keenan asked the first time he met Jillian. "I'd sell her for glue."

"I can't do that," Regan had said, aghast. She stroked the horse's mane. "Mom would hate me for it."

"But she can't hate you anymore," he said, not getting it. Keenan, game and good-natured as he was, was in a perpetual state of not getting it.

"That's a matter of opinion, entropy, and thermodynamics."

"Ghosts are bullshit."

"I have to sleep at night," she said, trying to extricate herself before she lost any more respect for her boyfriend.

But she didn't sleep, not always. This ranch was her only asset, and it was as dry as a sandbox.

==

The tall man's name was Pieter, and he was nervous. Regan watched him climb into the heavy machine, Sam right behind him.

"Can I hurt anyone with this thing?" Pieter asked, sliding into the worn leather seat behind the controls.

"You'll be fine, man," Sam said, gripping his shoulder. "Slow and steady."

While Sam was showing him the control panel, Regan slipped the "family heirloom" into Pieter's dirt pile.

The idea was that finding the heirloom gave the whole dig meaning—a narrative of sorts, and people left feeling like they'd really been a part of something. It became more than just getting in touch with your Little Boy Desires and moving dirt around. You were *helping*. You were heroic. That's how men wanted to feel, wasn't it?

Pieter had an accent she couldn't place. Sam jumped out of the excavator's cab. He nodded to her.

"He's a jumpy one," he whispered.

"Mm-hmm."

Pieter waved nervously at them and they waved back.

"Did you give him the heirloom?"

"Yep."

They stepped back and pretended to be in conversation. It took Pieter three attempts to get the bucket of the excavator moving in the right direction. After he moved a second load of earth, the bucket caught the pile where Regan had placed the medal.

"Wait!" she shouted, holding up her hand.

Pieter looked sick. "Did I hurt someone?" he shouted back at them. He pushed his sunglasses up into his hair for a better look.

"No, no," Regan said, pointing to the medal. "I think we've found something!"

Sam reached in and pulled out the medal, dusted it off, and handed it to Regan, who feigned awe.

She climbed up into the cab and showed it to Pieter. Even though she'd done this bit fifty times, she nearly believed herself.

"What is it?" he said, watching her rub dry mud from the object.

"My great-grandfather's war medal," she said. "Spanish-American War. My mother thought she lost it."

"Oh my God," he said, shaking his head. "That's *incredible*."

Sam waved to them as he turned to check on the other men.

Regan looked at Pieter's knee, bouncing up and down.

"Are you okay?"

"Sure," he said, biting his lip.

He clenched his jaw. The emotion welling up within him was so palpable she felt it in the way that one can feel the ocean pull back before a big wave.

"It's okay," she whispered.

He burst into tears, immediately trying to stop himself by clamping his own hand against his mouth.

"Just let it out," Regan said, as her mother had often said to her. "You'll feel better once the big feeling is outside of you."

"I don't—I don't normally do this."

"Of course." Suddenly the cab of the machine felt too hot, the sun baking them in the small space. The switches were worn, and the upholstery—dry in the heat—was cracked and uncomfortable against the backs of her thighs.

"It's just that they've all left me."

"Who?"

"My wife. My daughters. They moved out. She's sleeping with an emergency room doctor. He actually *saves* lives, she says."

"Oh."

"I mean—how could this happen?" he asked, turning to look at her. "Am I such a bad guy?"

"I couldn't say."

His shoulders were heaving, as if this was the first cry he'd let himself have. She sort of regretted doing the heirloom trick on Pieter. It had clearly triggered too many feelings in him. She felt uncomfortable and began to make a move to get out of the excavator cab. She tried to get into what the dominatrix called a Transactional Mentality. It's just business, Regan thought. I owe him nothing.

"You know what would feel good right now?" she asked, as she was poised to slide out of the cab.

"What?" Pieter asked, between his fingers, which were now covering his face.

"Smashing a car with an excavator."

"I don't know."

"Give it some thought," she said, and then she dropped to the ground. It was time to feed Jillian. She could see the horse pacing in her pen.

Jillian was always restless. The veterinarian said that horses were herd animals and that Jillian was lonely.

It's your own damn fault, Regan thought, watching the horse take another lap in the dry, amber-colored pen. You killed the woman who loved you most.

====

Regan recalled the time her mother was interviewed by CNN about building the Earth House. Sometimes, when Regan missed her most, she'd pull up the old footage on her computer and watch her mom walk the reporter around the ranch.

Her mother wore a pair of stonewashed jeans and a purple sweater, and a Stetson hat with a scrub jay feather tucked into the ribbon that circled the brim. Her frizzy auburn hair was wrangled into a side braid. Molly had an easy smile, and Regan could now read enthusiasm, naivete, and old hurt in her mother's blue eyes.

"It's a two-season situation," Molly said to the reporter, gesturing back to the house in progress. "There's the bunker for bad weather—I always sleep down there—and the small upstairs rooms. You can see I've repurposed glass bottles here, and that we grow our own food along this border."

The camera takes her in. Regan can feel the gaze of the newscaster, thinking of her mom as some idealist. It wasn't wrong.

"And you've done this all without a husband?"

Her mother snorted. She toyed with Jillian's mane for a second, then turned back to the cameraperson.

"At this point," Molly said, one hand on her hip, "a man would be ornamental."

It was Regan's favorite part. She'd inherited her mother's suspicion that at some point relationships with men moved from pleasure to pain, and never righted themselves again. Regan knew she was waiting for the turn with Keenan, maybe even watching it unfold this very week.

When the video ended, Regan often found herself wishing it continued. Wishing her mother could say more. There were, of course, the things her mother taught her without using words—that the darkness of life had teeth and learning how to fight it was more important than learning how to write a thank-you note or press tablecloths.

There was the house as her mother had left it—honest. The pink, gelatinous vibrator on the bed stand. The bottle of Lexapro. That was a strange and important gift, to know that the world was as fucked-up and lonely as it seemed. That a woman gathered pain and taught herself to bear it along the way.

Inevitably, Regan pictured Jillian in the horse pen, walking the perimeter. Walking off anxiety and grief. Atoning. Waiting for the right companion.

==

Pieter was unskilled, but man, she'd *never* seen someone go at smashing a car so intently.

"Cathartic," Regan said to his friends, who were clearly uncomfortable with Pieter's display of emotion.

"FUCK IT," Pieter was yelling through his tears. "Fuck her, fuck him, fuck everything!"

"Yes!" one of the men said. It was as if he'd broken some invisible, unspoken seal. Soon all the Hedge Funders were leering over the scuffed, orange highway barricade blocks, screaming from their guts, full of rage.

"FUCK EVERYTHING," Pieter screamed as the claw of the excavator scraped the roof of the car.

"FUCK IT!" the men shouted.

Keenan joined her at the barrier. She had three leering, screaming Hedge Funders on one side and Keenan on the other.

I'm going to leave you soon, Regan thought, feeling him near her.

That was what happened, wasn't it, she thought. People were engaged in a cycle of coming and going, perpetually deciding to stay or to leave. Sometimes they returned after a mental absence, you never knowing they'd left in the first place, lying next to you in the dark as she did with Keenan, thinking of life on the other side.

Sometimes the partner returned, like Sam scooping the blind and faithful Lucy Diamonds into his arms at the close of each business day.

Sometimes the partner didn't return at all, and you were left—like Jillian—in a state of grief and expectancy.

Her mother hadn't returned.

Pieter's wife hadn't, either.

"FUCK," Pieter shouted, each time he dented the hood of the blue sedan.

"YEAH!" his friends screamed, nearly foaming at the mouth.

"FUCK!" Keenan yelled, his voice breaking.

"You should try it," she said, turning to the Hedge Funders, knowing they would and she'd have enough money for rent. Knowing *she* would finish destroying the sedan, when they were gone and there was no audience.

Who wasn't angry now? Who didn't want to summon all that pent-up rage to split a metal machine wide open? Who didn't want to release all of that pain here in the waterless desert?

Inheritance

The taxi took the curves of the unmarked army road over the mountain, muffler rattling. Hayes rolled down her window. The air was heavy with fragrance, something like wild dill, yellow and blooming by the road, bright against the scrub and dry brush. She looked down at an expanse of clouds that she knew was hiding a deep blue stretch of ocean.

The clouds gave way to a clear view of the sea, a view that made her breath catch, though she'd seen it several times as a child when her family came for awkward visits with her grandmother Paulina, who lived in a small but extraordinary glass house on a cliff overlooking the Pacific.

The road flowed over the last of the mountain and into Highway 1. She'd been waiting for this moment for months: this smell, this light, this sense of freedom.

Surely her grandmother had felt the same way. In the early seventies she left everything—including Hayes's mother, Louise— for the coast of California. Louise had been in high school at the time, and as far as Hayes could tell, her mother held a grudge for life.

To Hayes, everything about Paulina's existence was a victory: the woman had exchanged church suppers for chardonnay at Nepenthe, pearl chokers for mala beads, hymnals for Henry Miller. She did yoga, drank spinach smoothies, and on one visit urged Louise to "loosen up and get a colonic already."

Now the cab came to a familiar curve in the road: the rusted limousine still parked in front of the local library, the sun streaming in bands through the tall redwoods, tourists pedaling rented bicycles in the middle of the highway. Private homes and ranches were scattered from the mountainside to the cliff.

"Could you pull over?" Hayes asked, eager to get out before it was clear which house was her destination. She wanted to keep her presence unknown, in case she decided to take her father's advice and forgo her claim on Paulina's property.

"It's an albatross," he'd said. "You can't afford the taxes."

Hayes paid the driver and stepped out with her backpack and suitcase. The driver lingered, but she waved him off, not wanting him to see her dragging her luggage down the dusty side of the highway.

The roadside smelled familiar—dry pine, chaparral, salt air. She hadn't been here in years; a fence had gone up between the road and the property. She tried the first of two keys, and the lock to the gate gave way. She checked to see if anyone was watching, then closed the gate behind her.

The house, a low-slung rectangle with a central chimney and floor-to-ceiling windows, seemed perilously close to the cliff, the drop-off steeper than she remembered. As she got closer to the house, she braced herself, as the sight of the ocean below made her dizzy. She left her bags on the sidewalk. Dry grass snaked up around the paving stones. Wind had overturned the trash cans. She righted them, then took the second key out of her purse and opened the door.

The light was extraordinary, so extraordinary that it had bleached the upholstery and art on the white living room walls. The living room had sleek gray couches and chairs, Pendleton blankets, a meditation cushion. She walked to the far wall and began opening windows, letting air rush through the house.

Walking through her grandmother's old life, she had the sensation of existing in an old home movie, appearing on someone else's television screen in muted color.

There was wine in the refrigerator and an unopened jar of cocktail olives that seemed too old to eat. Nothing, she thought, would be less sexy than dying of botulism while attempting to find yourself.

She poured herself a glass of chardonnay and walked out to the wooden lounge chairs on the patio. The wine tasted musty, but she drank it anyway. The cushions were leaf stained and slightly damp. Exhausted, she sank into them, watching the waves crash upon the rocks, amber clumps of giant kelp swirling in the distance.

During the childhood visits, Hayes's parents would retire to a motel and leave the kids with Paulina. She wrapped them in scratchy wool blankets and guided them to the porch to watch the sunset. Listening to the elephant seals barking on the beaches below the cliff, Hayes felt sure that her grandmother's was a happy, elegant life, one she might want for herself.

"Look for the green flash, just as the sun sets," Paulina said, pointing to the glow on the horizon. Hayes watched tirelessly but never saw the flash. It felt like a personal failing, reminding her that she did not belong to this windswept place the same way Paulina did.

Perhaps that would change.

Hayes had the urge to call her soon-to-be-ex-husband Michael, to tell him where she was. She'd escaped the condominium they once purchased together, her monotonous nonprofit job fighting food waste, and her parents' disapproval.

She didn't miss Michael's company as much as she missed the feeling of belonging to someone, a feeling she took for granted once married, as if she'd made it across an imaginary finish line her parents had coaxed her toward her entire life.

Michael, she thought, had been a wall holding off the dread that seemed to wash over her more each year, a dread she couldn't name.

Had Paulina felt the same way, perhaps the night after her second husband, a Brazilian director, died? Had she woken up alone and reached out for the warmth of a phantom body? Maybe she sat here with a glass of wine and felt, like Hayes did, impossibly small against the expanse of the Pacific. Exhausted by what it would take to live a beautiful life you could be proud to call your own.

==

Hayes had not been close to her grandmother. They did not share secrets, affection, or heirloom silver. She liked to think they shared an unspoken understanding that they were wired the same way—tempestuous, artistic, bookish—and that is why her grandmother had willed her the house. In the wake of her wrecked marriage, it felt like an affirmation.

The next week, Hayes did two things that seemed to her to be very Californian: she bought a beige 1984 Volkswagen Westfalia camper van for five thousand dollars and got a part-time job at a natural health clinic, where she booked Reiki appointments, colonics, and private yoga sessions for wealthy weekenders, women who came in with prominent cheekbones and designer athletic wear.

The clinic played Tibetan Bowl music, and Hayes felt the vibrational sounds pinging from one side of her skull to the other. She compared herself to the women who frequented the clinic—their unlined foreheads, the space between their thighs.

Their fear of aging was palpable, and she absorbed it into her growing fear of the future. In the mornings, when she woke up staring out at the sea, she had the nagging sensation that the world was changing faster than anyone wanted to admit. At night, the sunsets were so extraordinary—streaks of fuchsia and lavender—that it felt like a bright finale.

Saturday night, after getting home from the clinic, she brought her laptop to bed and ordered two pairs of expensive leggings, turmeric capsules, thermal facial mist, and a self-help book about radical acceptance. Two hundred dollars later, she felt hopeful.

She sat out on the deck overlooking the ocean with a wool blanket around her shoulders, staring out at the rocky crags. When the wind picked up, she went inside to read before bed, selecting a book on the sexual politics of plants from her grandmother's shelf.

She looked up at a painting of Paulina, hung on the wall opposite the bookcase. Her grandmother's white hair was lifted by the wind as she peered out from behind a row of purple iris. There was something almost smug in Paulina's face in the painting, Hayes thought. As if her grandmother had pulled one over on everyone, broken free from the system.

"Your grandmother must have been good in bed," Louise once said. "A woman didn't get million-dollar real estate with good conversation in *her* time."

It was conceivable. Hayes could feel her grandmother's potent spiritual residue here, as if the house still bore the knowledge of her movements and preferences—the pillows on the left side of the window seat, the chair tilted toward the stone fireplace instead of the light.

Once, for a project in elementary school, Hayes had been asked to write about a hero. She'd written about Paulina: *I like my grandmother because she does yoga in California and lives in a glass box by the sea.* When the project came home, her mother, Louise, pulled it from a folder and stared in disbelief at the illustrated report.

"Remember," she'd said, placing the paper back into the red folder, "you can only idolize someone you don't know very well."

=

Hayes had imagined her move to California—if only to squat in her grandmother's mid-century modern home for a few months—would have a whiff of glamour to it. As the days wore on, she felt herself fatigued by change: new colleagues, the time difference, a lack of easy coffee. The height of the house over the churning water.

One Friday night she climbed the winding stairs to Nepenthe, arriving early to claim a spot at the heavy wooden bar. It was one of Paulina's favorite places. The bartender poured generously, but sitting in the room full of people talking reminded her of how alone she felt.

Saturday morning she drove to the gas station, cranking the temperamental van engine until it turned over. Hayes always said she was bad at making coffee so that Michael would bring it to her in bed, a gesture that made her feel adored, and that was the feeling she coveted most. It was the *feeling* she missed, she told herself. Not the man.

Driving down Highway 1 was a pleasure, even if the fog was thick. She wore a sweater and cruised with her windows down because she liked the way it felt, but also because the interior of the van smelled like clove cigarettes and cheap, chemical air freshener.

As she drove, she passed innocuous shacks; small, million-dollar homes; and vans in various states of disrepair along the side of the road. It was easy to get priced out of housing here, and most jobs were hourly—hospitality or restaurant jobs. It was hard to tell if someone in a van was a waiter or surf enthusiast with a trust fund.

I'll date carefully, she thought. If at all.

She filled her grandmother's red thermos at the coffee pump, and left two dollars on the counter for Carson, the reticent but kind cashier with shoulder-length silver hair. He looked as though he might have done a lot of hard drugs in his time. He turned around from stocking cigarettes and gave her a slow wave.

She liked using her grandmother's things, eating from her

dishes, drinking from her wineglasses and thermos. It was a way of communing with Paulina, who now seemed like a vague character from a book she read years ago, someone who had to be continually conjured and reimagined.

Outside the gas station, a blond, middle-aged guy in a faded Talking Heads T-shirt was filling his own van with gas.

"You live in there?" he asked, smiling as she opened her driver's-side door.

"Yeah," Hayes said. She hadn't brushed her hair and was thankful she was wearing her expensive leggings. She took a sip of coffee; the liquid burned her lips. She winced.

"Better than spending your hard-earned money on a house that's going to fall into the sea," he said.

"Absolutely," she said, standing there with her hand on the door. Above them, a red-tailed hawk circled.

"We're early climate refugees," he said, smiling at her, as if this was a distinction that he was proud to claim. "Of course, people don't want to call it that yet. But this coast is still the most fucking unbelievable place on the planet, man, so we're here. What do you do?"

"What do I do?" She fumbled in her pocket for the van keys. She didn't want to talk about the health clinic, the white floating shelves with stacks of macrobiotic cookbooks and crystals.

"Yeah. For work."

She thought for a moment and repeated what she'd heard a beautiful woman at the health clinic say. "I work in fiber arts."

"Like macramé?"

"Sort of."

"Cool. Do you surf?"

She shook her head, taking note of the surfboard on the roof of his van.

"Cool," he said again, replacing his gas cap. "My name is Dave. See you on the road."

Hayes drove home, parking the van just inside the gate and carefully out of sight. That evening, after making herself a salad, she brought a towel to the outdoor shower and undressed. Standing naked in the rain, stars overhead, she expected to feel more satisfied—wasn't this the life she dreamed of when she was younger, and again when her marriage failed? She tweaked the rusted spigot, and the shower started. She turned her back to the warm spray and looked out at the ocean.

This house is the most beautiful place I'll ever live, she thought. But it was isolated, no neighbors within sight, squeezed between a highway and the ocean. Its windows were a constant invitation to look—to look so often, and at such beauty, that you forgot yourself.

She toweled off and walked naked back to the house, sitting on the deck for a few minutes, until she had the sensation that she, too, was being watched.

That night, the elephant seals were so loud they woke her from a deep sleep. Barking and grunting, they sounded like two people having uninhibited sex, crashing into each other in the dark after a few drinks.

She remembered how excited Michael had once been about sleeping in her childhood bedroom in Virginia. "Every man wants to fuck the younger version of his wife," he'd said, lifting her sweater above her head as soon as the door was closed.

She got up and shut the window. Hard.

=

It began to rain. The moisture in the air made her normally straight hair damp and wavy. The view to the ocean from the porch was choked with fog. Her van stalled out at the start of her coffee run. She wondered if she should rotate the tires; it occurred to her that it was now up to her to know these things.

Sitting down at her grandmother's desk, she was surprised to see that the contents looked untouched, as if her grandmother might return at any moment and continue her correspondence. There were ballpoint pens, travel packets of aspirin, unused stationery, and stacks of letters.

She pulled one from the stack, instinctively looking over one shoulder. Though she knew she was alone in the house, she recognized her transgression. She read the salutation—*Dear Pigeon*—and paused. Had Paulina abided such a pet name? The woman who refused to be called Grandma?

The letters were handwritten in black ink and signed Arnaldo. Paulina's second husband had passed away while Hayes was still young, but her mother had always called him *the Brazilian director* and nothing more, hissing the phrase as if it brought her pain. Hayes recalled a whiff of strong cologne and cigarettes, Arnaldo's easy smile.

She thumbed through several letters, some from an admirer named Charlie, whose cursive was minute and controlled. He embellished his letters with botanical illustrations, grapevines and pride of Madeira, flowers with phallic spikes.

Michael had written letters to Hayes early on, in that first year where his name was a neon light flashing on and off in her brain, when love felt balanced and mutual. Letters, she thought. Such a longer way of working up to sex. How coy and reticent they seemed in comparison to the nude photo sent via text, the shadowy gap between a nineteen-year-old's thighs that had appeared on her husband's phone screen one Sunday evening.

That night she drank half a bottle of cabernet and watched the rain move over the ocean. When the wind blew, the rain slapped the windows. Unable to sleep, she got up early and went for a walk, meandering down a steep trail until she reached a rock where she could look out at the sea.

Fog blanketed the flat ocean, and the sun was beginning to rise. There were small pools of rainwater in the sandy soil, as if the ground had been too dry to drink in the storm all at once. She listened to rivulets of water sliding down the cliff onto the empty beach below.

She hiked home, opened the back door to the house, and walked toward her van, parked between the house and the fence that lined the road. She saw that the van's back doors were flung open.

A man in a black neoprene wet suit was sitting in the back of the van, his elbows on his knees and his chin in his hands as if he was meditating in the golden morning light. She opened her mouth and closed it again. He looked up at her with kind brown eyes.

"I checked on the plants," he said, his voice matter-of-fact.

"Excuse me?"

He seemed to be in his late sixties and had a full head of white hair, a few days of white stubble on his face. He was handsome—she saw that immediately, even through her fear.

75

"The snapdragon and the arnica," he said, his voice trailing off, as if he had come to some awareness that he was in the wrong place.

"I don't know what you're talking about," she said, backing away.

"I didn't mean to scare you," he said, shaking his head. "I'll go."

He stepped out of the van and threw his hands up to the sky and walked toward the gate mumbling his apologies. He gave a casual wave goodbye and set off down the road, turning toward the library.

Shaking, she went inside and picked up the phone, cradling the receiver.

Who are you going to call? she asked herself.

The line was dead anyway. No one had paid the bill in years.

==

The lack of sun began to get to her. She felt as if there had been weeks without it, as if she lived in a terrarium with lush greens and blue light. This did not compute with her notion of California. The sky was often gray, and the ground was now soft from constant rain.

She wore her grandmother's pale blue satin robe in the evenings, and then the mornings, too. She found it on a hook behind the bathroom door. For years she believed that if she wore other people's clothes from the thrift store, she might take on their smells and personalities. When she used Paulina's pen, she imagined that it wrote with her grandmother's script, the memory of someone else's fingers.

She recalled her last visit with Paulina, when she was fifteen.

"I *love* your house," she'd said, looking for a way to connect with her grandmother, who was drinking a glass of wine and had her bare, freshly painted toes on the top of the wrought iron bistro table behind the house.

"Oh." Paulina shrugged, smiling as if used to the compliment. "This old bell jar?"

=

Hayes was moody at work. One morning, two women came up to the counter while she was reconciling the cash drawer.

"Excuse me," one said, smiling as she pinned her hair into a messy bun on top of her head, "but could you take a picture of us meditating?"

Hayes stood, stone-faced, with one woman's phone in her hand, while the two customers applied lip gloss, laughing as they settled into position. "Ready," one said, as if it worked that way. The woman closed her eyes and pursed her glossy lips.

That night, looking at posts online where the shop was tagged, she misread the woman's caption on the meditation photo: *I am working to bear my life.*

Her eyes adjusted: *better* my life.

Hayes wore the blue satin robe onto the porch and watched the sunset, still looking for the green flash on the horizon. Nothing.

She did not go home for Christmas but called her parents. She told her mother she couldn't afford the plane ticket until the divorce was finalized.

"The executors have written," her father said, taking the phone. "They'd like to know your current address."

"Tell them I'm living in a van," she said. "That I'm an early climate refugee."

"That's in poor taste," her mother said, apparently sitting next to her father on the couch. Hayes imagined them holding the phone between them and barking into it.

"Referring to oneself as a refugee?"

"No," Louise said. "Living in a van."

Her days became predictable. Hayes made small talk with Dave when they saw each other at the gas station some mornings. She took an online class in fiber arts during the evening; it was called Hanging by a Thread. On Friday nights she had an early drink at Nepenthe and came home to work on her art. She knotted up some long strands of alpaca wool that she purchased online and hung them from a piece of driftwood she'd found hiking the trails that wound through brush to the rocky beach. She removed the Paul Feeley print from over the mantel and hung her fiber work. When she looked at it again in the morning light, she took it down. Quickly.

"At first, your expectations may be higher than your ability," the instructor said in the last video. "Results take time."

Hayes noticed there were no photographs of her in the house. Or her mother, for that matter—just the oil painting of Paulina, and a framed black-and-white photo of Arnaldo in the bedroom. She reassured herself that Paulina was a minimalist, or perhaps Louise had been too bitter to send photos.

When she arrived home from work some afternoons, she felt as if someone had been in the yard. Leaves were swept, planters righted, the clematis pruned, rusted shears left to dry in the sun.

78

The following night she saw the man in the wet suit again, just before sunset. The suit was unzipped a few inches, and he was pruning the long-neglected grapevine near the dry cavity of the old pool. For half an hour, he whacked away at the ropy, gnarled vines. Whenever he turned his face toward the window, she had the sensation that he was crying. She did not want to confront or disturb him. She felt as if she understood—not who he was, or why he was doing this—just that he desperately needed to do it.

=

One early February afternoon she came home from work to find a yellow notice nailed to the wooden gate. *This dwelling may not be safe during heavy rains*, it said in a no-nonsense typeface. It was the typeface of warnings and deeds, of words that bound humans to one another, or split them apart.

There had been unprecedented rainfall, the heaviest wet season on record, Carson told her as she paid for her morning coffee. "Stay alert," he said.

Dave drove up in his orange van as they were talking. "That guy," Carson said, rolling his eyes.

"What about him?" she asked, sipping from her thermos.

"He only lives in that van when someone's watching," Carson said. "His dad is a somebody in telecom. Big ranch up the way."

"Go figure," she said, but the words stung. How long until he found out she was doing the same thing?

Lately she felt envious of her grandmother, jealous that Paulina had lived the last of the good lives on this coast, when the specter of climate change hadn't loomed over everything, when you could look at the purple iris or a sherbet-colored sunset without the compulsion to photograph it. When you could meditate without documentation.

One day the glass house would be ushered into the sea by a wave of mud, she thought. It would shatter on the rocks below.

Photos from a lifetime of newspaper images flashed in her mind: cars and trucks overturned, houses flattened, a soup of broken trees and belongings. The photo of the little girl in Colombia, trapped beneath her house in a pool of water for days, dying in the public eye.

That afternoon, she alphabetized aromatherapy bottles between greeting customers at the clinic: Rosemary, Sacred Mountain, and Thieves Oil. She drove home in the rain, drank, and went to bed alone. Just as Paulina must have done, it occurred to her. For years.

=

Hayes got up in the dark, the moon coming through various windows, illuminating the house, which was oddly permeable, always taking on the mood of the weather outside.

It wasn't that she had a difficult time being in bed without Michael. She had a difficult time being in bed alone with herself. She could smell fires in the distance, coming in on big winds.

She inhaled lavender oil to calm herself, then made a cup of turmeric tea. The thing with a placebo effect, she thought, is that you have to believe in what you're doing, and she was out of faith.

She was spending days at a time now alone in the house. The longer she was alone, the harder it became to be around others. She felt as if she was unlearning a language.

She sat down at Paulina's desk and riffled through another stack of letters, finding one in her mother's precise penmanship. She held it to the light from the desk lamp, her eyes still focusing on the words.

I know it's not easy on either of us, Louise had written. *But I think the kids should get to know you. I'd like you to meet them. We won't stay long.*

Hayes closed her eyes. She could not remember any time with her grandmother when she was a young child, only later, in middle school. It never occurred to her that Louise had been the one to push the relationship, that her grandmother merely tolerated their visits. At the end of her life, Hayes was the only one who corresponded with Paulina, writing her long letters, sending flowers to her hospital bed. Hayes's mother and brother had given up on decorum and obligation years before.

Paulina hadn't given her the glass house out of love, or likemindedness, Hayes realized. There had simply been no one else.

=

One night the seals stopped barking, and there was an odd quiet, then a sensation that the earth had started to shift.

Anxiety, she thought, reaching for the phantom body in the bed, for reassurance, recognizing the cold horror moving underneath her skin. She sat up and looked out at the sea, heart pounding, mouth dry.

"Monkey brain," her therapist had called it, a week after her separation was finalized. "When you feel primal panic coming on, begin tapping your face. Bring yourself out of the mind and into the body."

Everything is fine, Hayes told herself, tapping her forehead and cheeks. Everything is all right.

She put on a sweatshirt and opened her umbrella and walked out to the van.

I'll spend the night there, she thought. Further from the cliff.

She stood still, listening, detecting the faint sound of sirens. The rain bounced off the fabric of her umbrella. Then a crumbling sound. Rocks, she thought, gazing up at the mountain's expanse across the road. Rocks sliding over one another and crashing onto the road below.

She went inside the house to put on tennis shoes in case she had to run. I don't know what to do, she thought, panicking. I don't know where to go.

She came back outside and saw the man in his wet suit, leaning against the hood of her van. The curl of his white hair had tightened in the rain. Raindrops beaded on the neoprene.

"I know I'm not supposed to be here," he said, his voice strangely passionate. "But I wanted to make sure that you're okay."

"What?" She felt disoriented.

"I know there are other boys now," he said, "and that you've moved on. But I want to stay in your life. I'm not worried about the age difference."

"You aren't making sense," she said, bewildered.

He stood there, blinking, looking as though his head hurt. "When the weather turned, I got worried about you being here all alone."

"You must have me mistaken for someone else," she said. "I don't know who you are."

"I see," he said, closing his eyes for a minute. "Sometimes I get confused about time. I look back and I get stuck."

"Do you need me to call someone?" she asked. Her instinct told her she was not in danger.

"We should move," he said, reaching for her hand. "We can see more of what's happening from the road."

"But I don't *know* you." She let him hold her hand.

"I want you to be safe," he said. He was convincing. He looked toward the van. "Come on."

"One second," she said, darting back inside the house. She grabbed two steak knives from the kitchen and wrapped them in a towel, placing them inside her handbag. Her clothes and artwork were in the bedroom closet, but otherwise the house was clean, as if no one had been there.

=

Looking left and right from the road and seeing no imminent movement or damage, they decided to get into the van and drive.

"Let's find out where the slide is," the man said. He sat in the passenger seat, buckled up, and craned his head out of the open window, watching.

She was silent. She drove slowly and watched him as much as she watched the road.

"I'm going to drive to the gas station," she said, thinking that a public place would be best, even if it was four o'clock in the morning.

"Fine idea," he said.

The drive, which usually felt short, seemed to take longer than ever before. She pulled into the parking lot, her headlights panning the mist. There were two other cars there with lights on, and she assumed the drivers were as unsettled as she was. One man rolled down a window. "The slide came down just north of here," he said, pointing. "A quarter mile up the road. You can't pass."

The cashier wandered out from behind the store. He was wearing pajama pants and a T-shirt and walked across the gravel in his bare feet, lit overhead by a single streetlamp. She was relieved to see him, and started to roll down her window. Her companion, however, had already opened up the van door and stepped outside, greeting him with an arm around his shoulders.

"Good to see you, man," Carson said, returning the hug. "You well?"

"I'm all right," the man said. "Crazy night, huh?"

Carson turned his attention to Hayes, giving her a questioning look. She opened her eyes wide as if to say: I don't know.

He came to her window and rested his arms on the glass, leaning over in her ear. "What's going on?" he asked.

"I don't know him," she whispered. "He just shows up sometimes."

"Charlie's harmless," he said, turning to look back at the man, "but he has some memory-loss issues, I think. Early Alzheimer's, maybe? Great with plants, though."

"Are we safe here?" she asked, looking around.

"I think so. Do you want to come in for some tea?"

"I'll just stay here in the van," she said.

"That's fine," he said. "I'll call Charlie's wife, to let her know he's okay."

Hayes nodded. *Charlie.* She pulled the van closer to the streetlight. It felt safer to be away from the dark. She lay down in the back but couldn't sleep.

She envied Charlie, the lack of reality that lay ahead for him.

He could move within time, return to the truth that suited him best.

Why is it, she wondered, that we have to work so hard for the love we want? It comes from the wrong directions, the places you avoid. The places you have given up on.

=

She woke to the sound of voices in the parking lot. A woman, crying. "Why did you leave? Where did you go?"

Charlie was standing in the drizzle, looking bereft. The sunrise was dramatic; here, like everywhere on the coast, you waited for the golden light to land on you. Hayes brushed her hair with her fingers, rubbed the sleep from her eyes, and jumped out of the van, hoping she might offer some help.

"I found him last night," she said as soon as she was in earshot. "In my backyard."

Charlie looked up at her as she approached, his eyes sad. She wasn't even sure that he recognized her in the morning light. He offered a sheepish grin. "I'm sorry, everyone," he said, shoving his hands into the pockets of cargo pants likely borrowed from Carson. "I don't remember what I was thinking, or why it seemed important at the time." He turned to his wife apologetically. He reached for her hand, but she snatched it back.

"Let me guess," she said, shaking her head. "You went back to *her* house."

Charlie was quiet. His wife turned away and looked out toward the ocean.

"Where did you park your van again?" Carson asked, joining

Hayes. They both watched Charlie and his wife from a distance. "Was it near the glass house, by chance?"

"Just down the road from there," Hayes said, not looking him in the eyes. "What do you know about the house?"

"The woman who owned it had quite a reputation," Carson said. "She put advertisements in the local paper looking for young men to help in the yard. People started to read between the lines. It became—how do I say this—an apprenticeship. She was lonely, you know?"

You never really *know* anyone, Hayes thought, still staring straight ahead at Charlie's wife's car. Not your grandmother or yourself.

The man you love could climb in bed beside you, she thought, and return to another woman in the recesses of his mind, like Charlie did, or Michael, who must have spent many nights next to her thinking of the nineteen-year-old who was good with a camera, who had slender thighs.

"We should get you home," Charlie's wife said, turning to him underneath the streetlight, her tone softening. "I'll make you some eggs."

"I know you're tired of this," he said as she led him to the passenger-side door of her car. "I know this is hard on you."

Hayes backed away, feeling it was too intimate of a moment to observe. She hurt for them both. She was angry for them both. She offered a wave that no one saw and went into the store after Carson, who was now making a carafe of coffee. "It must be awful for Charlie," he said, straightening the filter. "Living in the past like that."

"Oh, I don't know," Hayes said, leaning against the counter. "Sometimes it's easier than facing what's to come."

The future was closing in, she thought. An enormous slide of earth and rock had surged over the road and into the ocean like a giant tongue.

The door chimed as she left. The van started on the first try. She drove south until she got to a place that felt safe, a place she no longer recognized.

A Taste for Lionfish

In twenty-four hours, Holland would be 3,894 miles away, outside Nome on Alaska's Seward Peninsula, setting up camp on a ridgeline near the red knot breeding grounds.

"You can't *wait* to get there," I said, trying not to show the hurt I felt. "Even with grizzly bears rooting through your trash—and mosquitoes the size of small planes."

Holland snorted and took a big gulp of her beer. "I have bear spray," she said. "And that weird mosquito-net hat. You won't miss seeing me in that."

"But I *will*."

Holland was setting up her Alaskan research station with a woman named Rachel. I could tell by Rachel's pictures online—mountain biking and bird banding—that she was a threat. She was tall, like Holland. The phrase "a handsome woman" came to mind, but that's the kind of phrase that gets a person into trouble these days. You can't say what you really think anymore, even if you're one of the good guys—and we all think we're one of those, I guess.

The trip was for Holland's seminal research project on red knot migration, the cornerstone of her PhD. She spent most of her day studying these russet-chested, endangered shorebirds. I liked them, too, but Holland woke up thinking about red knots and where they were in their migration pattern, how weather was going to affect them. When she sat next to a stranger at a dinner party, she told them the story of the Danish king Canute, potential namesake of the red knot, who demonstrated his lack of power over the tides and called it a testament to the awesome power of God. "That's where they forage," she'd say, always a little awestruck. "The tides."

After spending two years with Holland, I would forever have secondhand red knot knowledge. I knew that they were jump migrants, covering large distances all at once—some of the largest migrations in the entire animal kingdom. They were monogamous. The male knot tended the eggs, a fact which Holland loved.

How would I get through three months of picturing Rachel and Holland in a yellow tent together, banding birds, explaining their deepest thoughts and lives to each other in the absence of any other human?

"It's not forever," Holland said, shoveling peanut noodles into her mouth. She patted my arm, amber-colored eyes full of excitement, her thick, ropy braid tossed over one shoulder.

But I think we both knew it was.

Three months is a long time to be away from the person you love. It's time enough for someone to change, to let go. I knew, because it's what my mother had done to my father when I was fifteen, and we never saw much of her after that.

There is always the leaver and the left, and I understood what camp I was in.

===

It was not the goodbye I wanted.

There was nothing romantic about the odd glow of our bedroom at 4:30 a.m. as Holland knocked around the bathroom, brushing her teeth before her flight. She wasn't one to be careful or overly considerate about noise. She flipped on the lights and zipped her suitcase loudly. I envied her assured movements.

I had ambitions of waking up and making her coffee, of looking clear-eyed when I said goodbye. But I sat up with matted hair, wrapped my arms around her, and she was gone.

I heard her cab pulling away from the curb, rolled over, and let myself cry into the pillow—but just for five minutes. My father always said you could throw yourself a funeral when you were sad, but only for five minutes. Then you had to dust yourself off and move on, like he had, retiring to a sensible one-bedroom condominium in downtown Raleigh.

Holland had moved her furniture and belongings to a storage unit the week before. I taped up the last of our boxes, preparing them for the storage unit, gazing at the remains of our life, the carpeted hall littered with the debris of a move—bits of tape and cardboard, the top to the toothpaste. Our rental would go back on the market tomorrow. Who knew what came after that?

To fill the time, I'd signed up for my own research project. I wanted to have something going on, something tugging at my attention that would render me unable to answer the phone every time Holland called.

When you live among PhD students, you get used to them saying "my research" in a breathless, sanctimonious sort of way. And even though I found it grating, eventually I grew jealous. I told myself that many of Holland's friends were going to be making fifteen dollars an hour, living in a trailer on the edge of a national forest, applying for grants, hands raw from pulling invasive vines. Still, six months ago I saw a posting asking for environmental justice enthusiasts who liked to travel and ripped the flyer from the café bulletin board. I applied and got the job working on eliminating the invasive lionfish.

I threw my bags into the back of my Subaru, slammed the trunk shut, got on I-85, and headed toward Alligator, North Carolina.

===

I drove east for nearly eight hours, the flat roads flanked by pine forests and gas stations, and billboards for plastic surgery and tanning beds. The monotony kept me from thinking, lulled my brain into an exhausted fog. I stopped and got an enormous iced tea, the condensation dripping down my wrist and onto the upholstered seat of my car.

For the last six weeks, I'd been studying the invasive lionfish in preparation for this trip. I'd always thought it was an extraordinary-looking fish, with a permanent frown and several dazzling, venomous appendages. Native to Indonesia, the fish started appearing near Florida in the nineties—now they were destroying entire reef ecosystems. With no natural predators, they proliferate from Florida to North Carolina, releasing something like two million eggs a year.

My job was to convince people to start eating them. My boss at Invasivores—a new conservation organization—had given me a script. When I spoke to young people, I was supposed to say: "We're creating a new generation of Invasivores—people who hunt and eat invasive species in order to save native species. You can help save the planet by incorporating lionfish into your diet!" When I spoke to "ordinary folks"—that's how they said it to me, as if that's a box you might check on a census—I was supposed to say, "Lionfish are plentiful and free, and they taste great—soft white flesh, like a hogfish. They're poisonous to the touch but great to eat."

I got closer to Columbia, the town just outside Alligator. Men sat motionless in the sun in front of pickup trucks parked on the roadsides, signs advertising sweet potatoes, collards, and live bait. I had that new kid feeling, like I was starting at a school where I knew I wouldn't fit in.

A few minutes later I pulled into a long, sandy driveway off a road called Old Beach House Road. I found a two-story blue duplex on stilts, perceptibly listing to one side. I knew without entering that it was going to smell like an ancient underwater cave, like mildew. Houses like these take on so much weather, like getting slapped in the face repeatedly by hurricane winds and high tides.

"Hey there, sailor," a tall, skinny man said. He came out from the utility closet underneath the house in denim cutoffs.

"Hey," I said, wondering if he had my name wrong, or if "sailor" was a term of endearment. "I'm Lily, from Invasivores."

"I can tell," he said. "Let's get your stuff in the house before the weather breaks." He pointed at the charcoal-colored cloud on the horizon.

There were a few other houses on the road, but this wasn't a second-home hot spot like Nags Head. It felt honest and a little sad, like the end of the earth.

"Ward Williams," he said, shaking my hand too hard. He scooped up a suitcase and two bags—he was wiry-looking but strong, maybe in his early fifties—and bounded up the wooden staircase to the first floor of the beach house.

Inside, the white paint was speckled with black mildew, and the drywall had some damp spots. He showed me to my room. "I'll let you get settled," he said, "and then we can meet up in the living room and talk logistics."

I smiled and closed the bedroom door, swallowing down the dread. I slung my bags into the corner of the room and arranged my toiletries on the rattan chest of drawers. I could hear Ward bustling around in the living room, and I went to join him, afraid of being alone with my thoughts another minute.

"How'd you get into fish?" he asked, handing me a Coors Light.

Was I really even into fish? It was hard to say.

I cracked open the Coors and took a sip. "My dad kept two forty-gallon aquarium tanks in the waiting room of his dentist office," I said. "He used to pay me three dollars a week to clean them and arrange the faux coral in the bottom of the tank."

"Oh," Ward said, grinning. "You started off as one of the bad guys."

I laughed because he was right. It wasn't cool to talk about aquariums in conservation circles, not unless you were breeding natives or something earnest like that. In fact, it was thought that lionfish had first gotten into the waters around Miami after a hurricane wiped out an aquarium tank left on a seawall, sweeping the poisonous fish into the sea.

Ward finished off his beer in a long gulp and opened another. "This was my mother's house," he said, as if apologizing. "I never would have picked white carpet."

"I hear that," I said.

"Do you ever think—man—*how* am I related to my parents?" he said, shaking his head, taking another long sip of his beer.

"All the time," I said, thinking about the mother I never saw, who now sold cosmetics at a mall in Texas.

"But the thing is—the older you get, you just *feel* it in your bones," he said. "And in your words. Can you feel it?"

I must have cringed because he laughed. "But I've got a decade or two on you, sailor," he said. "You still have time to change so much that your ancestors can't catch up to you."

He stood up, walked to the fridge, and pulled out another beer. "You may have assumed I have a drinking problem by now," he said. "And you'd be right. But I'm harmless. I sleep it off. Can I get you one before I turn in?"

I shook my head.

"See you in the morning, then."

I was left alone for a minute. Or, it was me and a giant blue marlin over the fireplace, an unlit cigarette cradled in its open mouth. I stared through the windows at the seemingly infinite darkness of the ocean. Now that Ward was gone I could hear the waves and the wind.

I checked my phone, but there was no word from Holland.

=

In the morning I threw on a T-shirt and shorts, pulled my hair back, and set out to buy groceries. I found a local bait shop that offered pontoon boat tours, beer, and a dusty-looking set of packaged foods. I bought some soup, crackers, and Pop-Tarts, knowing I would eat all of the latter first before I touched anything else.

"Who are you out here visiting?" the clerk asked, eyeing me. She looked to be in her sixties. Leathery skin, sweet smile, blue eye shadow. A wall of cigarettes and lottery tickets behind her head.

"I'm studying lionfish," I said. I liked the way that sounded, even though it wasn't entirely true.

"Gross little devil fish!" she said, blinking her mascara-laden lashes. "What do you want to know about them?"

"Well," I said, taking a deep breath. "They're plentiful and free, and they taste great—soft white flesh, like a hogfish."

"They're *poisonous*," she said, giving me the eye. "Like being stung by a jellyfish, I've heard."

"True," I said. "But they're fine to eat."

"You can have them all for yourself, honey," she said, breaking into a smile. She put my groceries into a plastic bag.

"No bag for me," I said, beginning to empty the contents.

"You're one of those world savers," she said, shaking her head. "Staying over at Ward's, I bet."

"Yes ma'am," I said.

"We always know if a world saver is in town, they've come to stay with Ward." She leaned down as if she was about to tell me a secret. "He's about half-cocked, if you want to know the truth," she said. "His family's been big landowners around here for generations. But Ward's as crazy as the day is long. Just hell-bent on punishing himself for something he didn't do."

I nodded. I was curious but couldn't bring myself to ask for more details.

"You be safe," she said. The door chimed as I walked out with an armful of groceries.

It was already hot out, and the inside of my car felt oppressive. The air was thick. I drove back to Ward's with the windows down, passing a few roadside stands, people walking dogs. Folks out here looked tired, as if they were waiting for something better to happen but knew it wouldn't.

Congratulations, I thought, turning into Ward's driveway. You escaped the development boom, and now it's too late—everyone knows rising seas are going to wipe these places off the map, and you never have to deal with inflated condominiums and homeowner associations and mini-golf.

But I guess it's not much of a consolation to know that this is the best it's going to be. That better isn't coming.

I put the groceries on the shelves and in the mini-fridge in my room. I took my bike out of the trunk and assembled it in the driveway. There was no sign of Ward, but Holland had written. "Here," she said.

It was the simplest thing a person could declare—their arrival, the location of their body. It hurt me enough that I decided not to respond, to cause her worry if I still could. To register my absence in some way.

Numb, I pedaled the long flat roads. Invasivore had instructed me to look for fishers—you weren't supposed to say fishermen anymore—and to approach them casually before making my pitch.

I passed overgrown lawns, abandoned churches, recently

mown family graveyards. Seagulls called out overhead and the sun bore down into my skin.

You could really ride out life in a place like Alligator, talk and act like it was still the old times. But it was no longer the old times.

I saw some men fishing from the local pier, and I biked closer to them, but they were deep in conversation. Who was I to interrupt? I went home.

I paused on the side of the road to respond to the text from my Invasivore coach. "How many converts today?" she asked.

"One," I typed.

"The day isn't over yet!" she wrote. I'd never met her face-to-face. My coach was a robot, for all I knew.

Ward was organizing some heavy ropes underneath the house when I biked into the driveway.

"Afternoon, sailor."

"Afternoon." I hopped off and rolled my bike to a shady spot, leaning it against one of the house's stilts.

"Did you hear about the storm coming in?" he asked excitedly. "It's still three days out, and just a tropical storm, but it could intensify. Some are thinking it will cut in near Wilmington, which would give us some big surf this way."

"I didn't know," I said. "I've been a little checked out the last few days."

"That's to be expected, sailor." Wade's eyes were brighter than they had been last night. "But there's so much to do around here. I might need your help with some plywood later, if the forecast holds."

"Sure," I said.

"For the windows," he added. He removed his sweat-stained

cap and brushed his hair back out of his eyes. "This is when it gets exciting. This is when we can really start to *feel* something again."

==

That night I could hear Wade moving around the house. I was sure he didn't sleep.

I hadn't slept, either. The grief I'd been delaying for weeks washed over me that night, and I imagined it ebb and flow with the wind and current outside. I curled into a fetal position and gritted my teeth, letting the loss of Holland seep in and settle. The funeral.

In the morning, I made a bitter, strong cup of coffee and went out on my bike again, swigging from my thermos as I pedaled. Fuck, I said to myself, over and over again.

This time I biked to the marina, where several people were fishing. Three men and one woman—each a few feet down from the other—had cast out. I walked up to the first man I saw. He had a white plastic bucket by his feet, and when I got closer, I could see a few inches of seawater inside.

"Excuse me, sir," I said.

"I've already given my soul to Jesus," he said quietly. "You can try someone else."

"It's not that," I said, my cheeks flushing. "I just wanted to talk to you for a moment about lionfish."

"I don't have much time for lionfish."

"Did you know you can eat them?" I asked. "And that it helps save native fish?"

"Like swallowing poison, I'd guess," he said.

"The white meat is just like hogfish."

"Excuse me," he said, turning to me, "but I can't talk to every college girl with a mission these days. I'm going to get back to my fishing, if that's all right with you."

"I understand," I said. Humiliated, I walked back to my bike. I knew my coach at Invasivore would be disappointed in my conversion numbers. Maybe I'd inflate them a little. That idea came from my fear of failure more than my desire to earn the conversion points required for the purple Invasivore hoodie and water bottle.

Holland used to say that she didn't fear failure, but I think that's because she came from an unbroken home and plenty of money. She'd never had to experience it, not the real kind. That's how she got to be the type of person who could withstand the threat of grizzly bears by her tent. That's how she got to leave others behind. Risk was relative.

When I got back to the beach house, sweaty and sad, Ward was there with a fresh buzz cut.

"I went to the barber. Great guy. A hundred years old. Can't see well, always has a country western film going on the television. I never let him do a full shave because—you know—he might cut something important." He touched his neck.

"It looks nice," I said.

"You have to stay prepared," he said. "Speaking of—we should nail the plywood in tonight."

"Sure thing," I said, following him inside.

"How's your work going?" he asked, handing me a beer.

"I'm no good at it," I said, feeling miserable.

"That's to your credit, you know?"

"How so?"

"It's not honorable work," he said, his face suddenly growing serious. "You're out there trying to tell someone else how to live. You're trying to tell these poor folks how to fix a rich folks' problem. Do you know what it takes to catch a lionfish? A spear, or a net and a Kevlar glove. It's not on the folks around here to eat the lionfish nobody else wants. It's not on them to make it right for everybody else." He was practically leering at me. I stepped backward.

"It's to help protect native species," I said. "A grown lionfish can demolish an entire ecosystem in days."

"It's more than that," he said. "It's *always* more than that."

"If you hate the idea, then why do you rent out your room?" I asked, feeling defensive.

"I don't mean to come on so strong, sailor," he said, wiping his brow and gathering himself. "It's just that guilt is all around us, you know? All around us."

He was carrying a hammer and I felt uncomfortable. I also knew he was right.

"You should probably get out of here in the morning," he said, fishing for something in his toolbox. "Not because I don't like your work but because the storm is going to come in and it will be hard living out here for a bit. You should evacuate before they say to. The traffic gets awful."

"I'll do that," I said coldly.

That night I packed up my room, having imaginary conversations with Holland, the same way I'd done for years with my mother. I could see Holland slipping a silver band onto the thin leg of a red knot, then looking up in the cool summer air at Rachel. I could see my mother packing her station wagon, not able to take one more day with my father and me. We were holding her back from the life she wanted to live, with powders and perfume. With freedom.

When you worry, nine days out of ten, that you aren't any good, that you can't keep people in your life, the anxiety plays on a loop. It's a never-ending story. It's the snake biting its tail.

=

I woke to a strange darkness. Disoriented, I checked my watch to see that I'd slept in. It was ten minutes past nine. I realized Ward had boarded the windows and blocked the morning light. I had slept through his hammering.

I loaded my car with my belongings. There was no sign of Ward. I walked from the front of the house onto the wooden boardwalk to look at the ocean, which was now kind of emerald-looking underneath the darkening clouds and rogue rays of light. The water was wild and whitecapped.

I stopped at the bait shop on the way out of town for some coffee.

"Is he out there already?" the cashier asked, the same woman as before.

"Who?"

"Ward."

"Where would he be in this weather?" I asked, thinking she meant on his boat.

"You still don't know?"

I shook my head. She lowered her face as before. "He ties himself to the front of the pier when the storms come in."

"What?"

The cashier shook her head. "Yes ma'am. It's hard to believe but sure as rain that's what he does. He ropes himself onto one of the lead pilings, and he just takes wave after wave to the face, sputtering and half drowning himself and whooping in delight."

"Are you kidding me?"

"It's an awful thing to see," the cashier said. "Just awful. The Weather Channel filmed it once. Drove his mama nuts when she was still alive. He said he was doing it to make amends."

"For what?"

"For his family owning all that land and enslaving people. That was over a hundred years ago, his mama would tell him—but he wouldn't listen. Like he was some sort of Catholic out there, punishing himself for the crimes of others."

I paid for my coffee and took it back to my car. I sat in the driver's seat for a long time. I could picture Wade out there in the wild surf, like a strange figurehead on a boat, mouth open, the salt water pummeling his face and stinging his eyes, running through him.

"I just don't think that's how asking for forgiveness is done," the cashier had said on my way out.

But I'd never met anyone who really knew how to do it, anyway.

I made a U-turn and drove back to the pier. I guess I wanted to see if it was true.

I heard Ward hollering before I got close. I held on to the edge of the railing and looked down at the top of his drenched head. The rain was persistent and the surf was high, but there he was, soaking wet and roped to the wooden piling. The rope wound around his chest and hips, and his legs dangled into the water. When the waves came—and they were breaking all over the place—they crashed into his face, and salt water and snot dripped from his chin. He sputtered and whooped, in some sort of altered, if not ecstatic, state.

It was horrible to see, and I regretted bearing witness to it. I wondered if I was somehow responsible for his well-being. I turned back to my car and called the police. "We know about that one," the dispatcher said. "There's not much we can do, legally speaking, if he doesn't want help and isn't endangering others."

"He's going to die out there," I said.

"Hasn't yet. And, honey," she added, "this is off-the-record, but sometimes you just have to let people like that go. If he wants to drown himself, I'm not sure we can stop him." The line went dead.

I spent an hour sitting in my car, rain hitting the windshield.

I went back out to the edge of the pier. Spray from the waves came up over the railing. I was scared. "Ward! Get down from there," I yelled. His body was more still now, with less fight in it.

But then he took out a knife and cut his ropes, plunging into the water below.

I gasped.

His head rose between the crests of two waves. He dove under. Eventually he came up just before a big wave, and the water took him to shore. He crawled up the sand on all fours.

I ran to where he was lying on his side, almost fetal.

"Hi, sailor," he mumbled.

"What the hell are you doing?"

"Suffering," he said plainly. "And to think—what I experienced out there doesn't come close. Not to a month of what they put up with from my family. Not even a day.

"Can't make it right," he said, crying. "Which is why you have to do better than you're doing. You can't go around telling people how to solve your problems. *You* solve them. *You* get in this god-damned ocean with a spear and catch the invasive fish. *You* clean up the reef. *You* get down on your hands and knees and do the fucking work. *You* suffer for once."

He gagged and vomited seawater.

"You need help," I said.

"We all do," he said.

I stood next to him, waiting for him to say more, but eventually I accepted that he was okay. I walked back to my car. I drove out of town, past the kudzu-covered trees and churches and the bad strip malls with tanning beds. I thought of Holland wearing her mosquito-net hat, staring out at the nests of vulnerable birds on the Seward Peninsula, content. I thought of my mother painting another woman's face with rouge, driving home to an apartment I'd never seen, content.

The trick was to believe in your choices. Once you let the doubt in, it ate you alive. Once you started trying to be good, you could only see the ways in which you weren't. I guess people like Ward and I knew that, and we'd never be at peace. And that was sort of the point.

That summer ended on a sad note. I drove home to Raleigh to have dinner with my father, who'd retired from dentistry and kept his aquariums near the dinner table. He didn't ask a lot of questions when I showed up.

"Did you ever forgive Mom?" I asked. "For leaving us?"

"Of course," he said. "That's water under the bridge." But I could tell by the blank walls of his home and the placid expression on his face that he hadn't. He'd just given up the fight and

Peaches, 1979

The telltale yellowing of the leaves.

The soil so dry it felt coarse in her hands.

A knot of doom in her gut warning her the harvest was going to fail.

Darcy prayed for rain, and in the morning walked the rows of contorted trees, sipping coffee and applying a strip of orange paint to any dead trunks the way her father had done before he died two years ago. Peaches needed the hot nights, but they also needed water, and the farm had gone weeks now without meaningful rain.

Shit, she said to herself. My first year in charge and the orchard withers into a pile of sticks.

That evening, after work, Darcy turned the key in her father's old Chevy truck, the steering wheel still hot enough to burn her hands. She headed toward the Weeks Farm, a Christian boardinghouse for women a few miles from the town center, off Route 29. Her older sister, Beth, had lived there for several years, and Darcy was perpetually overdue for a visit.

She had something on her mind, other than the parched family orchard.

There'd been a string of murders in town—three—and Darcy was getting nervous about Beth living away from home. She was kind but vulnerable. Big blond hair, dimples. Beth bought every bogus magazine subscription, filled the offering plate at church, and said yes to every creep who made a pass at her. Was she not the easiest of targets?

Darcy rolled the truck windows down. Warm wind riffled through years of registration papers and fertilizer receipts paper-clipped to the sun visor.

The light was falling, and the blue hour came on. It was always Darcy's loneliest point—that elegant hour, when she wanted more for herself. Better company, a different job, a family she didn't have to look after. If only she'd stayed away from Gaffney after college. She'd give any ambitious young person that advice now—don't go back home, thinking you can leave again. Your stoic father will up and die of lung cancer, your evangelical mother will beg you to keep things going, and your good-for-nothing brother will pawn the family silver and sell fireworks out of the truck he lives in. Beth, well, who could fault Beth for anything?

Darcy drove past farm stands, clapboard churches, kudzu-strangled billboards, and old white houses with blazing pink azalea bushes out front. Her auburn curls were pulled back in a loose ponytail. She pushed her sunglasses up onto the top of her head as the light faded. The truck's turn signal was loud, a coarse, rhythmic ticking that stayed in her mind even after she flicked it off.

Darcy came to the turn and knew the Weeks place by its barren and browned pastures, discarded tractors, sun-bleached American flag, the caved-in barn roof. As she slowed the truck she noticed a cow lying alone in the mud. Its neck looked funny, abnormally sunken toward the ground. Was it dead?

She stopped and stepped out of the truck. As her foot pressed into the dry grass, a few flies circled up from the earth, and she swatted them away.

"You okay?" she called out, knowing it was a stupid thing to say to a cow, dead or not.

The cow did not lift its head or try to rise, but she thought she saw it breathing, a barely perceptible rise and fall in the rib cage. Then she saw its back leg move upward and come to rest on swollen udders. What could she do? Maybe I'll tell Miss Barbara, she thought, getting back into her truck and pulling farther up the dirt driveway. A barn cat dashed in front of her as she parked next to the dilapidated house with cinder block stairs and salmon-colored siding.

She knocked on the front door. No one answered, so she opened the door and called out. "Beth?"

There was a light on in the kitchen, and Darcy walked down a dark, carpeted hall to find Beth and another girl sitting at a table. The house smelled like beef broth and cigarettes. Beth stood up from the rickety kitchen table, smiling. Her thick blond hair hung down to her shoulders, and bangs fell across her eyebrows. She wiped her hands on her jeans and reached out to give Darcy a hug. Beth had gotten heavy over the years, the angles of her face now soft and rounded. Recently Darcy had taken her to Belks to find new jeans and underwear. "No one watches what she eats," Darcy complained to their mother. "She has Cheetos for lunch and microwaved fettuccine for dinner."

"I didn't know you were coming!" Beth said, beaming. "Want some ice cream?"

"No thanks," Darcy said, looking around at the bare-bones kitchen, the row of slightly open cereal boxes, the cluster of brown bananas dangling from a hook. "I came to check on you."

"Check on me?" Beth blinked.

Darcy paused. Of course Beth didn't read the newspaper. Maybe her sister didn't know about the Strangler, and maybe she didn't need to. She got scared so easily. Shit, Darcy thought.

"How was work this week?" Darcy said instead. "Tell me about it."

Beth exchanged wary glances with the other girl at the table, who went back to reading what looked to Darcy like a children's chapter book about a cruise ship. The refrigerator hummed loudly.

"It was sad," Beth said, looking down at her feet. Darcy noticed the cream-colored linoleum floor was warped and peeling.

"Sad how?"

"We had to take the stomachs out of the baby cows and put them in the freezer," Beth explained.

"Don't worry. I washed my hands a lot," she added.

"I know you did," Darcy said, feeling queasy. She had the feeling that Miss Barbara worked the girls too hard—and in exchange for what? This falling-down house that smelled like a sewer?

"Do you want to come up to my room for a bit?" Beth said, smiling. Darcy knew Beth was proud of her room. She'd helped her paint it yellow—was it four summers ago? Time was folding in on itself here, and her promise of getting Beth back home seemed flimsy and distant.

They walked up the stairs together. The walls were bare except for a generic landscape painting of a forest clearing that someone had plastered a smiley face sticker onto.

They opened the door to Beth's room. There was a single, unmade bed, over which hung a portrait of Beth when she was eleven, in a black leotard, tap shoes, and a peach blossom in her hair.

It had always bugged Darcy that her mother didn't keep the portrait of Beth. "I can't bear to look at it," Dee told her once. "I had such high hopes for her."

Beth took a few steps and then paused in the center of her room. She looked back at Darcy, then at the clutter on her floor, then at the closet. Darcy sensed her distress.

"What's wrong?" she asked, touching Beth's back, wondering if her sister felt embarrassed of the dirty room.

"Nothing," Beth said, turning around, forcing a smile. That's what Beth did—she smiled. It was supposed to set others at ease, Darcy knew, but it only made her sad to see. It was one of Beth's only tools in life, for protecting herself or getting out of uncomfortable situations.

Beth picked up the candy wrappers and the soda bottle from the floor and put them in the garbage underneath her desk. "Sorry it's a mess in here," she said.

"Don't apologize," Darcy said. Her eyes landed on a hair dryer on top of the bureau, still plugged into the wall. It was the old black one her mother, Dee, used on them, when they sat to-

111

gether on the bathroom floor with their heads hung, Dee's impatient fingers tousling their hair. Darcy had a pleasant memory of the heat hitting the back of her neck.

"I should get you a new hair dryer," she said.

"It still works," Beth said, shrugging.

God, Darcy thought. Don't you want anything for yourself?

"How would you feel about coming back to the farm for a while?" she asked.

Beth hesitated. "You know I want to. But you always work so hard, and Mama don't want me there."

"We'll show her how good it can be," Darcy said, holding Beth's arm as they sat down on the bed. "We'd all have a nice time, share the chores."

"I don't mean to hurt your feelings," Beth said, smiling, "but you always get my hopes up when you talk like that."

Darcy couldn't find words to fill the hot silence. She wanted to do better by her family, but it was hard to push herself and them up and out of trouble. It was hard to spend time with people she loved but didn't enjoy when she was tired from work and short on cash.

"How's the orchard?" Beth asked, tilting her head.

"Dry," Darcy said, looking down at her lap. "Real dry."

"I pray for rain," Beth said earnestly, patting Darcy on the back. "Every night."

"I know you do. What about Daniel?" Darcy asked, looking pointedly at her sister. "Do you hear from him?"

Beth ran her fingers through her hair and looked outside the window, out into the fading light. Darcy could tell she didn't want to talk about their brother.

"Does he ever call or come by?" she pressed.

"No," Beth said. Then, out of nowhere, she asked again, "Do you want some ice cream?"

Darcy shook her head no, then saw her sister's mud-encrusted tennis shoes lined up next to someone's boots by the wall.

"Have you had any friends over recently?" Darcy asked, worried Beth was getting taken advantage of. Again.

"No!" Beth said, blushing. "I just, uh, borrowed those."

"Do you need boots?" Darcy asked.

"I get by fine," Beth said. "Sometimes the girls and I tie grocery bags on our feet."

Darcy winced. She was starting to feel responsible for her sister in a way she'd never felt before. Beth shouldn't live like this. It had been her mother's decision, but now it felt like hers.

"How're you and Mama getting along?" Beth asked, sweating.

"Not very well," Darcy said.

"I know she's hard," Beth said, her big eyes radiating sympathy.

"We fight like dogs," Darcy said, with the same matter-of-fact voice she used when trying to act like the man of the house they all missed. But maybe that wasn't the right model. Maybe her dad hadn't been so great after all. Years of hard drinking, a bad temper, and not much in the way of emotional connection. But when he died, a void had opened up and Darcy stepped in. Sometimes it gave her purpose to help her family and take over the orchard, and she prayed that feeling would only grow, because right now it didn't feel like enough.

"Where's Barbara, by the way?" she asked. "I saw a dead, or nearly dead, cow on my way in."

"Miss Barbara's laid up at the big house right now. She isn't well."

"Is she taking care of you? Do you have enough spending money?" Darcy asked, leaning toward her sister. "Do you need me to run to the grocery store?"

"I'm fine. Stop worrying!" Beth said, smiling. "You're the younger sister, remember?"

"I'll call tomorrow," Darcy said, rising to her feet. She hugged Beth tightly. Her sister smelled like baby powder and flowers, like a little girl. When they were young, they used to sniff perfumes at the drugstore while their mother shopped for toothpaste and lipstick. Beth loved the smell of White Shoulders, and once spilled half a bottle on the front of her shirt at the store and burst into tears. The family car had smelled like White Shoulders for a long time.

As she pulled away from her sister she noticed Beth's dry and blistered hands.

"Next week I'm going to take you to the nail salon," Darcy said, nodding at Beth's fingers. She hated when she made promises like these.

"I'd love that," Beth said, squeezing her arm. "If you can find the time."

"Good night," Darcy said. "Lock the door after I leave, okay? And call if you need something. Please."

"You take care," Beth said, standing at the front door.

Darcy felt unsettled driving out. The boots by the door. The Strangler at large.

The cow was still when she passed it this time, no breath filling the chest. Who would remove it? Would anyone?

Darcy drove too quickly over the uneven gravel driveway back out to 29. She turned down the radio because the advertisements for mattresses and used cars for no money down made her angry. It wasn't the message as much as the urgency in everyone's voice.

We're paying attention to the wrong things, she thought.

Her mother, Dee, had used a similar urgency when they were children and the lack of rain threatened the peaches. *If you care about your father and this family, then you should get on your knees every night and pray to God for rain.* Sometimes, when the rain didn't come, Darcy threw the Bible across the room, and it landed like a tent on the carpet.

—

The next afternoon, Darcy hustled alongside the workers in the orchard, a hot sun overhead. She reached into the back of the pickup and lifted a gallon bucket of gray water. It sloshed onto her T-shirt and bare knees as she lugged it to the base of a peach tree and poured someone's shower water onto the trunk. The ground was so dry the water pooled on top of the soil before filtering down to thirsty roots.

She didn't want to fail her family or the farm. Failing was expensive and embarrassing.

The fumes from Bruce's truck exhaust mixed with the smell of her body every time she lifted her arms to grab a bucket of water. Bruce, her lead farmhand, was obsessed with Nicolette Larson and played "Lotta Love" several times a day from his running truck, singing in a falsetto as he watered trees alongside her.

The stupid jazz flute part came on.

"Last time I can take this song today, Bruce," Darcy said, her tone too sharp. She was hot, and the small of her back ached.

"Okay, boss," he said, smiling. Large beads of sweat clung to his nose. He clamped a cigarette between his teeth. They'd gone on one date in high school—a slasher film at the drive-in—but that was a decade ago and now they were just two humans trying to make life work in a small South Carolina town. Every now and then there was a short flash of interest, lust, something, but heat and hard labor had a way of dampening things. She wished she liked him more. Maybe one day.

Bruce had cut the lower half and sleeves off a white Hanes T-shirt, and Darcy could see a trail of coarse blond hair running from his navel to the waistband of his khaki work shorts. He was the kind of man with a big, easy smile you couldn't pin anger on. Former military. He had a drinking problem, but it didn't get in the way. Yet. She glanced at the pile of empty Coors cans in the bed of the pickup.

"You seen the papers today?" he asked. He was standing behind her as she lifted the last gallon bucket, sweat falling from her forehead across her eyes. He reached into the cab of his truck with one long, deeply tanned arm and pulled out the paper. He pointed to a black-and-white police drawing of a man with thin lips and wide-set eyes.

"He's strangled three women within ten miles of the police barracks. Now that's *crazy.*"

Darcy knew immediately who it was. Her heart began to race.

She hoped she was wrong.

No, she thought. I *have* to be wrong.

"Kinda looks like your brother," Bruce said, eyeing her.

"That's *everyone* you'd see at Deval's," she said, turning away with the bucket. Deval's was a convenience store with a small café that sold reheated rotisserie hot dogs and beer. It's where all the farmers, landscapers, and hourly workers went for coffee and lunch. She hated going in there because her father's old friends sat smoking in a corner, and they'd get real quiet when she walked in.

"I dunno."

Darcy watched the cloudy water swirl around another tree trunk. She was quiet, thinking about the drawing. The eyes.

"It's not your fault if the orchard fails this year," Bruce said, assuming she was upset about the trees. "Your daddy had bad years, too."

"You think people would see it that way?" she asked, exhausted. She slammed the tailgate of his truck shut.

"They don't care that you're a lady farmer."

"That's *all* they'll talk about if I mess up."

Bruce cleared his throat. "What do you hear from Beth?"

She appreciated his attempt to change the subject.

"I'm going to get her out of the Weeks place as soon as the harvest is over with."

"Beth's a good girl," Bruce said, nodding in approval. "Never meant anyone no harm."

"I wish Mama could see it that way."

"You're the woman of the house now, ain'tcha?" Bruce said, clapping her on the back before getting into his driver's seat. She heard him crack open a warm beer and rewind Nicolette Larson as he drove through the two-track dirt path out of the orchard and onto the access road. He'd grab dinner at Deval's, linger with his friends for a drink, then head on to Highway 29 and back

117

to his trailer in Cowpens, and show up at the orchard at 7:30 a.m. sharp the next morning. They both knew she couldn't get on without him.

Darcy walked back to the split-level ranch her family had owned since the sixties, where she now lived with her mother. It was an eight-minute walk she could do in her sleep. She entered the house and walked straight toward the bathroom for a shower.

Dee was in her recliner, watching the television on top volume. "Look at these pictures!" she cried out without turning around. "An angry rabbit attacked Jimmy Carter. While he was fishing!"

"Mama."

Darcy liked Jimmy Carter. Dee couldn't stand him.

"It's true! He's so ridiculous out there—can't even fend off a little rabbit."

Darcy ducked into the bathroom. She turned on a cold shower and stepped in, enjoying the shock, rinsing her hair. She was determined not to take her mother's bait.

When she walked out of the bathroom in pajamas, Dee was standing at the sink doing dishes in bright yellow gloves, watching the second television she kept on the counter in the kitchen. Darcy saw her mother was staring at the police drawing of the Strangler, which had made the five o'clock news.

Dee looked up from rinsing the lasagna pan to address the television directly. "He's not bad-looking."

"You can't say that about a serial killer," Darcy said, wincing. She looked at her mother's face. Had she seen the resemblance?

"Why the hell not?"

You *know* why, Darcy thought. But neither of them wanted to say it.

"I guess he has stupid eyes," Dee said quietly. She scrubbed the pan vigorously, staring into the soapy water.

"Don't you think the Strangler looks like Daniel?" Darcy blurted out. She'd been holding it in all day, and it came out of her like a lightning bolt.

Her mother's eyes widened behind her thick glasses. The corners of her little smoker's mouth curved downward.

"I *told* you," Dee said, gazing into the darkness of the trees, blowing a stream of smoke into the night air. "That man has stupid eyes. Daniel doesn't have stupid eyes."

Darcy's brother, Daniel, had been in and out of police custody since he was fifteen, and was selling fireworks and pickled eggs at a truck stop on Route 29, the last she'd heard. She figured he was also into some hard drugs. Last time he'd come around, he'd taken a drawer full of silver and the cash from Dee's purse.

"Have you seen him lately?" Darcy asked.

"You won't let him in the house anymore," Dee said, scowling. She exhaled. "How could I see him?"

Darcy sensed Dee had always loved Daniel best of all. He was the youngest, and when he was a baby he'd screamed every time he left Dee's arms, and that had meant something to her. It showed loyalty, Dee said.

What it really showed, Darcy thought, was a sense of entitlement.

Later that night Darcy sat at the kitchen table in a pilled white bathrobe doing her checkbook. She liked to keep an immaculate checkbook; to her, it felt like setting her world right, controlling what she could.

She was staring out of the sliding glass doors that led to the deck when she thought she saw a man standing in the yard. She gasped and ran to the window.

"What's gotten into you?" Dee asked, scowling.

"I thought I saw a man out there. Looking at us."

"We're not much to look at anymore." Dee made her way to the glass doors with a pack of cigarettes and a lighter. "You can't let the news get into your head."

"You're not going out there!" Darcy said, holding her arms out wide to block her mother's path.

"You think someone's gone bother messing with an old lady?" Dee asked, pushing past.

Darcy didn't want to admit that yes, that's exactly what she thought.

"*You're* supposed to be the smart one," Dee said, lighting her cigarette and taking a draw. Defiant, she leaned casually against the railing in a light cotton sweater, short khaki pants, and scuffed white tennis shoes, red-rimmed glasses, mouth pinched around the cigarette.

Darcy, heart pounding, stood protectively out on the porch with her mother while Dee finished her cigarette.

Later, as Darcy reconciled the last entries in her checkbook, she again had the sense that someone was watching her through the window. She stared out at the dark night.

Dee filled a glass of water, preparing herself for bed.

"I saw Beth today," Darcy said. It felt like a confession.

"And?" Dee drank a sip of water, staring at Darcy.

"And I was thinking she'd be safer here."

Dee rolled her eyes. "If she comes back, she'll be your responsibility for life. You'll *never* get rid of her. You'll find her behind the azaleas with her legs spread, one of the workers on top of her," Dee continued.

"That's not true," Darcy said, starting to shake with anger.

"It's happened before. Don't think you'll find another Mrs. Weeks, willing to take in a girl like Beth."

"Have you seen the way she lives, Mama? Do you know what they have her doing for work?"

Dee marched to her bedroom and slammed the door.

Minutes later Darcy could hear her mother having a coughing fit; she usually had three or four each night. Dee hadn't given up cigarettes after her husband's lung cancer—in fact, she'd added half a pack per day, as if hastening toward the same end.

Her parents hadn't even liked each other when they were living, she thought. Why rush to be together again?

That night, lying in bed between worn floral sheets, Darcy thought about a sentence Daniel had written about himself in his high school yearbook. "People say I'm one of those tortured geniuses," it said beside his picture. But as far as Darcy knew, no one had ever mistaken her brother for a genius. And he wasn't all that tortured, either.

"It's because your father liked to use DDT around here," Dee once confided after they lived alone together. "He chased the crop dusters to huff that stuff, and I don't think it did wonders for any of y'all."

Darcy slapped a mosquito on her arm and wiped her hand on her bedsheets. It was hot, but she was too afraid to open her windows.

The papers said the Strangler had a three- or four-day-old

beard and was over six feet tall. What if one day they mentioned a tattoo of a copperhead on his forearm? Darcy wondered.

But it wasn't Daniel, she assured herself. The killer just *looked* like Daniel.

Feeling foolish, she got up to turn on the lights and check underneath the bed and in the closet, the way she and Beth used to do when they shared a room. Confident she was alone, she climbed back in bed.

Darcy, her mind falling toward sleep, recalled her brother at nine years old, knocking the wind out of her mother with a baseball bat, swinging it at her back when she wasn't looking. Dee had crumpled onto the grass, glasses flying off her face onto the lawn, too shocked to scream, rows of hot-pink peach blossoms swaying behind her.

=

Darcy and her mother always ate their oatmeal in front of the kitchen television. They could turn from the television and look out at the morning from the big bay window. Bruce and his team were already outside, lugging hoses and buckets into the orchard. Dee eyed them as she swiped a spoon through her oatmeal and riffled through the paper.

"You don't think it's one of our fellas killing folks, do you?" she asked, looking down the bridge of her nose.

"Mom."

Darcy watched her mother take in stingy mouthfuls of food. Wrung-up little mouth, she thought. Pinched from clenching cigarettes and being angry all the time. Dee was bad with criticism of any kind; she took it all personally. Tell her she put too much butter in the green beans and she wouldn't serve you any. Tell her you're allergic to the fabric softener and she'd stop doing your laundry.

Dee straightened her shoulders and lifted her chin. "I was thinking last night," she said. "Thinking about calling on Daniel." She looked at Darcy for a reaction. "For security purposes. He's good with guns."

"We don't need him around here causing trouble," Darcy said, annoyed. "We're already short on cash."

"I'd give up a few dollars to stay safe."

"*I* can keep us safe."

"We need a man or a mean dog."

"I'm late for work," Darcy said, feeling as though she was going to explode, just like her father had done routinely throughout her childhood, pushing his chair back from the table, swearing, throwing plates.

She stood up and placed her unrinsed bowl in the sink, a passive-aggressive way of leaving work for her mother, underscoring her place in the pecking order. Tax season and too many dead trees had drained her; she felt justified in her anger. Her family was impossible! But by the time she reached the barn she felt guilty, and imagined her mother scrubbing dishes and thumbing through books she'd already read, alone in their house, smoking cigarette after cigarette on the back porch. Waiting.

=

When Darcy got back, Dee was making shortcakes, pressing her fluted biscuit cutter into the dough with aggressive strokes. Peaches were boiling down to syrup in a pot.

"Those look good," Darcy said, standing next to her mother. She was trying to make peace, and maybe Dee knew it.

"In case Daniel comes by," Dee said, a gleam in her eye. She broke an egg into a glass bowl and whisked a drop of water into it, and using a yellowed brush applied the egg glaze to the pastries, giving them a strange sheen underneath the fluorescent lights.

"You called him?"

Dee nodded, a defiant look on her face. "It's still my house," she said.

"What did he say? Where has he been?"

"Lord only knows. He didn't answer."

"I don't think he has a phone anymore, Mama."

"I called his friend and left a message."

Darcy poured herself a bourbon and orange juice, the drink her father had made in the evenings when he was tired or coming down with a cold. She leaned against the counter and watched her mother arranging the pastries just so.

"I don't want him here," Darcy said, bringing the glass to her lips.

Dee didn't respond. She just kept brushing the pastries with egg glaze.

Finally, Dee turned around. "You know he's killed again," she said. "A woman behind the Winn-Dixie."

Darcy felt her blood go cold. "You think it's Daniel, too?"

"No, stupid. The Strangler."

Darcy put down her drink and walked out to the orchard.

Bruce was cleaning up and was drinking a beer by his truck. He waved her over, somehow still cheerful after eight hours in the hot sun.

"You all right?" He handed her his beer can.

"Mm-hmm," she said, lifting the can to her lips. The beer was a little warm, but somehow still good. Somehow still able to remind her of drinking in a field as the summer sun went down at eighteen, smoking a cigarette in a hammock. Unburdened.

"We work too much," he said, swatting at a mosquito. "And now we're too ugly to make it in Hollywood."

"Speak for yourself," Darcy said, punching him in the stomach, his sweat clinging to her fist. Was there a flicker of interest? It had been so long since that feeling had been stirred up inside her. Now, as years ago, the spark between them felt faint and anemic. She wanted a spark in her life. Any kind of spark would do.

She said good night and turned toward the house, eager to get inside before dark.

She locked the door behind her. Did Daniel still have a key?

In the morning the biscuits her mother had made were still there, untouched on a silver tray, hard as porcelain on top, soft and rotten-looking on the bottom, swimming in a pool of gelatinous fruit.

=

Darcy had orange paint on her fingers; she'd discovered six more dead trees on the south side of the property that morning.

The leaves were sun scorched, and much of the fruit had turned brown and mummified-looking, not unlike the skin of ancient men people pulled from those peat bogs, she thought.

Some trees were still producing fruit, and the barn was half-full of crates brimming with fat peaches, not quite ripe, the white fuzz catching the small rays of light that peeked through the barn slats.

Bruce was taking stock of things when she reached him. Fruit flies swarmed his truck, which he'd loaded early before it got too warm to handle the fruit. Handling the fruit was everything—one bruised peach could spoil a bunch.

"Careful," she said to a man throwing a crate inside the truck bed, an admonishment she knew was more about her anxiety, and maybe an attempt to reassure herself of her authority. Bruce and his men knew how to load the peaches. They'd done it a hundred times the year before, and the year before that.

"It's going to be all right," Bruce said. His skin was already glistening.

It wasn't a great harvest, not even close—they kept estimated yields per year written on the wall of the barn for comparison—but it might be enough to get them by. But they couldn't have another year like this, Darcy thought, certainly not two.

"I'll keep food on the table," Darcy said, swatting a bee away from her face.

"Hey," he said. "I was thinking. Do you want to see a movie this weekend?"

She looked at him funny, like she couldn't hear him. "What?"

"A movie."

"Would you take a maybe?" She wanted to go to the movies with him, but not in the current state she was in—worried, exhausted, a stress breakout on her chin.

"From you? Sure."

Later that morning, Dee unfolded the paper and spread it out in front of them. She took a big swig of coffee, winced at its heat, and pointed her finger at the headline as she swallowed.

This time the Strangler had taken a twenty-three-year-old nurse who lived alone, not five miles down the road from the Weeks Farm. She worked the late shift and hit the grocery store afterward, and the police figured he'd followed her to the store.

"I'm going to get Beth right now," Darcy said, standing up from the table.

"You just wait and see," Dee said. "You'll never—"

"What's so hard for you about having her here?" Darcy snapped.

Dee looked down at her lap. Darcy could hear the chatter of the workers out back, the clink of footsteps on metal ladders.

"You think I'm mean," Dee said, eyes still downcast. "But you can't imagine how hard it is to see your own child like that. So easily hurt. I got to the point where I couldn't take it," she said, starting to cry.

"Well, *I* can take it. We have to."

Darcy turned her back on her mother, and let the kitchen door slam behind her.

—

The cow was still motionless in the mud as Darcy drove by the Weekses' pastures, but she didn't stop.

She parked in front of the farmhouse, underneath a lightning-scarred willow tree that moved a little in the breeze. When she opened the front door, she sensed that the house was not entirely awake, though she could hear a television or a radio on in a room somewhere. She stepped over a dish of food that Beth had probably left out for the cats.

The bright morning light didn't flatter the house. There were magazines and catalogs piled in the foyer and hallway. The kitchen stank of rotting bananas, waterlogged carpet, and mildewed shoes.

"Beth," Darcy called out on the staircase. She could feel the stairs heaving underneath her steps.

Beth's bedroom door was closed. Darcy sensed a commotion, the sound of two people moving frantically, perhaps just awake.

"Beth?"

Beth opened the door and stood, backlit, in an overly large T-shirt with a dolphin on it. Darcy was shocked at the sight of her sister's saggy knees and dimpled thighs.

"You surprised me!" Beth said, scrunching up her nose.

"Beth," Darcy said, stepping forward, "is someone with you?"

Beth shook her head. Her eyes were wide, maybe red, maybe filling with tears. Her blond hair was matted on one side as if she had been sleeping hard.

"Where is he?" Darcy said, starting toward the closet. "Is he in here?"

"Don't," Beth said, holding up a hand. "Don't go in there."

Darcy pushed past her sister and opened the closet. She felt her breath catch as her eyes adjusted to the figure hugging his knees before her.

"Daniel," she said, looking at her brother.

It was eerily quiet, except for the dull sounds of a television somewhere in the house.

"Why are you hiding?" she asked.

As he began to stand, she felt fear move through her body. "Why are you here?" she asked, backing up a little. She tried to keep her voice firm and authoritative.

"I needed a place to stay," he said, rising to his full height. "What's the big deal."

He was around six feet tall, unshaven, his dark hair grown long and curling on his neck and behind his ears. He wore a black T-shirt and a baseball cap. But everyone wears a baseball cap, Darcy told herself. Everyone.

"I'm sorry," Beth said between sobs. She stood behind them with her face in her hands. "But he needed help. He said he was homeless."

"I'm between jobs," Daniel said, clearing his throat. "I just come and sleep on the floor at night."

"Have you been taking her money?" she asked, looking from Daniel to Beth. She kept the tone of her voice as unemotional as she could. She wanted the facts, but she didn't want Daniel to get angry.

"Yeah, I owe her some money," Daniel said, shrugging. He had dark rings underneath his brown eyes. Darcy could smell his body odor.

"He's good for it," Beth said encouragingly. "And I like helping him."

"How much has he taken?" Darcy asked. Looking into Beth's eyes, she knew Beth had no idea how much. "How long has he been sleeping on the floor?"

"I like having him here. He makes me feel safe. He doesn't cause trouble."

Darcy took a deep breath. Who was she to say what they could and couldn't do? Who was she to arrange the lives of her adult siblings? She walked over to the big window and looked out at the backyard, and farther out, the pastures. The dead cow was still there. Darcy figured it would be there for a long time.

She became aware that she was uncomfortable having her back to her brother and turned to face him. "What do you get up to these days?" she asked, the tension in the room as thick as spoiled milk.

"Nothing much. Still selling fireworks, but I went out on my own."

"Out on your own how?"

"From the back of my car."

Darcy nodded. He'd been in trouble before for selling stolen merchandise.

Daniel smiled as if something ridiculous had just occurred to him. Even though a few teeth were missing, he could still turn on the charm. "What—you think I'm that killer they been talking about on television?"

Darcy tried to keep her face as plain as possible. "No," she said.

"Liar. You never did think too highly of any of us," he said accusingly. "Did you?"

"All I did was come here to check on Beth."

Beth smiled at both of them.

"You thought I might come up here and cut my sister into pieces and leave her body with the cows, didn't you?"

"Shut up."

"You and Mama got to turn off that TV."

"Shut up both of you!" Beth said, her slow and pretty face breaking into tears. "We're family. Ain't none of us going to cut the other up."

She reached for both of their hands. Darcy stared at her feet.

They stood there in Beth's dirty bedroom, listening to a fly hit a windowpane over and over again.

"I heard the cows last night," Daniel said, moving away from his sisters and rubbing his eyes.

"That's because they separate the moms from the babies,"

Beth said, her face solemn. "I asked Miss Barbara once. I wish I hadn't."

"They were loud."

"It'll stop soon. It only lasts for a few days. They sure do hate being apart."

Darcy realized she hadn't been in the same room as her brother and sister for a long time. It made her think of a day when her father lifted them into the bed of his truck and went for a drive. He'd hit Route 29 going fast and the wind swept the saliva out of the kids' mouths. The sun was hot but setting, and the ribs of the truck bed scalded their skin. Beth had held on to Darcy, who was still small, maybe ten or eleven at the time. Daniel was on his knees, leering dangerously over the side, when her father took a sharp turn and they all tumbled into one another, knocking heads, laughing.

"How's life with the old witch?" Daniel asked Darcy.

"Oh, don't say that," Beth said. "She's our *mother.*"

"She made you shortcakes last night," Darcy said. "With peaches."

Daniel grunted. "How's the orchard?"

"One bad year away from a for sale sign and a bulldozer," Darcy said calmly. "Maybe two. Wait long enough and it'll be a housing development."

Beth clutched her sister's arm, and Darcy could feel her rough and blistered skin. Mom is right, she thought. It's easier not to watch. It's easier not to take responsibility.

But she knew she was going to put both of them into her car and drive them home. Feed them. Make sure they were okay.

"I miss Mama's shortcakes," Beth said, sighing.

In the distance a cow was lowing, calling her calf through a barbed wire fence. Darcy's mind was already drifting away,

131

thinking of where she could get a mean dog. She thought of credits and debits, of water in and peaches out. Of women and cows and broken necks.

"You know," Daniel said, looking out at the dry yard behind the house, "I've always hated peaches. But I still have the habit of praying for rain."

==

Dee dumped a box of spaghetti noodles into rapidly boiling water.

"I guess you just think you can show up and I'll make magic happen," she muttered. She lifted the lid of her saucepan and dumped a can of crushed tomatoes over browning hamburger. She poked at the meat with her wooden spoon. To Darcy, it smelled like childhood. Like a warm summer night with peaches baking in the dying sun. Someone cutting grass, a neighbor grilling, a child crying in the distance. It activated the pit of her stomach, the old unhappiness. The past that none of them could explain or touch. The anticipation of a fight brewing in the house.

"Mama, ain't nobody confusing those dry noodles with magic," Daniel said. He chewed on a toothpick and rocked backward in the kitchen chair.

Beth covered up her laugh too late, and Dee turned to glare at her. The three children were sitting around the kitchen table, in the same spots they'd always had. The caning was a little loose in the chairs now. Bite marks on the furniture legs from a long-gone dog. Beth sat in the center across from Dee's place, and Darcy and Daniel on either side.

"You three just think I'm here to look out for you for life,"

Dee said, turning her back to them again. "Like I'll just keep picking up after your messes."

"I haven't made a mess, far as I can see," Daniel said. He cracked open a warm Coors he'd found in the garage. Darcy stared at the copperhead tattoo, now faded on his forearm.

Beth stood up and put an arm around her mother's shoulders. "Why don't you sit down, Mama?" she asked. "Let me finish dinner."

"And burn the sauce? No, thank you," Dee said stiffly.

Beth shrugged and returned to the table. Darcy swallowed a sip of water that tasted swampy to her, as if it had been sitting just underground. Her stomach was knotted up.

=

Dee didn't say much as they were cleaning up after dinner. Daniel was pulling out blankets for a night on the couch. Beth was brushing her teeth, her duffel bag slung into a corner of Darcy's room.

"Happy now?" Dee asked through clenched teeth.

Darcy didn't answer.

=

The next morning Darcy walked into the kitchen, blinking in the light, to pour herself a cup of coffee.

"He's gone," Dee said bitterly. She had an unlit cigarette and was walking toward the back porch.

"Did he take anything?"

"You know he left because you were so awful to him. He knew what you thought of him! That he was some deranged killer, capable of strangling women and leaving them in a pile of trash behind the Winn-Dixie."

"Don't pretend like you didn't consider it yourself."

"You know they have a lead now? And it's not Daniel. But you just go on thinking you're better than all of us!" Dee said, lighting her cigarette indoors. "You think you have life figured out. That you're going to save us."

"Who else is going to save you?" Darcy practically spat.

"The good Lord himself!" Dee's cigarette dropped from her lips and fell to the floor. She mashed it into the carpet with her foot and stormed out onto the back porch.

"Good luck with that one, Mama," Darcy yelled. She was still wearing her bathrobe, but she slipped on sandals and stomped outside into the orchard, grabbing a can of orange spray paint.

The sky was sherbet colored, and the air was already hot. Darcy could smell the scent of peaches rotting on the ground. The wasps were increasing in number.

She heard voices in the barn. It was too early for workers to be there. She was scared. As she got closer, the voices sounded like moaning, as if someone was in pain. What if the Strangler was in there, pressing a wire into another woman's throat? What if her mother was mistaken or the police had the wrong guy?

Adrenaline coursed through her body, numbing her tongue. Darcy lifted the old metal latch and ripped the barn door open, only to find Bruce on top of her sister Beth in the back of his pickup truck. Beth's pasty white legs were thrust upward.

Both were stunned and just stared at her, Bruce in a modified push-up position, balanced precariously over Beth.

There was a quiet moment, the three of them in the hot barn

with the flies and peaches, the morning sun coming through the dry slats of the barn.

Darcy started spraying the truck—and then Bruce's back and Beth's legs with orange paint. The can, nearly empty, hissed. She threw it on the ground and ran back through a row of peach trees toward the house, bathrobe flapping open, the hot air streaming around her body, sweat beading on her forehead and chest, dripping into her eyes. She screamed in anger at the trees until she stopped, breathless and hunched, in the middle of the orchard.

She thought of the dead cow in the Weekses' pasture, how it had wandered away from the herd, putting itself in danger. Dying slowly and alone.

Just how wrong would it be to save myself? she wondered, looking up at the watercolor sky. And only myself?

Indigo Run

Women must destroy in themselves,
the desire to be loved.

—Mina Loy

1752

*B*y *noon the ocean surged into the city. Pines arced danger-*
ously in the wind and snapped. Waves crashed into the gen-
eral store, claiming ledgers and bursting swollen sacks of flour.
Schooners broke anchor and sailed onto East Bay Street. Winds
brought down the gallows with eight asphyxiated pirates still de-
composing in the public square, eye sockets eaten away and teem-
ing with larvae.

A group of men rode a detached roof down the swirling brown
tidal river, reaching for branches, hoping to reach marsh or solid
ground. Marlon Glass was one of them.

He felt certain that his young wife and son were dead, and
that he would soon join them. He'd watched as the water took
them away, watched as they clung to one another in desperation,
flailing. Drowning each other.

He looked at the other men alongside him. He reached out in vain as his stable hand slipped from the roof, fingers dragging down the wooden beam until he was swallowed by the water, hands reaching toward the sky.

The roof began to come apart, splintering. The roar of the water was deafening; the motion disoriented him. Marlon saw a cow, swept into the current beside them, eyes bulging. The mast of a ship thrust upward from the curl of a wave. He prayed, mumbled, shouted, and took in mouthfuls of bitter water. He was alone now, legs dragging in the water, swept along by the river. His nose stung, and his hands were raw and cut open from clinging to slate shingles. The water tossed him against a small building, a tide mill.

He came to consciousness in the woods of an old plantation, belly down on a sandy trail near the peach orchard, a stream of blood dripping from his broken nose. He vomited a great deal of water and drew himself, shaking, to his knees. He stayed like that for a while, wishing himself dead, kneeling, shouldering an enormous emptiness that broke for just a moment into peace. The birds were calling. The eye of the storm was upon them. He could feel the pounding of the water and the churning of the earth underneath the places where his body touched the ground.

He sensed movement in the bushes and remained still. He breathed slowly through his mouth, through his pain. A small white doe stood alone in the path, her ebony hooves impossibly perfect. They locked eyes. It was the longest second of his life.

Two years later, he purchased the abandoned plantation and christened it Stillwood, even though the fruit trees were salt burned, the oaks undermined and heart shaken. His new wife, Bettina, a curious woman with pale hair and light eyes, slept

under a tent of gauze to avoid insects and spent her days culti-
vating camellias, placing japonica and sasanqua cuttings in the
dappled shade.

1

1954

Skip Spangler stood in the grove of overgrown peach trees, where she could look down the sloping lawns toward the dark Ashley River and the dilapidated family mansion.

She pressed her thumb into the soft skin of a rotten peach as the storm gathered on the horizon. Heat lightning lit the cumulus clouds from within.

She liked bad weather. Dramatic weather. The kind you could watch unfold like a movie. The kind that made you feel small and ridiculous compared to the wind and the angry water.

As a child, she used to grab piles of jasmine blossoms and throw them into the air, pretending it was snow, which she didn't see until she was twenty. She could remember the silken, wet petals in her fists, then white confetti against a blinding blue sky. Those were the days when she could sense another world outside Stillwood, but couldn't reach it, except through the books in her father's library.

She'd read about a storm in New England in the early 1800s, where fences, rooftops, and cattle horns glowed blue with static electricity. Your own fingers, she imagined. *Glowing.*

Skip had waited most of her life for a storm like this to come to Stillwood. Something savage and biblical, redemptive. She wasn't much of a believer but thought of Psalms. Preacher Noble, long dead, once said the Lord could lift high the waves and still a storm to a whisper. And all the wicked would shut their mouths.

Preacher Noble also said Skip talked too much. Not as much as you drink, she'd replied, and her mother had slapped her for *her* wicked mouth. Hard.

The sting of her mother's hand made her feel nervous and alive. Plus, she'd always known herself to have a streak of wickedness. She figured she deserved a little wrath when it came her way.

She tucked a strand of chin-length hair behind her ear. Prematurely gray. Whitecaps formed on the river. She watched the shutters clap against the siding of the old house.

She was the last of a line of women born at Stillwood. Time had reduced the others to faded portraits and penciled lines in the brittle vellum pages of the family Bible. *Born, died.*

Skip was not sentimental like the women before her; she was tired of lugging the past around. She spent most of the year far north, living in a cabin surrounded by a grove of silver maples near Maine's Saco River. She managed a rarely visited wildlife sanctuary, a floodplain forest filled with ferns and songbirds in summer.

She was ready to be free of her family home, but didn't sell it for fear that someone would renovate it, strengthen its foundation, and open it to the public. Put a woman in a hoopskirt out front talking about how things used to be.

For now, Stillwood's manor sagged on a knoll, three miles south of where the ferry used to run over a narrow bend of the tidal river.

You could drive a horse down the ancient rutted roads that

paralleled the Ashley River—but the farm was vacant, the pastures overgrown, the peaches left to rot on the ground. The air smelled of soil and sulfur. The water flowed from the Great Cypress Swamp toward the city, past the sloping lawns of old plantations. Guernsey cattle lowed in the distance, ankle-deep in the cool marsh. Trains whistled. The faint lights of Charleston burned into the night, brighter every year.

People wrote to Skip, requesting to get married on the banks of the river by the old plantation. She turned them away. Stop being crazy, she told them. Who wants to shuck oysters and dance at a mosquito-drenched place like this, where so many humans suffered?

She intended to let the place rot. She'd rather give it to the birds than the brides.

The Preservation Society sent an urgent letter every month. "Save Stillwood before it's too late!" In an op-ed in the *Courier*, they claimed she, Skip Spangler, was erasing history, a landmark that belonged to the public. A fire engulfed an outbuilding five years before, and the president of the society accused her of starting it. "I only *wish* I had the courage," she wrote him, against her lawyer's advice.

Skip looked to the lavender sky, wondering if this could be the storm to do the job. Stillwood was a stubborn house, proving its mettle against hurricanes and termites decade after decade. Rain rusted the eternal tin roof. The porch sagged but could still bear weight. The marble statue had lost one arm but rose from the center of an empty pool, covered in lichen, reaching for the sky.

Skip, like her mother and grandmother, was born in an upstairs bedroom. Her mother's siblings, pronounced dead at birth, were buried beneath the magenta *Camellia japonica*, brought to America by French botanist André Michaux in 1780, and cultivated by the first Glass matriarch, Bettina.

If Skip was sentimental about anything, it was the ancient camellias, crepe myrtles, live oaks, and tea olives. *Osmanthus fragrans.* The heron rookery. The shade of the forest, the sun on the river, the old female alligator with the wallow hole by the forgotten rice field. The buzzards that circled her den, looking to clean the last of her kills.

That alligator must be fifty years old by now, Skip figured. Did she also spend her later years wondering what life would have been like on a different river?

Skip's mother and grandmother had been proud to hail from this place, to live in this house.

Remember, they said, it's best to go a little hungry, never keep score, and hold Christ close to your heart.

Yellow jackets and ants were feeding on the bruised peaches by Skip's feet. The wind picked up, and the rain began.

Practice the art of polite conversation, Skip thought, throwing her peach onto the ground. And know that a woman can die of thirst beside the ocean.

2

Two elderly sisters spotted the Virgin Mary above their cottage on Folly Beach while shucking corn. Betty and Letty Sims claimed the hatch to heaven must have opened in the clouds over their clapboard shack with the yellow door. The *Courier* declared it the Lowcountry Miracle.

It had been a tumultuous time in the city. Race riots spilled from sidewalks, the front steps of Folly Baptist. The week before, white sailors shot two Black men, chasing them down and pulling them from the barbershop, and the entire city had erupted in violence. Naval troops were forced to patrol the streets.

Letty Sims felt the entire city was like a pustule, and the ugliness needed casting out. "We give the devil his work here," she told Betty over their nightly card game. "No shortage of souls to feast upon."

The men had come back from the war in bad shape, missing limbs, mumbling in church, beating their wives at night. A plague of locusts with red eyes emerged from the ground, clinging to trees and quivering on porch columns.

"The worst places are in need of the best blessings," Letty said to the papers when she explained the way the Virgin Mary had come to her on the fifteenth of May. "The clouds parted, and it was the face of pure forgiveness," she said, making sure the reporter wrote that part down.

Betty accused her of being dehydrated and spinning yarn, but Letty *knew* she'd seen the golden countenance of Mary peering down at them as they husked the corn and plucked the worms from the tips. Letty was insistent, so Betty gave in to believing.

Letty's loyal dog, an elderly copper-colored spaniel, leaned against her bare knees as she spoke to the *Courier*'s reporter. Letty took a strong pour of whiskey in her midmorning coffee and ran her tongue across a chipped front tooth as she spoke.

"This is the kind of place where if you sip from the wrong bottle, or worship at the wrong altar, the darkness gets into you," she told the reporter. "It's in *all* of us, you see, and the

Virgin Mother appeared so as to forgive us. To offer us a way out."

The *Courier* cut that part, to her disappointment.

Sonny Lee, the enterprising proprietor of the nearby Calhoun Beach Club, paid Letty a visit the morning after the *Courier*'s article about the Lowcountry Miracle. He arrived on foot, sweating profusely, sand in his leather dress shoes.

"Morning, Miss Sims," he said, calling through the screen and rapping loudly on the door until Letty came. The spaniel lunged at Sonny but was deflected by the screen.

Betty dipped a pickle in mayonnaise. They were listening to the stock car race on the radio in the kitchen, nursing flat colas. "Don't open the door," she whispered. "He looks like he's selling something."

"Say your peace," Letty instructed, tapping on the wire mesh. "I won't buy nothing."

The dog lunged again.

"Goddamn!" Sonny said, falling back a step. "That screen going to stay put?"

"I reckon," Letty said, irritable. She held the dog by his rust-colored scruff.

"These sightings of yours," Sonny said, wiping his forehead. "Do you think we could make 'em a regular occurrence? Say every second Sunday?"

Letty looked at him suspiciously. He showed her an envelope of cash and slid it underneath the door.

A broken engagement thirty years earlier had left her dependent on the money she could make sewing and altering gowns. Betty had a bad heart. Letty didn't like the idea of lying, but her fingers hurt when she held the sewing needle. Her eyes and back ached. The dog had worms.

She felt all along that life should have been better for her, that God owed her a little last-minute grace.

"It could be a monthly payment," Sonny said, winking. "A miracle on installment."

3

Helena-Raye Glass smoothed her eyebrows with petroleum jelly and a small metal comb. She pressed Pears deodorant powder into her armpits and between her modest breasts. She dabbed Dorin of Paris rouge to her cheeks, chin, and the lobes of her ears. She'd read about that last part in a magazine. *Preserve the fleeting flush of youth*, it said. *Slap your cheeks to find your most authentic color. Look at yourself in the mirror and say: what a pretty girl!*

What a pretty girl, she muttered, feeling ridiculous.

She'd never been the kind of woman to focus on men or makeup. She preferred stomping around the riverbanks during low tide with a bucket of oysters, or climbing the large branches of live oaks, but her mother had worked to tame all her wilder instincts. Belching, scratching, shooting rifles, failing to brush her hair, ripping her tights, objecting to polite hugs, failing to offer a visitor a glass of cold tea.

For years, her mother, Mary-Grace, had said Helena was the kind of girl who would marry up. When she was eighteen, Helena believed in her beauty. But now that her reputation had taken a hit, and two years had passed, she felt a hint of desperation. "You can't afford to miss the boat," her mother warned. "And it's pulling away from the dock."

Helena brushed her teeth, rubbed her lips with a washcloth, and applied Tangee lipstick, blotting once. She was hungry, having skipped lunch in anticipation of dinner at the Calhoun Beach Club.

"If you can manage to control your appetite," Mary-Grace said, "please do."

Helena came downstairs to wait for her father, Percy, to escort her to dinner. Mary-Grace, who was hosting friends in the parlor for a temperance meeting, pulled her aside. Helena could feel her mother inspecting her outfit, her waist, her shoes.

Vases of gerbera daisies and gardenias decorated the table. Helena reached for the plate of deviled eggs, but her mother grabbed her wrist.

"I think the barn needs another coat of paint," Mary-Grace whispered, one eyebrow raised.

Helena cursed her mother inside her head and added another swipe of lipstick before joining her father at the front door. *What a pretty girl!*

4

Struggling through his second term of medical school, Win Spangler fantasized about his summer plans. His father's secretary mailed him a clipping about the Lowcountry Miracle. *Your father strongly suggests you go*, she wrote. *His friend Sonny owns a resort on Folly. We've booked a room for you.*

Win's father was the kind of man who thought religion was contagious. He believed that if Win just hung around it long enough, he might catch it, like a case of smallpox.

Win didn't care about the Miracle, but the resort sounded like good rest. Fifteen miles south of town, the Calhoun Beach Club was a luxurious, sprawling Victorian with turrets, a hundred rooms, a wide veranda, and a good reputation among industrialists like his father. According to the brochure, there was a casino, billiards room, and a music hall with red velvet seating.

He'd read that Folly Beach was prone to bad winds and shipwrecks, and had been many things in the past: a plantation, an encampment for Union troops as the Yankees tried to take Battery Wagner. But now it was a place of good concerts, dancing, and women—things that had been in short supply in medical school.

Win walked from his last exam into the open door of a hired car. He slumped against the door, sleeping so hard that his face ached when he woke up to the sight of a bellhop in full uniform opening the door to let him out.

He had the habit, he knew, of falling from the high of dreams to the sorrows of reality, plummeting from optimist to pessimist. His relationship with his father whom he'd once revered. His older brother he once admired. The Lord, his occasional Savior. Lillian Wood and her auburn braids. Cecily Betts's bow-shaped lips, which he kissed behind the barn in ninth grade. Two years of cello lessons. Now medical school.

Win cleared his throat and blinked his eyes. It was late afternoon, hot, and bright. The island felt remote, as if he'd traveled a great distance. Pines and palmettos grew up from the sand. He spotted a lighthouse at the end of a jetty.

Another bellhop held the door for him as he entered the

Calhoun Beach Club. The ceilings on the first floor were fifteen feet high. Huge windows overlooked the beach and sea beyond. Gaslights flickered, and the furniture shone with polish.

Win took his key and walked straight to his room, knowing his luggage would follow. Pale coral paint covered the walls; the color made him feel warm. He organized his books on the desk and flung his windows open because the room was unbearably hot, but also so that he could hear the sea. He sat on the edge of his bed looking out at the water, wave after wave. He fell asleep in his clothes on top of the bright white coverlet and slept for twelve hours. He woke staring at a fly on the white shiplap ceiling.

His first thought was that he might fail out of medical school, and no donation could solve it. His second thought was that he needed a haircut. His wiry brown hair grew fast, and once it was a half inch too long it started to rise and curl from his head, untamed, as if betraying the refined image he worked so hard to project.

The next morning, he caught up on his neglected correspondence, eating pastries in bed. There was gumbo and she-crab soup for lunch in the dining room, with chocolate mousse for dessert. An attendant left lemon cookies by his door when he skipped dinner, having fallen asleep again. That night an enormous bowl of rum punch made with peaches, lemons, and black tea was set out in the lobby.

He fixed himself a glass and took it outside, where he watched strangers walking on the beach. He felt somewhat restored, but lonely.

He couldn't bring himself to open the textbooks for next semester. They mocked him, a tidy stack on his desk.

The next morning, Win sat in a white rocking chair next

to the owner of the inn. Sonny Lee, a once-handsome friend of his father's, was balding and heavy; he had a weakness for banana pudding, beauty pageants, and high-stakes horse races. He sipped his morning brandy from a crystal tumbler, blinking his small eyes.

"Drink up while you can," Sonny Lee said, pretending to toast him.

"What do you think about this holy hatch in the sky, sir?" Win asked out of politeness, shielding his brown eyes to look at the shrimp trawlers headed into harbor after a morning of fishing. Their nets were gathered, and gulls circled the ships.

"The Lowcountry Miracle?" Sonny looked at his hands as if in deep thought. "It's a ruse. Two idle spinsters who need a good turn in the sack."

He took a sip from his glass and relaxed into the back of the chair. "But they're damn good for business. I'm booked solid. Do you know how much I can charge on Second Weekends?"

"Plenty, I'm sure," Win said, covering a yawn. "Any price for a room near a ladder to the Lord is a bargain."

Sonny laughed and recrossed his legs. Win could see sweat in the creases of his clothes. "Eat, Drink, and See Mary, I say."

"I suppose I should stand underneath the heavenly ladder on Sunday?"

Sonny clapped Win on the thigh so hard it smarted.

"Yes, son. All you have to do is *go*. You don't have to *believe*," Sonny said, gazing up at the heavens. "But it's fun, trust me. I'll give you a small flask, and you can ride in the wagon of young folks. It's what you're here for, right? The company of young folks?"

"I'm here recovering from an unimpressive year at medical school," Win said, touching his temples. "And because my father thinks a woman from South Carolina will make a fine, God-fearing bride."

Sonny cleared his throat. "No need to be so on the nose about it, son. Here in the real South—no offense to you Texans—we think a little spit and shine on the truth is all right. Makes it easier to take, really."

Win thought for a moment of home, the dusty hills of the family farm, mountains of bison skulls waiting to be ground into fertilizer, slick hand-painted signs for Spangler Sugar, his father peering at monthly ledgers after supper. He never wanted to be that kind of man, the kind who fell into monotony. He craved travel and innovation. He was interested in the future, not tradition.

His father was interested in sugar and fertilizer, and the money it made. "There's a good living in sugar and shit, son," he'd once said.

"Before you take a bride," Sonny Lee continued, "get yourself some practice. Don't rush. The practice is the fun part, if you know what I mean." He laughed.

A choral group filed onto the sundeck in front of them and began to sing "O God, Our Help in Ages Past." The earnest middle-aged women clustered together, shoulder to shoulder as they sang, a few holding parasols to shade them from the sun. Win noticed their red lips.

"I think I've enjoyed about enough of *that*," Sonny said quietly, nodding toward the choir and rising to his feet. "I prefer to watch girls lounge on the sundeck. These women sing to the Lord like cats in heat. See you at dinner tonight, I presume?"

"Absolutely," Win said.

The women finished their hymn. Win nodded politely at them and rose from his chair, heading into the club for lunch.

Win walked behind the maître d' to his usual table by the French doors. He scanned the room.

There *was* someone who'd caught his eye earlier in the week. She was tall, slender, and had blond hair and a nose that turned just slightly up. There was something crisp in her green eyes, something dignified in the way she held her head. She appeared to enjoy a jovial relationship with her father, who rarely left her side. Noticing Win's interest, Sonny had leaned over to whisper in Win's ear. He reported they were from a prominent farming family in the area and came to the club to dine and swim.

"Helena Glass's father's a little short on money," he said. "Rice isn't what it used to be here. He didn't adapt quickly; his wife wouldn't let him. And Helena-Raye is *unnaturally* fond of rifles."

"Anything good you can say?" Win asked, smiling back at his father's friend, who changed jackets three times a day to prevent guests from seeing patches of damp sweat on his clothes. A cloud of cologne followed Sonny throughout the inn.

"She's a strong swimmer and does well in local pageants. Nice legs, if that's your thing."

"Could be," Win said. Sonny slapped him hard on the knee and laughed.

"A bit of wildness in her," Sonny added quietly. "And you know that can go either way. A good time for a *short* time, if you ask me."

Win watched Helena Glass at lunch that day, as she brought a scallop to her pink lips. He wanted to be the scallop on the tip of her fork, to be brought to her mouth and consumed. She ate lightly, dabbed her lips with a napkin, and cooled herself with an apricot-colored fan, which she left at the table when she departed. Win rushed to pick it up but did not call after her, though he'd intended to. It seemed to burn in his hands.

He held the fan, closed up tight like a razor clam, its gold clasp fastened. He slipped it into his pocket, nodded at the maître d', and continued up the carpeted staircase to his room. He placed the fan on the top of his bureau next to several rocks, one of Sonny Lee's silver monogrammed cuff links, and an antique nickel he'd swiped from his father. He'd had the habit since he was a boy, taking things that didn't belong to him and arranging them neatly in his private space, tiny altars that spoke to his desire to possess things, to study them, to evoke a richer sense of their owners. Growing up, he had a neighbor—a fruit importer—who had a weather-beaten travel trunk, Turkish rugs, Grecian kraters, and enough near-death experiences to captivate the table at several dinner parties. The man made his own father seem dull, stagnant, and small-minded. While his father spoke of the power of deep roots, Win found them smothering. He longed to lose himself on another continent, though preferably not on a warfront.

Win took a restless, hot nap on top of the hotel's good sheets and woke with the idea that he should get some air. He sat up and rubbed his eyes. The sun was merciless, but he liked the sound of the waves. He rose, washed his face, and strolled the long boardwalk over the white sand dunes toward the water, watching the pelicans sail overhead. He heard footsteps behind him, and turned to find the girl who liked rifles. She wore a white muslin summer dress and made unflinching eye contact. Pale freckles spread lightly across her nose and cheeks.

"I believe you have something of mine," she said, her pronunciation of the word *mine* and its emphasis on the *i* rattling something within him. He felt stirred, anxious. Her voice had a surprising raspiness to it, as if she were slightly hoarse. He liked that she wasn't perfect, that her voice indicated mischief.

"Yes," he said, collecting himself, straightening his posture. "I brought it up to my room for safekeeping."

Her eyes trailed to the sea as he talked. She had a knowing but distracted manner. The pelicans flew low over the water, and they both watched in silence. One of the birds dove for a fish and broke the spell.

"Unfortunately, I can't join you there to retrieve it," she said, locking eyes with him again. "You'll have to bring it to dinner tonight."

He nodded obediently. As she turned on her heel and walked back down the boardwalk to the clubhouse, he felt a warm blush of humiliation spread through him. He decided that this evening he would redeem himself, show his good upbringing. He had, after all, sat through hours of etiquette classes and ballroom dance lessons. Better put them to use, he thought.

===

He arrived at dinner early, as the pianist was warming up with scales and a scant rendition of "Get Out and Get Under That Moon." "Oh boy, give me a night in June!" one of the waiters sang as he laid silverware on tabletops in rhythmic fashion.

"Hush, Jimmy," said another waiter, who was watering the centerpieces.

The pianist began playing "Every Day Will Be Sunday When the Town Goes Dry."

"Goodbye, Hunter," Jimmy sang along. "So long, Scotch."

Win walked over to Jimmy, who looked up at him, then quickly went back to his work. He was a skinny young man with dark skin and kept dishing out silverware in rapid movements. Sonny Lee staffed his hotel and bandstand with men from the local fields. They picked beans and cotton during the day, worked the kitchens at night.

"Could you deliver this to Miss Glass this evening?" Win asked, showing Jimmy the fan.

"I don't really have time." Jimmy turned back to his task.

Win wrapped a few bills around the fan and extended it, confident the waiter would change his mind.

"Fine, fine," Jimmy said, pocketing the fan. "You want a rose on the tray with it or something?"

"Sure," Win said. He felt stupid.

"She gets an awful lot of presents, sir," Jimmy said. The hint of compassion in the waiter's voice mortified Win, who went out to the veranda and watched the water until he was sure she was seated.

Was he doing this wrong? Probably. No one had told him much about women.

He made his way to his own small table by the far wall. He watched from across the crowded dining room as Jimmy approached Helena with a tray balanced on one hand. He set down a small glass vase with a pale yellow rose, and the fan. She grimaced, or at least Win was pretty sure she had, and he felt too sick to eat his shrimp cocktail.

Sonny sat down with a big exhale, sweat gathering on his brow. "I'm whipped," he said, moving a large hand toward Win's plate. "Running over hell's half acre. Are you going to eat that?"

"All yours," Win said, sliding the crystal dish toward Sonny.

"You're staring too hard." Sonny popped an entire shrimp into his mouth.

"Excuse me?"

"At her." Sonny wiped bright red cocktail sauce from his mouth. He smacked his lips when he ate. Win envied the way his father's friend seemed to enjoy himself. Sonny was voracious. It seemed like life kept serving him what he wanted.

"Just appreciating what she has to offer," Win said. "It's nothing serious."

"With the price of cotton and rice down in this drought, I imagine a sugar scion looks mighty good."

"What are you suggesting?" Win asked, leaning forward. The waiter set down two plates of shad and a dish of lemon wedges.

"That you think clearly." Sonny slid his fork into the flesh of the fish. "That you *practice*."

"Thanks for the advice," Win said, "but rest assured that all women are temporary commitments while I'm in school." He knew he was too far gone to avoid another interaction with Helena. But he was going home in two days. If anything, that would keep him safe.

As soon as there was a break in the music, Helena walked over to him with an athletic stride, navigating a cluster of young girls with satin ribbons in their hair. She wore a pale blue drop-waist dress with a long strand of black pearls and held the closed fan in front of her. "Thank you," she said, "for delivering this to me." She slapped him on the wrist with it.

"Excuse me, Miss Glass," Sonny said, rising politely. He folded his napkin and gave Win a knowing look. "But I must make sure the kitchen is in order for dessert."

Helena looked pointedly at Win. "Aren't you going to pull the chair out for me?"

He jumped up to help her into the chair and pushed her gently forward. Nearby, the waiters were assembling a table of cream puffs and thick slabs of caramel cake.

"People say your daddy makes a lot of money in sugar." She rested her chin on her hands and looked sweetly at him, as if she'd practiced saying inappropriate things her entire life.

"People say you can shoot the beak off a pigeon," Win said, trying not to let his eyes linger too long on hers. "Is it true?"

The girls with satin ribbons held hands and began to dance in a circle nearby, laughing.

"Why don't you come out back and see for yourself?" Helena grinned. Her coy manner attracted Win. This was not the southern bride his father had in mind, and that was precisely the reason she had such an intoxicating effect. Her hair was pinned up, and he could see a slight dusting of translucent powder over her freckles.

Ten minutes later, he stared in disbelief as her father, well shaven except for a silver mustache, unlocked the small enclosure where grouse were kept for dog training. The setting sun bathed the hunting quarters in orange light.

"Percy Glass," the man said, grasping Win's hand, squeezing it tightly.

"Winston Spangler," Win said, trying his best to squeeze back with equal force. "The third."

"I see Helena here roped you into her party trick," Mr. Glass said, dropping the handshake. He wore a well-made dinner jacket and silk pocket square, and combed his silver mustache with a forefinger.

Win looked into the man's eyes. As folksy and kind as Helena's father was, he seemed remote.

Helena's father reached into the pen and then held a quivering grouse against his chest. It was bigger than Win expected, brown with a mottled chest. He made the mistake of looking in the bird's shining eyes, admiring the downy feathers displaced by the man's fingertips.

"You don't need to—"

"Here, Daddy," Helena said, interrupting Win, a rifle in her right hand. "You hold that bird and let me get situated. Just back up a little," she said, waving him off.

Win felt squeamish, like the first day he'd pressed his scalpel to flesh, and winced.

"You're going to turn a loaded gun toward your own father?" Win couldn't help but ask. His eyes widened as she brought the gun in front of her body. She took a deep breath and lowered her shoulders, squaring off. Her finger found the trigger.

"Oh yes. Daddy taught me how. Didn't you, Daddy?"

"We had to find a way to discourage suitors," her father said, nonchalant, scowling at the bird as it wriggled.

The element of performance was not lost on Win. It seemed as though the two had done this routine before. At least they think I'm worth the effort, he thought.

Mr. Glass held the grouse out in front of him at arm's length, his fingers wrapped around its neck. The bird squirmed. "Go on, now, Helena," he said. "She's getting ticklish."

Helena raised the pistol. "One shot for marksmanship," she said, firing at the beak. Win covered his ears too late. The bullet ripped into the bird's small head. "And another to end suffering."

Win flinched as the second shot rang out, and watched as the grouse exploded onto Mr. Glass. He dropped the remnants of the bird into a heap on the ground, then peeled off his blood-speckled dinner jacket.

"There," he said, rubbing his hands, then clapping them together loudly. He walked toward Helena and Win as if nothing untoward had happened, jacket slung over his shoulder. "I'm going to get cleaned up and leave the night to you two young people."

"Thank you, Daddy," Helena said, kissing her father gently on the cheek.

"One day she's going to learn how to split a playing card," Mr. Glass said over his shoulder. "Like Annie Oakley."

"Let's stroll on the beach," she said, turning to Win, who was stunned but offered her his arm. She took it. They walked the boardwalk over the dunes in silence, nodding politely at other couples. He guided her to a wooden swing with an uninterrupted view to the ocean. The sound of waves crashing took the place of conversation.

She opened her small handbag and pulled out a tube of lipstick, running it along her lips in a practiced motion.

He realized that the polite ambivalence he'd always treated young women with would not work. Helena did not waste time feigning innocence. She was magnetic.

"I like your voice," he said.

"Oh," she said, looking down to search her purse again. "It's a sad story."

"Tell me."

"I accidentally drank a large sip of bleach," she said, "when I was two."

"That's awful."

"According to my mother, I've always found trouble without looking too hard."

Win crossed his legs and slapped a mosquito on the back of his neck.

"Do you like it here?" she asked, inching closer to him until the sides of their bodies touched.

"As much as I like it anywhere," he said, shrugging. He envied her confidence.

"Could you ever live here in Carolina?" she said, tucking a loose strand of hair behind her ear. "That's what I really mean."

"I haven't thought about it," he said, flinching a little at her forward manner. "My family's in Texas."

"What's Texas like?"

"I don't know. Dry?"

She played with a gold bracelet on her wrist. "What are your plans for the future?"

It was the exact question he'd been asking himself. He paused.

"I suppose I'll finish medical school," he said. "But when I'm older, I want to travel." He paused. "I'm also a collector."

She stared at him blankly. "Of what?"

"I'm interested in other cultures." He didn't want to admit that he hadn't started collecting anything of substance yet.

"I suppose that's better than cutting people open. Is there much money in other cultures?"

"That's not one of the things I worry about." He shifted uncomfortably on the wooden bench. He could see her freckled arms, and liked them.

"I see," she said, raising an eyebrow. "And why put together a collection? What's the point?"

"I haven't thought out the details," he said, shrugging. "If we're going to make advances in medicine and commerce in the South, we need to see variation. We need bigger minds."

"*I've* never traveled anywhere," she said pointedly. "Is my mind big enough for you?"

He sat up straight. "I didn't mean it like that. I mean—I haven't traveled much, either."

She looked down at her shoes for a moment, white leather oxfords with laces. "We should do something else before we get tired of each other," she said. "Come on."

She pulled him off the bench and back up the boardwalk to the club. It was a warm night, and the buildings glowed. He could make out silhouettes of guests dancing in the large windows, the murmur of their conversations and the local orchestra's music. Their gaiety seemed foreign to him, as it had his entire life, as if the fun others had was just out of reach. He'd always wondered: Were all these people happy, or just better at pretending than he was?

Helena's hand was warm. The skin-to-skin contact was pleasant, the sliding of damp flesh with a few grains of sand between. She pulled him toward the shadowy maintenance area where the men who swept the boardwalk and raked the sand retrieved tools during the day.

"I want to show you something," she said, tugging him into a dark stable that smelled of hay and rotten wood. "This is where they keep the old mannequins. The ones they model bathing costumes on."

Moonlight fell across three ivory mannequins, two female and one male. They had smooth arms and placid porcelain faces. He walked closer for a better look. Their bodies were the color of eggshells, jointed, and stuffed with horsehair. Their delicate mouths and dark eyes gave them a sweet expression.

He reached out to touch the male's arm. It was soft, like the expensive silk hosiery his mother once ordered from Paris.

He could see Helena's pensive face in the light. She chewed her lip and looked like she was thinking.

"I have an idea," she said, closing in on one of the female forms. "I want you to help me lift this gal right here. Let's call her Loretta."

"Do you think it's okay to move her?"

"Don't be chicken."

"I'm being *reasonable*."

"Loretta is an ideal woman, really," Helena went on, ignoring him. "She's obedient and available. She has Hollywood dreams, Lowcountry circumstances."

He rested his fingers on the mannequin's neck. He was apprehensive about whatever Helena had in mind. His brother had once told him: *The only real risk we have in this life is our reputation.* His father's money was good for getting out of trouble, and the brothers had benefited from the special status accorded them, missing class as they'd liked, turning in assignments late, and sleeping through Sunday school.

"You take her shoulders, and I'll get the feet." Helena stood back and appraised the mannequin's rigid body. "Ready?" she said, bending down to reach for the ankles. "One, two, three, lift!"

Win held the mannequin easily with one arm. He could feel Loretta's breasts, firm and conspicuous, pressing against his hip.

"Where to?" he asked.

"The old house," she said, "where Betty and Letty claim heaven opens up."

"Why there?"

"Why not?" Helena said, shrugging. "And don't get me started on those two. They need money like the rest of us, and half the county is embarrassed about their scheme, while the other half is mad they didn't think of it first."

"So you don't believe it?"

Helena put one hand on her hip, still holding Loretta's ankle with the other. "I've seen Letty whip her dog raw with a switch. Now, tell me—if the Lord's going to choose a place to let down a ladder, is it going to be a house where a red-faced woman beats a dog?"

He thought it odd a woman who had no reservations killing a bird for sport should object to a whipped dog.

"The only reason people are supporting this Lowcountry Miracle," she said, "is because they need it so badly. And it's making some people, like your friend Sonny Lee, *piles* of money. Let's move close to the dunes," she whispered.

It was awkward walking in the sand with the mannequin. They stumbled and muffled their laughter but fell into reverent silence as they approached the dark house. It was hot. Helena's hair had come down. The ocean seemed louder, and the sea oats bent in the slight breeze.

"Let's put Loretta on her knees," Helena whispered. Her hair blew across her face.

The mannequin's knees didn't want to give, but when they did, they made a loud crack as if they had broken. Win froze. A minute later, after no one had stirred in the house, Helena began repositioning the mannequin. "I think she should raise her hands in prayer," she whispered, pulling the hands to a position just underneath the mannequin's soft chin.

"Dear God," Helena whispered. "Forgive us our trespasses and let your will prevail in our lives.

"They won't stay," she complained as she tried again to get the mannequin's hands in position. The sand shifted underneath their feet. Loretta was now front and center of the Lowcountry Miracle, kneeling in the low, grassy dunes between the beach and the old cottage.

He tried interlocking the rigid thumbs, but the arms fell to the mannequin's side. He looked down to see Helena pulling the laces from her oxfords. She tied them together into one long string and circled the mannequin's wrists. "There," she said, leaning back to admire her work. "Prime position. Devout and ready for the Second Sunday Sunrise service."

They turned away from Loretta's bound and naked form, which looked to Win like a crude human sacrifice, and ran back toward the Calhoun Beach Club. Helena's shoes wouldn't stay on without the laces. She took them off, laughing with her head tilted back and her blond hair loose, and handed them to Win, who held them for her until they reached the boardwalk, holding each other's arms, gasping for breath.

Farther down the beach, there were fires crackling and small groups of people strolling toward the water.

Helena smoothed her hair and dusted the sand from her legs, then reached out for her shoes and smiled. "Save a seat for me on the wagon tomorrow," she said, reaching out for his hand and letting hers linger for a minute before withdrawing, finger by finger.

He watched her move toward the light, and the dancing people. He felt, for the first time in years, that he too had a small portion of happiness.

5

Early the next morning, Win opened the doors to his balcony and let the warm breeze pour into his room. He sat with his feet on the railing and thought about Helena. She felt alive and available, an antidote to the gloom of the last few years. After struggling through medical school, Win felt as though he deserved this lightness. This desire.

Win went downstairs, where he drank strong, black coffee and stood by the wagon that would soon take the Calhoun Club patrons to the Sunday Service. The wagon was painted bright white, and the bench cushions were covered in blue-and-white-striped canvas. A stable hand hitched the horses, and Win heard the jangle of brass and soft swearing as one of the horses shat, and the mess was quickly shoveled away.

Religion had never affected him the way it did his father, who kept a preacher on staff, an old friend named Sam Noble, a former football player turned minister who liked liquor and long funeral orations.

The sun beat down on the back of Win's neck, and he was hot in his suit. Couples stepped into the wagon, and he nodded at them. Sunday mornings had a whiff of solemnity here, a break from small talk about sports and cotton yields. The men were freshly shaven, and the women smelled of soap and folded their light dresses underneath their bodies as they sat, dabbing the sweat from their brows with linen handkerchiefs.

Helena's father escorted her to the wagon, nodding to his friends. She looked sullen but beautiful in a freshly ironed white cotton dress. Mr. Glass and Win shook hands.

Helena sat down next to him and scowled. "Why didn't you tell me you were leaving tomorrow?" she asked.

"It didn't come up," he said, bewildered. He could smell her floral perfume. Gardenias.

"I don't *want* you to leave." She turned away from him with her arms crossed over her body. He squeezed her shoulder, hoping to make her smile, but she only glared straight ahead.

He looked at the sweep of her blond brows, the slight dampness on her cheekbones. He didn't want to leave, either.

An older man in a beige linen suit with a thin, serious face and soft voice boarded the wagon and stood above the passengers. "I'm Reverend Walter Paul," he said, "and I'll be guiding you to the space of the apparition."

The small crowd nodded respectfully.

"I want to caution you that we had vandals last night," the reverend said gravely. He clutched one of the wagon railings for support.

Win didn't dare look at Helena.

"Are you sure it wasn't a sign from God?" Helena asked in a saccharine voice, tilting her eyes up toward him.

"Positive," the reverend said, squinting to look at her. "Though the Lord does work in mysterious ways, especially in our new age. Let's move on to the house, shall we?" He made a sign to the driver, and the two draft horses began to pull the wagon toward the sisters' house.

The horses' hooves kicked up sand. The men and women in the wagon were quiet. Win studied the dunes until he saw the mannequin. Loretta looked broken and obscene in the sand, as if she'd been left to beg for her life.

"The morning light has not been kind to her," Helena whispered.

The wagon came to a stop. Win could see a small, decrepit beach cottage with peeling paint, fifty feet behind the dunes. Soon the two sisters came out and stood silently on their porch, straight-faced and plain. They looked exactly as Win had expected—dour and old-fashioned. The people in the wagon murmured. One sister wore a yellow housedress and the other, calico. Minutes passed. Win swatted flies. Helena fanned herself for a while, then turned it on Win playfully.

"You've forgiven me for leaving tomorrow, then?"

"Never," she said, sliding closer to him.

After twenty minutes, one of the sisters pointed to a break in the clouds, and the wagon passengers gasped.

"Oh, they're liars," Helena groaned. "All of them."

She didn't talk much on the ride home, but he liked the way her body felt next to his. He searched for something hopeful to say but couldn't find it.

"We'll write letters," he suggested.

She rolled her eyes. "I'm not the letter-writing type," she said, and tapped the flask in his pocket.

"Here?" he whispered.

"Yes," she said with a startling frankness in her eyes. "Don't be uptight."

He handed it to her, worried Sonny would hear reports of him giving scotch to a woman. A young, unmarried woman.

She closed her eyes for a moment as the drink went down. "Could we arrange time tonight?" she asked, looking up again at him.

"An assignation?" he asked, raising an eyebrow.

"Don't call it that," she said, scowling. "You make it sound like work."

"I'd love to."

"In old stables after dinner, then."

==

The clatter of the dining room seemed frenetic that night, the clanging of the silverware like bells, the laughter of the young girls hovering over the pie station painfully loud. There was too much salt on the fish or maybe not enough. Win couldn't trust his senses.

He knew where Helena was in the large room without looking. He gave up eating and wiped his mouth, crossed and uncrossed his legs. What kind of meeting did she have in mind?

He got to the stables too early and felt foolish, standing there with the two remaining mannequins. In the dark his anticipation mixed with shame, but he couldn't turn away now. And what would he be turning away from? He wasn't sure he could name it.

Moonlight leaked through cracks in the barn roof.

The door opened. He heard her footsteps coming toward him on the old barn boards.

"You're here," he said, feeling inept. He worried that she knew more than he did about what was going to happen.

Helena laced her fingers around his neck and leaned into him with the full length of her body, tilting her head toward his so that their lips met. She touched the side of his face and pulled away for a moment, looking into his eyes before moving again toward his mouth.

She pulled him out of the stable and to the beach, moving as if she knew he would follow. As he stumbled in the sand behind her, he felt as though he could see sparks where he stepped.

At a pitch-dark place behind a dune, she kissed him again. The warmth and wetness of her mouth surprised him. Then she pulled away, abruptly.

"What's wrong?" he asked, wanting her to stay close, wanting more.

Helena didn't answer. She shook her head and looked out at the water.

He kept quiet. He could feel her thinking again, but the want inside him was growing.

She sighed and reached for his belt.

"What are you doing?"

"Please," she said, eyes determined, fingers working faster. "We might never see each other again."

He kissed her neck and the top of her breasts, let his cheek rest on her warm skin.

It happened quickly, the undoing of his trousers, the hitching of her skirt. The feeling inside him shifted from awkwardness to urgency. He didn't know what to do, but his body seemed to have some idea, and as they moved together they toppled into the dunes and his teeth clenched. He had a sense that he had blacked out from release and pleasure, that his ears were full, that he had found the feeling he'd been missing his entire life, a sense of oneness, an explosive quiet.

Then, coming to, he realized half of her face was in the sand. Her body had gone stiff beneath him. He rolled away from her. "Oh God," he said, reaching for her hand. "I'm sorry."

She picked herself up and brushed the sand off her dress, ignoring his reach. "It's always the same," she said, spitting sand from her mouth. She seemed to glare and smile at him. He couldn't make sense of anything. He sat down on the beach and brought his forehead to his knees, catching his breath. When he looked up, she was gone.

6

Helena coiled herself into a knot on the cool tile of her childhood bathroom at Stillwood, where she'd brushed her teeth and combed her hair for nineteen years. Where she spent afternoons practicing smiles in the mirror, and styled her hair with piping hot tongs and curling fluid.

"Play your best hand at the club while you still have your looks," Mary-Grace had advised one morning over breakfast. "We're in the final month of our membership." Percy was hiding from his creditors, leaving letters and bills unopened and unanswered on his desk. Sonny Lee had given him a one-month grace period in which to come up with his late annual club dues.

Well, she'd gone and done what her mother had asked, hadn't she?

Helena expected bravery from herself, but felt terrified. She didn't really think it would work this way, so fast. The mechanics of sex were still coming together for her.

She threw up again.

Damn it.

June Wheatley, the young housekeeper with wide-set eyes, mousy hair, and large, clumsy feet, came to the bathroom door. She had pale skin and a space between her teeth and believed ardently in the Lowcountry Miracle, cutting out newspaper articles and saving them in the pages of her Bible. June had been orphaned years before and had what Mary-Grace Glass called an "unhealthy attachment" to Helena. "She'd rather be your sister when she should be folding your clothes," she'd said.

June exchanged a look with Helena, who wiped her mouth, still crouched by the toilet.

"Lord, have mercy," June said. "I'll get you a cold washcloth." She turned from the door. The old house echoed with her heavy footfalls, the weight of her big bones.

Women know.

7

Old rice plantations were nestled along the Ashley River. The columned houses rose above the marsh grass, kept up by old southern families trying to find their place in the changing order of the world.

Win Spangler arrived at Stillwood just before cocktail hour. He'd heard that people on River Road lived in the past, but even he was shocked by the cotton blowing across the road, men and women crouching in the fields, the mules pulling carts underneath the boughs of large oaks. The woods on either side of the road were dark, except for the light that fought through the thick brush and caught on the white petals of dogwoods.

The driver paused at the driveway, then got out to open the wrought iron gates. A wooden sign, painted black with gold lettering, hung from the branch of a live oak. It read STILLWOOD, 1798.

They drove down the winding private road, through a magnificent old maritime forest, past horse pastures, a peach orchard, old shacks, and lush gardens with camellias in bloom. Finally, the manor itself came into view, the brown Ashley River twisting like a snake behind it.

The facade of the old house had been freshly painted for the wedding, though Win could see that the sides were peeling and had been quickly whitewashed. The Federal-style house was three stories tall with a portico and pediment out front. There was a brick foundation, a double stairway tumbling down from the porch, and copious ironwork covered in ivy and fig vines. A circular drive arced in front of two brick columns with gaslights and a walkway that led to the front of the house.

The driver opened his door, and Win got out, breathing in the humid air. Intuitively he walked toward the brick veranda on the side of the house, which overlooked the river. He stared down at the terraced gardens that sloped toward the brown water and the huge live oaks leering over the riverbanks and rice ponds.

Dear God, he thought. Help me make this work.

The reality of his situation began to bear down on him like the heat of the late-afternoon sun. So much had changed in a few months. Helena had reached out to him at home in Texas, to explain that she'd missed her cycle and conducted a urine test. "I have some news," she'd said, in that raspy voice of hers.

Win had decided on what he felt was the most honorable path: proposing to Helena, and leaving medical school.

Helena burst through a side door of the house and threw her arms around him. She was wearing a red dress and looked the same as he remembered: fresh, blond, athletic. But she was not the same.

"It's good to see you again," he said. A small part of him

wanted to turn and run. But another part of him was hopeful. Maybe they could be happy.

"Funny how things turn out sometimes," she said, her green eyes searching his, as if looking for reassurance he could not provide.

"Perhaps just a little faster than we'd planned," he said politely. He felt like they were two strangers in a store, talking about the price of apples.

"You can still make love to me when I'm pregnant, you know," she whispered.

He cleared his throat, embarrassed. The truth was that he was afraid of hurting her, and the child she was carrying.

The housekeeper—an unnaturally tall young girl—brought out a pitcher of punch for them. Her hair was parted starkly down the center of her head, with what looked like mathematical precision.

"June's been with us since she was twelve," Helena told him as the woman walked back to the kitchen. "Her parents worked the fields, but they both died of the flu. Mama gave her an attic bedroom and warned her not to confuse charity with affection, or she'd send her to the textile mills. I don't think she's ever been farther than twenty miles from this house her whole life."

"Got it. Anything else I should know?"

"Let's see," Helena said, touching her brow. "We count egrets instead of sheep at night. You can use any swear word but *goddamn*. Never challenge Mother in public. Steer clear of conversations about the Lost Cause. Don't hang around Indigo Run after dark. Any vice you need you can probably get behind Matthew, Mark, Luke, and John's bait shop, but don't let Mother catch you back there. I think that's it."

"Oh," she said, holding up a finger. "And remember that Mother *never* uses the powder room. Toilet talk offends her honor."

Win laughed, pushing down the fear rising within him that he had gone and done a stupid thing that was going to define his life.

Helena's parents, Mary-Grace and Percy Glass, descended onto the veranda, well-dressed and fragrant. Win felt a new part of his life beginning in a place where he had never intended to live.

"Welcome to the family home," Mary-Grace said. She had two strands of pearls around her neck and large rings that seemed almost burdensome on her thin frame.

Win kissed her on the cheek and shook Percy's hand, fighting off shame. He felt as though he should apologize for Helena's pregnancy, but there seemed to be an unspoken agreement among all of them to proceed with a brave face. He reached for Helena's hand. They drank punch until the sun set. "You're doing fine," she assured him.

"Thanks."

She leaned over. "I suppose I should also tell you that my parents are second cousins and they prefer not to mention that part," she said quietly. "My guess is that they don't like each other that much, but my mother wanted to keep her last name and the family home."

"Interesting," he said, embarrassed.

For a moment, he lingered in the central hallway of Stillwood, which was painted a crimson red, even the ceiling. A grandfather clock kept time nearby. Wedding pictures and portraits of the family's Confederate soldiers, grandfathers and great-uncles, lined the red walls. The space seemed to close in around him, as if he was standing inside the central artery of the house.

It's going to work out, Win thought. He was putting on a brave face for Helena, but also himself.

Mary-Grace gathered guests around the dinner table before supper to show them her father's brass rice scales and tell them the history of the house. She wore a plum-colored dress and stood with authority at the head of the table. Her freshly tinted auburn hair fell past her shoulders, curling upward just so. A pressed, white linen tablecloth covered the Chippendale table. Monogrammed silver shone from the place settings.

"Mama and Daddy were good people," Mary-Grace said, looking directly at Win. "You can be proud to call Stillwood home."

He smiled back at her. His day had been full of false smiles. I'm a good man, he kept telling himself. This is what good men do.

Standing with her fingertips on the tablecloth, a proud smile tugged at Mary-Grace's lips. "The house was nearly burned when Union troops came up the Ashley River," she said, turning again to Win, "but my great-uncle Lindley Glass set out smallpox flags around the perimeter of the place, and they left us alone for days.

"Eventually," she continued, clearly satisfied with her family's cleverness, "Union soldiers burned the north wing as my mother moved silver to an empty grain silo, all the while cursing the Yankee boy who beheaded the garden statues and set the water buffalo free. Granddaddy *did* have an experiment with water buffalo, believe it or not, but the Yankees ate five of them. *Ate* them! We have the oldest camellias in the state, and the gardens," she paused for effect, "are French."

"How's a South Carolina garden French?" Win whispered.

"It just is," Helena whispered back. "In spirit."

"The gardens are world-renowned," Mary-Grace went on. "Wisteria, azaleas, gingko, jessamine. We have four seasons of flowers. Senator Calhoun *loved* to walk our gardens when he visited—he was a friend of the family."

"They're eaten up in it, aren't they?" Win said as he and Helena went outside for a brief smoke after dinner. They stood on the veranda, looking out at the river's brackish water, where schooners and barges once moved rice, and now moved fertilizer.

"In what?"

"Being from here. It matters to them." Win lit Helena's cigarette first, then his own. He exhaled slowly.

"My family was powerful before the war," Helena said, exhaling. "They lost standing and want to regain it. That's all."

"That's all," Win said, pausing as if to savor the idea. He laughed and took another drag from his cigarette.

Helena pointed out a shape in the river, a deer swimming to the marshland on the far banks.

"Seems to me a haunted sort of place," Win said.

"The past matters here," Helena said.

"All the parties, peach brandy, and water moccasins a man could want," Win said, raising an eyebrow before they rejoined her family inside.

"We hunt in the morning," Percy told him, grabbing him forcefully on the shoulder.

"I'm sorry," Win said, holding up a hand. "But might I pass on the invitation this time? I'm exhausted."

"Of course," Percy said, though he was clearly disappointed.

Whenever he spoke to his future father-in-law, Win felt as if he was looking for the man inside but could only find manners.

He stepped into the crimson hallway and glanced at the portraits of Helena's ancestors, feeling the pale eyes of Lindley Glass follow him into the parlor.

"One last toast for the evening," Percy said, beckoning Win into the dining room.

"To family," Percy said.

"To family," Win repeated.

"Of course, Helena can't debut at the St. Cecilia Ball as we'd always planned, but it's an excellent match between prominent southern families," Mary-Grace said, sipping from her drink. "Just not as local as we'd hoped."

"Jesus Christ, Mother," Helena said, touching her temples.

"Don't take the Lord's name in vain, Helena."

"Was there a coconut cake?" Win asked as disarmingly as he could. "I could've sworn I smelled one earlier." One day into his new life, and he couldn't deny his dread was growing. The old plantation was a world unto itself, and Win knew, in that moment, it would never really be his.

==

Win and Helena married on a warm October day. The sun was bright, and the lawn parched. White ribbons were tied around the trunks of large trees, and June set bunches of wild sweetgrass and roses out on the tables. Win's father had sent the family preacher, Sam Noble, in his place, and the man arrived with a chess set, flask, and a funeral oratory he'd adjusted for the wedding service.

"Should I be offended that your family didn't come?" Helena asked, turning to him, lace running the lengths of her arms, a long veil flowing from a crescent-shaped pearl comb. The cut of her gown obscured the fact that she was pregnant, but wouldn't for much longer.

"My father's frail," Win said. "I told you that." He didn't want Helena to feel hurt. The truth was that his father was enraged. Win suspected Sam Noble was there to report back on the state of affairs at Stillwood.

"You know," Mary-Grace leaned in to whisper to Win, "I like the looks of Mr. Noble. That old minister of ours is into the brandy lately, and I was thinking that maybe your preacher Noble would like to stay on with us? A token from home for you?"

"That's something we could discuss," Win said, hopeful his mother-in-law was just being polite. Plus, he knew Preacher Noble was into worse than brandy.

"Helena," she whispered. "Don't forget to hold your belly in when you walk the aisle."

"You too," Helena whispered back. Mary-Grace glared at her.

The wedding party fanned themselves underneath branches covered in resurrection ferns. Helena said they could go for a hundred years without water, and then come back to life with one good rain. Win looked at her face, hoping to catch a glimpse of hope or happiness, something that would reassure him about the future. She compulsively ran her hands over her growing belly, as if in disbelief, as if reminding herself the child was still there.

He stared at the curling, browned ferns as they waited for guests to be seated. A few rows of chairs had been set up in front of the river. He reached for Helena's hand and squeezed it. She squeezed back.

Percy escorted them to the edge of the river. Win, Helena, and Preacher Noble stepped into a small wooden boat, which

Percy pushed gently from the banks. A band played from the sandy shore. Ushers passed woven baskets full of rice. Mary-Grace wept into a linen handkerchief.

"Great will be your glory in not falling short of your natural character," Preacher Noble told them. He was thick necked and balding, and he looked at the couple with serious brown eyes.

It occurred to Win that it was precisely his natural character that had caused him the most trouble.

That morning, the *Courier* had praised the intricacy of Helena's dress, the thousands of pearl beads hand sewn by Letty Sims.

"I do," Helena said, bringing a hand to her brow. The sun was in her eyes, and it looked to Win as if she was crying. Her veil trailed in the southerly flowing water, and a single drop of sweat fell from her forehead.

That night, when they were finally alone, Helena followed a long-standing Glass wedding tradition: the gifting of a family pistol to her husband.

"What's this?" Win asked, opening the antique wooden box.

"The idea," Helena said coyly, "is that you'll shoot yourself before you leave me." She laughed, presenting it to him on her outstretched palms. Engraved on the side of the barrel: *till death*.

It was a flash of the woman he'd fallen for at the beach club. Irreverent and dangerous. He liked it.

Win locked the gun in the top drawer of his desk. "I swear on my life," he said, turning to her, earnest and slightly afraid, "I will always be here for you and our child."

He was beginning to know the heat of her skin, the smell of her perfume. He enjoyed the way her hoarse voice sounded when she sang, the way she exchanged glances with him when her mother said something off-color.

"In times of plenty and in times of famine," Helena said, suddenly serious. "Young and old."

"Always."

8

Helena roared like a lion, two days into a grueling labor. She'd had a fruitless night of contractions and was livid.

She thrashed in the heirloom four-poster bed, the same one the Glass women had used for three generations. Her long blond hair was damp with sweat, even though it was a cool spring morning. A small wedge of sunlight fell across the pale floral wallpaper.

"For God's sake, Helena, stop groaning," Mary-Grace said, leaning over the bed in a pink day dress. She dabbed Helena's forehead with a washcloth. "Arm yourself with prayer and bring your child into the world with dignity."

"Go to hell, Mother," Helena hissed, trying to catch her breath. She clenched her fists. "This is all your fault."

"I hardly think so!" Mary-Grace stepped back from the bed, posture rigid. She tucked her thick auburn hair behind one ear. She'd freshened her lipstick before the doctor arrived.

Helena glared at her mother, whose belief in decorum was absolute. Mary-Grace had worn large heirloom jewelry to the occasion, pearl necklaces and cocktail rings that weighed down her thin neck and fingers.

"You can't take it personally," Dr. Lloyd Harris, the slow-talking town physician, said quietly, placing a calm hand on Mary-Grace's arm. "I've heard much worse."

"Stop *looking* at me like that," Helena said, crushing her eyes shut.

"Like what?" Mary-Grace said, offended.

"Like I'm going to die."

"Well, stop *acting* that way."

"Ladies," Dr. Harris said, sweat beading on his bald head. "Arguing won't do."

Two years earlier he'd spent weeks in a damp trench along the river Meuse with a bayonet strapped to his back. Everyone in town knew the doctor didn't do his best work in a loud room. His nerves were bad. Helena wished there were another doctor in town.

He stepped away from the bed and spoke quietly to Mary-Grace. "I think we need to secure her wrists," he said, pulling the restraints from his bag. "I'm afraid she'll fall off the bed."

"No," Helena said, moaning and wrapping her arms around her own body, as if to protect herself. "I won't let you."

But she felt too tired to fight, and Dr. Harris gripped one wrist, then the other. His hands were rough and dry against her skin.

"Why do you hate me?"

"We're *helping* you," Mary-Grace snapped, looking down at Helena with her sharp blue eyes.

"Hush, hush," Dr. Harris said. "It'll be all right." He wiped his forehead as he sat back to observe his work.

Helena swore, spat, and rubbed her wrists raw on the leather restraints, fighting the waves of pain in her body. "I *want* to die," she said, looking them both in the eyes. She meant it. God, how she meant it.

"Summon Preacher Noble," Mary-Grace called down the

stairs. The minister arrived within the hour and stood, hulking and quiet, drinking coffee in the shadowed corner of the bedroom.

Dr. Harris injected Helena with morphine.

She entered a timeless space, where she could not think, or see. There was a blind urgency to release the pressure in her body, to complete the act, to find relief.

Finally, Dr. Harris wrenched the baby from Helena's body with forceps. She had long ceased screaming and now dry-heaved over the side of the bed.

"It's a girl," Dr. Harris said quietly.

Helena, feeling both empty and full, groped the air for the child. "Give her to me," she whispered, holding out her arms.

The baby was delivered early at home, Mary-Grace claimed to friends, though Sally-Anne Spangler was a healthy eight-pound child with full cheeks, born exactly nine months after her parents met. Blankets and infant gowns had been hastily embroidered.

Mary-Grace spoke to Dr. Harris in a hushed voice in the hallway the next morning, while Helena listened from the bed. "Lloyd, I worry the child was conceived in lust and not good Christian love," Mary-Grace said. "What does it mean for Sally-Anne?"

"Mama," Helena called out hoarsely. "I can *hear* you." Sally-Anne began to cry.

What do I do? Helena wondered, looking at the whimpering baby. "Shhh," she said. "Shhh."

"Don't worry," Dr. Harris said, laughing uncomfortably, pausing in the bedroom doorway. "Sally-Anne is a child of God. Born on a Sunday, no less. She has a charmed life ahead, I'm sure."

"What a perfect baby," Helena whispered hoarsely, knowing it was something all mothers said. She meant it nonetheless. Despite her love of her daughter, her body had torn badly during labor, and in the following days a deep melancholy settled over her. She bled in shocking amounts and was incontinent. Her breasts swelled with milk, and she felt feverish all over.

"Why didn't you tell me?" she asked her mother, who was folding a blanket at the foot of the bed the next morning. She felt betrayed.

"Tell you *what*?" Mary-Grace said, stopping midfold, looking at her daughter. Sally-Anne began to cry in her bassinet.

"How violent it would be," Helena said, starting to cry herself. "How everything would change."

"You were already pregnant."

"No one told me," Helena whispered.

What a horrible secret women kept, she thought. It was perverse of them not to warn everybody else.

"No one told me, either," Mary-Grace said as she placed the baby onto Helena's breast. Helena winced and bit her lip, turning away from Sally-Anne to stare out of the window at the *Camellia japonica*, a shell-pink April Blush with a sunny yellow inside.

The afternoon sun taunted her. She wanted to walk toward it and keep going. She had the horrible feeling that life was now behind her.

"You'll be beautiful again," Mary-Grace said quietly, touching her daughter's blond hair. "Just give it time."

"That's not what . . ."

"Just give it time."

"I declare," Win said cheerfully, holding his daughter for the first time. "She's lovely."

"You have to say that," Helena said flatly, unable to access her normal range of emotions.

Win was thin, energetic, freshly shaven. He'd assumed she would bear him a son, whom he'd planned to name after himself—but call Skip. "I mean to imply any misfortune will simply skip over our child," he'd said in a grand way that irritated Helena.

Though there was no son, the nickname stuck.

Win handed Skip back to Helena, who was reclining in bed. She cradled the baby, feeling an odd mix of deep love and terror.

Win brought a stack of books for her to read. She looked up at his soft brown eyes and starched shirt and sighed.

"You don't like these books?" he asked, running a hand through his wavy hair. His eagerness annoyed her, made her feel as if he was atoning for something. She could see him looking her up and down, worrying over her, wondering why she didn't get out of the bed.

Some days, he still seemed like a stranger.

"Perhaps other titles?" she said, thinking of how young he looked and how old she suddenly felt. She closed her eyes, fatigued. She'd lost the energy to be appealing, to feign curiosity in her new husband's whims.

"I'll read to you, then."

He was resolute and sat perched on the bedside for an hour, droning on. "I'm tired," she said, but he stayed with his daily program.

"It's something constructive I can do while you convalesce," he said.

Helena withdrew. The ringing of the grandfather clock—

a sound she'd grown up with—woke her in the night. The sound of her mother sucking on butterscotch candy enraged her. Skip's long crying jags made her cry, too. Sometimes they lay in the bed, skin to skin, crying together.

=

"Don't leave the window open," Helena whispered to Win when he came in late one evening to check on her. "She'll come in."

She was not fully awake.

"Who?" Win leaned down for the answer.

"The hag." Helena turned to face him, her green eyes staring through his. "The Night Hag will walk up from the river on her scaly chicken legs, climb through the window, and leap upon your chest until you can't breathe."

"My God, Helena. That's just a story people around here tell."

"Close the window," she said.

"All right, but it's going to get hot in here." He pulled the window down tight. He did it to pacify her, she could tell. He wasn't the type of man who could believe in anything past his own experience.

"She can enter through a keyhole," she said, gripping his arm, "and ride a man like a horse."

"Settle down, darling."

"You'll see."

=

Dr. Harris paid weekly visits from his office in Charleston. He provided a sleeping tonic for Helena, whom he said was suffering from a bad case of nerves. "We don't want to move into the territory of hysteria," he cautioned, handing her the first dose.

Helena put the spoon to her mouth and cringed at the scent, the bitter taste.

"She needs rest," Dr. Harris told Win and Mary-Grace. "Paraldehyde is gentle—I used it myself after the war."

Helena didn't like the taste of the tonic, but she liked the way it numbed the sharp edges of her sadness. Her feelings receded like a tide. Sadness became nothingness.

In the morning, she brushed her lips against the softness of her daughter's forehead, breathing her daughter in: sweat mixed with something floral. Southern heat on fresh skin.

Skip was wrapped in pink muslin that accentuated the flush of her cheeks.

Fatigue quickly overcame Helena again, and she wanted to sleep. She called for June to take the baby.

Win came in to lie next to Helena, sipping iced tea, stroking her hair, reading to her from his favorite adventure novels. Men on pirate ships, men in love.

Helena now slept in twelve- and fourteen-hour shifts and did not enjoy nursing Skip, flinching when her daughter's small lips searched for her breast. The baby began to lose weight, her features sharpening, legs shrinking. Helena's milk began to dry. "I'm sorry," she whispered to Skip.

Dr. Harris was called into Helena's bedroom on a Sunday afternoon. "I recommend a wet nurse," he said. "As soon as possible."

"Shouldn't it come more naturally?" Win asked, turning to Helena. "Couldn't you try harder?"

She could see the disappointment on his face, the seed of resentment blossoming within him. It was growing within her, too. The whip-poor-wills called after sunset, too close to the house this year: *Poor will, poor will.* A bad omen.

Butter softened on the counter. Cotton was planted in the Glass fields. Mary-Grace read the society column out loud each morning over her lukewarm coffee, as if to remind them all where they were not but could have been: visiting friends in the city, graduating from the medical college, attending the St. Cecilia Ball in a new dress.

Helena watched Win riding her horse through the fields. He said he was watching the farmhands shovel oyster shells back into the river, feeding the beds. She knew he was lonely. So was she.

Dr. Harris promised to bring a suitable nurse soon.

Helena kissed her daughter's forehead. "I will get better," she said, holding Skip, whose eyes were swollen from crying. "And I will raise you to be stronger than I ever was."

9

"Another day and we might have lost the child," Dr. Harris whispered as he showed Marie Olsen upstairs to nurse her charge. "The mother's milk has all but dried, and the baby is thin and lethargic."

The petite gray-eyed woman nodded, taking in the bloodred hallway and photographs of soldiers as she trailed the doctor upstairs. The scent of roses and old plaster. She comforted her infant son, Ase, who was slung over one shoulder. *Shh, shh.*

What kind of place was this? she wondered. It looked like something from a history book. A bad one.

"Where are you from again?" Dr. Harris asked.

"Norway."

Marie knew she'd confused him, showing up at his office with her lace collar and regal posture, command of several languages, and no money or husband. Her waist-long hair was twisted into a chignon, though a few loose curls always managed to escape.

She settled her sleepy son in one of the nursery's twin beds while Dr. Harris lifted Skip from the crib. "This is Sally-Anne. They call her Skip," he said, offering the child to Marie.

He stood over her for a moment as she sat down in the rocking chair and began to unbutton her blouse.

"A moment alone, if you please," she asked, looking up at him, tired.

Dr. Harris cleared his throat, as if surprised by her directness. "Certainly," he said.

She heard his footsteps as he descended the stairs, and exhaled in relief.

Marie looked at the small, dehydrated infant in her arms, blond hair beginning to curl upward from Skip's head, cheeks patchy from crying. "You poor girl," she said, clucking her tongue. "You must be so thirsty."

But Marie's milk would not let down. She was anxious in this new place, tired from travel. She moved Ase onto a blanket in front of the rocking chair and nudged him gently with her toe. He woke and began to cry. The milk came, though she felt guilty giving it away to someone other than her son. "Soon enough, *elskede*," she whispered.

She guided Skip's mouth toward her breast, shut her eyes, and felt tears slide down her own face. When she looked up a moment later, a young woman in a white cotton nightgown was standing in the door frame, freckles dotted across her nose, her eyelids heavy. There was something ghostly about her; was she sleepwalking?

"Thank you for feeding her," the woman said before closing the door and stumbling back to another bedroom. "I wanted to, but I couldn't."

The mother, Marie thought.

She glanced around the nursery, a large room on the third floor with walls papered in red toile, and two twin beds. There was a fireplace, a shelf of books, and a rocking chair. A little worn, but comfortable.

"Would you like some coffee?" Win asked when she returned downstairs, her sleeping son resting comfortably over one shoulder. Win was lanky and seemed like he was only playing the part of man of the house.

Marie shook her head, not wanting to appear needy. But yes, she very much wanted a steaming cup of black coffee.

"Did you make the trip alone?" he asked, drinking a sip from his mug.

"It is just us," she said, patting Ase softly on the back. She'd resolved not to speak of her reasons for leaving home.

"I hope you'll be happy here," Win said, setting his mug on a side table so he could escort her to the front door. "We'll ready a bed in the nursery for you tonight. Dr. Harris says Skip needs all the feedings you can manage. In the meantime, I'll look for a more permanent home for you and your son."

"May I ask after the mother?" Marie said, thinking of the woman she'd seen. Dr. Harris had told her nothing about the family, other than the fact that the husband would pay her well.

Win took a deep breath and leaned against the door frame,

looking pained. "Helena had a challenging labor and prefers to convalesce in her room," he said.

"It is a difficult time for a woman," Marie said knowingly.

The next two weeks exhausted her. Skip was ravenous, feeding every two hours. While Marie acknowledged the baby's need to make up lost meals, she was taxed, and not making enough milk for Ase. Neither child was satisfied, and both cried constantly.

What have I done? she wondered. But Marie trusted her ability to outsmart the situation, to work or think her way out of it. Plus, she'd quickly developed a soft spot for the girl.

"Patience, little Skip," she said, bringing the child into her arms to comfort her. "You will get everything you need."

The first installment of cash was most welcome; it was all she had. She thumbed through the bills—the money was still foreign to her—and tucked the envelope into her fine leather luggage, filled with relief and shame. If her mother or husband could see her like this, taking this sort of work, beyond desperate—the thought nauseated her.

Better times will come, she told herself.

The following week, Marie moved from the nursery into one of the tenant cottages on Indigo Run, a rough dirt road where Stillwood's farmhands and sharecroppers lived in cabins built for the rice plantation's slaves. Upon first glance, the living conditions seemed unfathomable, two rooms split by a crumbling central fireplace.

The past felt uncomfortably close here, as if it were being kept at bay but ready to rush in at any moment and take root again.

"Most of the help comes up the path from Indigo Run," Win explained. "It's a shortcut right to the kitchen door."

Marie flinched at the word *help*. She was not used to being talked to this way. She looked at Win's eyes and realized that he believed himself to be kind. She'd known men like this at home, men who were not fully intelligent, nor fully good.

Remember, she cautioned herself. This is only temporary.

She was still astounded by what she'd done—leaving home in the darkness, selling a pearl brooch for a ticket on the boat, purchased under an assumed name. The captain headed for Charleston was the only one who would accept her bribe. She'd never heard of the town but was desperate enough to take a chance. She vomited for two days straight in her shared cabin. From the port in Stavanger, the boat sailed around the tip of Scotland to Port Glasgow, then headed to Halifax Harbour in Nova Scotia. She considered fleeing at each port, but the captain told her to wait until she saw the sun shining in America. Somehow, she'd managed. She was stubborn. Too stubborn.

It was hard not to think about all the different lives she could have had. One at each port. One in her old life, wearing the starburst brooch of pearls. Now, here.

She didn't think she'd chosen well. But, as her mother used to say: the book was not yet written.

Marie didn't know how to cook or keep house, but at least she knew how to care for a child. When she'd taken a lethargic Ase to Dr. Harris's office after the boat docked, and admitted she was penniless, the doctor assured her that her son was simply fatigued, and approached her with the idea of serving as a wet nurse. "I know a good family in great need," he'd said.

Stillwood, she hoped, was merely a short stop on a longer journey. At least it was *something*, she thought. A landing place.

She rocked Ase to sleep in their new cottage when her shifts were over. Even though she was fond of Skip, Marie was always eager to get home and relax in her own space, humble as it was. The housekeeper June rang a loud bell when Skip was in need of an emergency feeding at night, and Marie would sling a sleeping Ase over her shoulder and take the path to the back door that led into the kitchen, where June would be waiting with a crying Skip.

It was an utterly foreign way to live, beholden to the whims and needs of another family.

Down the road, toothless Confederate veterans peeled potatoes and rendered lard. Skinny cows wandered past, and barefoot children sat hungry on sloping porches. The tabby houses had crude, peach-colored walls made of crushed oyster shells, with bright blue doors. The houses were so small that life seemed to spill from them in the form of laundry lines, children, and deer strung up to bleed out.

A neighbor, hair wrapped in a cotton cloth, brought her a bowl of rice and turtle meat for dinner. Her name was Mim. Marie turned her head so that Mim wouldn't see her cry. She was dumb with gratitude, at a loss for how to speak and act in this new world. The English she'd been taught by her tutor didn't match the way the people on River Road spoke, the drawn-out words, bloated vowels, and soft *r*'s.

"Thank you," Marie said, regretting she had nothing to give in return.

How different Indigo Run was from home—the amber-colored grass gone dead in the hot sun, the thick leaves of the magnolia trees that seemed to clap against one another when the wind blew, the wet fields, the reeking marsh, the men singing in the fields who seemed to carry both suffering and joy inside themselves.

=

In the evenings, when Skip was full, Marie tiptoed into Helena's bedroom and deposited the child into the bed with her mother, to give them time together. Anxious, she would check on Skip two or three times to make sure Helena had not rolled on top of her child.

One night, Ase asleep and Skip still nursing, Marie was turning the pages of Henry James's *Roderick Hudson* when Helena walked into the dim room and sat at her feet.

"Tell me a story," Helena said, leaning her forehead against Marie's knee. It was as if the woman had slipped backward in time, perhaps falling into the patterns of her childhood, which the upstairs still bore the markings of: ribbons for riding and swimming, worn books, delicate dolls.

"You should go back to bed, dear."

"Not until you tell me a story," Helena whispered. Her breath had a strong medicinal scent.

Helena would occasionally wander into the nursery this way, not fully conscious, and ask for Skip. Marie, now attached to the girl, could hardly bear to let Helena hold her daughter when she was in this unsteady state. Skip now slept in Marie's arms as if she were her own. Marie cradled the children two at a time, holding them to her bare breasts, which she sometimes smeared with honey in order to heal her cracked skin.

She felt as if she had given a part of herself to Skip, and that there would always be a powerful bond between the three of them.

"Let's see," Marie said, thinking back to the newspapers she'd read during the week. Win set them in a basket in the nursery after he was done reading them.

Marie usually arrived early for her shifts at the plantation house, carrying Ase, keeping an eye out for the latest reading material. She ate open-faced fish sandwiches for breakfast and drank black coffee until four in the afternoon, reading the previous day's paper as she could. She'd decided that the only way to survive this strange time in her life was to lose herself in books and news of the world.

"I read recently of the heath hen," Marie said, remembering Helena's love of hunting birds. "Not a bird I know, but one that has disappeared."

"And what of them?" Helena asked.

"Large fires raged across the scrub where they lived. The heath hen could escape by simply flying away, but she did not."

"Why?"

Marie found herself patting the top of Helena's head, attempting to comfort the woman. She was not without compassion for her, and played with her blond hair a little, lifting a long strand of it and letting it fall again across the woman's neck. The house was quiet until nine chimes from the grandfather clock in the parlor broke the peace.

"I hate that clock," Helena mumbled.

"The birds were loyal to a fault," Marie continued. "The hen would spread her wings over her flightless chicks, refusing to leave them as the flames came closer."

She did not add the detail of the charred bodies left behind in the field, the image of which had put an ache in her heart.

She placed a hand on the thin woman's back and encouraged her to stand. "Let's get you to your room."

"That's a terrible story," Helena said. "You're trying to scare me."

"Only back into your right mind," Marie whispered. "You must fight whatever has hold of you."

"I've tried."

"Try harder."

=

As the months wore on, Marie fed the children and read them stories in the upstairs nursery while dinner was served. Ase and Skip began to nap in the same crib, reaching for each other as they woke. She sang them traditional Norwegian songs her grandfather had taught to her, about a man who skins a crow.

Marie watched others' lives unfold from the nursery window. When she was holding a baby, she felt invisible, as if others assumed every part of her mind was focused on the children.

It wasn't.

She'd been raised with strong self-interest and curiosity about the world, two traits she could not suppress, even under her current circumstances. She studied the family and the fields with a perverse sort of intrigue, as if they might help her understand this place, and her role.

Helena spent the mornings walking in the garden, often settling on a bench near a live oak that overlooked an old rice pond. In the afternoons, she retired to her room.

Mary-Grace spent Saturday mornings in bed, eating bacon from china on a wicker tray, with her bedroom windows flung open. She planned menus, read the paper, and called Helena to her side to gossip. Helena usually fell asleep next to her.

Win retreated to his study after meals, where he smoked and read medical journals. After dessert, Mary-Grace embroidered pillows while Percy stood on the marshy riverbanks alongside the long-legged fishing birds, counting egrets.

The bobcat crept from her den to hunt rabbits. The candles went out, and the house went to sleep.

It was as if they were all waiting for a rock to pierce the un- naturally still surface of the water.

==

Ase and Skip rolled across the nursery floor, fought over books, drew circles on the wallpaper in red crayon, and wrestled at Ma- rie's pale feet. She fed them stories about fjords, walruses that clung to cliffs with tusks, a giant with no heart, and a troll who sent a young boy on a fool's errand to milk lions in a great garden.

"There is water in the world so clear it can hurt your eyes," she told the children. Skip was nearly two years old, and Ase was closing in on three.

Well over a year into her tenure at Stillwood, Marie struggled to acclimate to the heat or manners of the Deep South, the hu- midity and the yes ma'am. The drama of Stillwood's oval stairway and trompe l'oeil ceiling in the dining room was not so differ- ent from her childhood home, but the people that inhabited the place were. She flinched at June's religious fervor, Mary-Grace's social pages, the amount of sugar lumped into tea and coffee. There was the bizarre manner in which the men in the field and the homeowners related to each other, in some moments inti- mate and others brutally condescending.

Could they not see themselves, tiptoeing around this old drama? Stuck in the trench lines of history?

Still, she loved the trees and wading birds, and enjoyed her routine with the children, the time she had to herself while they napped. She found herself fantasizing about the future. What would she do next? Could she take Ase and the money she'd earned and move back to Norway, or perhaps New York?

Occasionally, Win listened at the nursery door when she played with the children. "I like your stories," he said.

She didn't mind him there and offered a smile. "Do you want me to tell you a story?"

"Please."

"Do you know Chaucer's work?"

"I must have forgotten."

"The gardens here make me think of his poem 'The Parlement of Foules.' He describes a dream garden, a place where you can only go when you are asleep. Birds have gathered in this night garden to choose their mates."

"And?"

"And because it is difficult, they decide to put it off until the following year."

He laughed and returned to his study.

She was surprised by the satisfaction she was able to take in this new life, its rhythm and stability, the love that flowed naturally between her and the children. Only occasionally did she let a soft swear slip—*helvete da*—when a child knocked over her tea or the stack of books near the rocking chair toppled over.

Skip was now as nearly dear to her as her own son. The one luxury she allowed Ase was the hindmilk, the fat at the end of feedings. She knew it was time to wean them both.

When the children fought—and they fought as ardently as they played now—Ase would win, as he was the largest and ten months older than Skip. Pale haired, bright eyed, a fast learner. Marie wondered how long it would be until he realized what she'd done, how she had disadvantaged him by leaving their life in Norway.

Skip, though smaller, was wily and determined about the things that mattered to her: books, a stuffed horse, stories with Marie, and time with her mother. She loved sour tastes and stole lemon wedges from tea and iced water, and was prone to climbing—stairs, trees, tabletops. She made direct eye contact when spoken to, knocked into furniture as she moved through a room.

"High-spirited," Win called his daughter.

"Accident-prone. Helena was the same way," Mary-Grace said, listening to Skip babble on the front porch one day while playing at Marie's feet. "All that boyish energy. She'll have to rely upon her looks, if that's the case. Let's hope those come out okay." She laughed a high little laugh.

Marie lifted Skip's face toward hers with one finger. "*I* can see the intelligence in your eyes."

"I was thinking Skip should call me something instead of Grandmother or, God forbid, Granny," Mary-Grace said, sipping her iced tea. "I was thinking Grand-mère. What do you think?"

Marie nodded, suppressing a smile. Mary-Grace lived in fear of humiliation or looking pedestrian.

"Of course," Marie said. "An elegant choice."

That fall, the children played underneath the pecan tree, napped side by side, collected cicada exoskeletons, pulled each other's hair, kissed each other's dirty cheeks. They made mud pies, pretended to fish, and counted the turtles that sunned themselves on fallen cypress and tupelo.

Undoubtedly, Skip loved Ase more than Ase loved Skip. Anyone could see that. Perhaps it was their ages, Marie thought, or perhaps Skip accepted the situation, while something deep within Ase resented it. But she ran after him whenever he moved, peered over the books he read, copied his expressions, and gazed at him tirelessly with big green eyes.

Marie forced Ase and Skip to hold hands when they walked, somewhat unsteadily, to the water. They were bound together and squeezed each other's fingers until their knuckles turned white.

=

One evening, on her way out of the house for the day, Marie knocked politely on the door to Win's study and asked to borrow another book. She stood in the doorway in her lace collar, silhouetted, sand-colored hair falling down from her chignon. Win rose from his desk.

"Does anyone read more than you?" he asked.

Marie laughed. "Not here."

"Come in," he said, gesturing toward the shelves. "Take anything you want."

She set the sleeping, towheaded Ase down in an armchair. He curled into the furniture, used to being moved in his sleep. She browsed with one finger, dragging it lightly across the spines of Win's books.

She imagined, suddenly, that she was dragging her finger across his body.

She could feel his eyes on her back as she scanned the titles.

"Bring home as many as you need," he said, drawing closer.

She turned slowly toward him and took a deep breath. It had been a long time since she'd seen desire in a man's eyes.

"Thank you," she said, taking a book from the shelf nearest her shaking hand, her eyes still on his.

That night she felt pleasantly miserable, ruminating over the look on Win's face, the sudden closeness of their bodies. His naivete suddenly seemed inviting—his attention, erotic. Surely, they had much in common as outsiders on the farm; they both loved books and walks by the river. Perhaps Win needed her company, someone to talk to.

Or maybe it was more elemental, an animal urge they both needed to satisfy, and there were so few choices. Perhaps they had to mask it in something genteel. After the last few years, she felt cynical when it came to love.

Poor Helena was nothing but a ghost in the house, a sleepy and dwindling presence everyone moved around, tolerated. There were days when she didn't leave the bed, nights when she called out so loudly she woke the children, gasping for air and screaming. How could any man be expected to be loyal to a woman who hardly existed in the waking world?

Marie knew both the mistake at hand and that she would make it. She could see—only for seconds at a time—her faulty logic, as if looking over one's shoulder at a familiar face in a crowd only to lose it again. Here was a man that she should not love—he was not made of the right ingredients, he was married, and he could not make her happy for long.

But her loneliness was big enough to eclipse wisdom; it woke her in the night. It had teeth.

=

One early winter evening, after tucking Skip and Ase into twin beds in the nursery, Marie descended the stairs with a book to return. She knocked on the door and found Win at his desk in the dim library. His dinner jacket was thrown over a chair, and he wore a white shirt with the sleeves rolled up. Her eyes were drawn to the gold ring on his hand. He looked up at her, the light from his lamp catching his face, and put down his pen.

"I heard your footsteps," he said.

She closed the door. There was a rich, quiet moment. He walked over to her and grasped her shoulders, heat passing through his fingers into her body. She felt for a moment as if she would be sick.

He hovered over her, tall and intoxicating.

They made love behind his desk, her thin fingers in his hair, his mouth on her neck, the children and his wife asleep upstairs. Every night for a week they found one another, reckless and starving. She loved how desperate he was; it flattered her. He grabbed the back of her head, pulling her hair when they kissed. He licked the length of her stomach and thighs until she pulled him into her. He often forgot himself and moaned too loudly until she gave him her fingers to bite down on.

In the weeks that followed, they left notes for each other in the library, tucked carefully between the pages of the books they passed back and forth.

"I do not feel entirely myself," Marie wrote. She felt stupid and awake.

"And I feel less alone," he replied.

On the evenings when they could not find time together, she

leaned in before whisking the children to bed. "Meet me in the night garden," she said.

The imagined tryst was often better than reality.

10

M arie slipped into Win's study most nights, after the children were settled in the twin beds, quilts pulled to their chins. It was winter, and everyone went to sleep earlier.

She read to him while he worked. Win admired her accent, the airy way she said *from* and *storm*. When she read, she slipped off her shoes and sat in the chair with one leg tucked underneath her body. He could feel her in the house during the day when he wasn't with her—he recognized the sound of her footsteps upstairs, let his eyes linger on the apple core left on the top of the trash after snack time with the children.

He followed her into the kitchen, where she peeled an orange. "They will help keep our eyes bright," she said, peeling more for the children, elegantly licking the juice from her fingers.

He reached over to take her hand, and just as he slipped one of her fingers into his mouth, June bustled into the room, holding a mop. Suddenly the flavor of Marie's skin mingled with the taste of copper. Guilt.

Marie kept a calm face as she withdrew her hand.

"Don't make trouble," Win said to June, hands now by his side, after the silence had become untenable.

"No sir," June said, looking him squarely in the eyes. "I'm not one to get in anybody's business."

She stared him down, her face saying something different than her mouth. Her deep loyalty to Helena was clear.

"Thank you, June," Marie said. Then she bent down, picked up the children, and walked upstairs to the nursery.

Every few months he tried to break himself of Marie, the scent of oranges and honey on her skin. They would meet at five in the morning when the roosters crowed, then only on Thursdays. Occasionally, on a righteous kick, he'd go weeks without being alone with her, but then he began to realize the heightened pleasure of indulging after deprivation, and he would meet her in the gamekeeper's cottage and drop to his knees, begging as she smiled knowingly at him and raised the hem of her skirt to her waist.

"I came to this country to escape shame," she told him once, sitting demurely on the blue velvet armchair in his office. "I won't give in to it now. We should enjoy pleasure where we find it."

He put his arms around her and rested his face in her warm neck. He realized guilt was a thing you could bargain with. He felt it the next morning, passing by Helena's room. Her door was ajar, and he could see her sitting up slightly in bed, her elbows on her knees and her head in her hands. Mary-Grace sat beside her with a hairbrush and dish soap, working the tangles in her daughter's hair.

Once a week, June changed the sheets. Today Helena had to be coaxed from the bed while the woman worked, brisk and deft fingered, muttering a quiet prayer. Win stood in the hallway waiting for June to finish.

"Whose salvation are you praying for?" Mary-Grace asked, bitterness evident in her voice.

"Yours, mine, and hers," June whispered, nodding to Helena,

who slumped against her mother, licking her chapped lips. "This is not the life she wanted. She should be out walking the river with her gun or riding a horse through the marsh. She should—"

Mary-Grace made a disapproving *tsk* sound. "That's enough," she said, giving June a stern look.

The maid walked off with an armful of sheets.

"You need to pull yourself together," Mary-Grace said to Helena, forcing the brush through her hair. "You can't live like this, sleeping your days away in this dark room. And that foreign woman so close to your husband. Helena, *do* something."

"I'm trying," she whispered. "But I'm so tired."

Win cleared his throat and stepped in to say good morning. The two women turned their eyes to him briefly—they were the same eyes. The sheet had pulled away, and he could see the angry flesh of a bedsore on Helena's exposed hip. She yanked her gown down to cover it but said nothing.

"She's *fine*," Mary-Grace said. "She just needs another week or two of rest."

After a minute, Mary-Grace continued brushing. The sound of bristles ripping through hair filled the room.

11

"Just sit back and keep quiet today," Mary-Grace said to Helena as June buttoned up the bodice of her salmon-pink antebellum dress. Mary-Grace held up one hand and swayed a little, catching herself on the bureau. She closed her eyes for a moment.

"It's tight," she said, a hand at her waist.

"No, ma'am," June said, starting toward the bedroom door. "You haven't been eating. I'm getting you a slice of buttered toast."

"I can dine with the Lord," Mary-Grace said, humorless, "when I'm dead."

She picked at her sleeves, slipping them down just so on her shoulders. She straightened her posture and looked squarely into the full-length mirror, then back at June. "Finish me up. Hurry."

"Do you want your coat?"

"The dress looks better without it," Mary-Grace said, turning to the side, the crinoline turning her lower half into the shape of a bell.

"You'll freeze to death."

Helena watched the familiar dance, feeling as if her thinking was in slow motion. Her mother was preparing for the sixth Running of the Silver, a historic reenactment of the Union troops invading the grounds of Stillwood in 1865.

Mary-Grace would do as her grandmother had allegedly done, whisking an armful of the family's silver to the silo, or at least where it had once stood. A farmhand would dig a pit in the sandy soil, in which Mary-Grace would bury the silver, cursing the advancing Yankees, who were the three ugliest men in the neighborhood on the three ugliest horses. She made *sure* of that.

"I want the men with bad teeth and poor posture," she told Percy. "Cast the roles appropriately."

Percy, playing his role as Lindley Glass, had set out the smallpox flags, which the faux-Yankees carried in one hand as they galloped into the backyard, angry at having discovered the ruse. The group would then proceed to the springhouse to sing "God Save the South."

Mary-Grace left to gather the silver, and June brushed Helena's hair. She felt like one of the mannequins from the Calhoun Beach Club, stiff, uninterested in her appearance.

"You have to try harder," June said softly to her. "You can't go on like this."

Helena didn't say anything. The words were lodged too deeply in her body.

"I have to go prepare lunch," June said. "I'll get you settled outside in a nice chair."

Helena eased onto the patio, where about twenty-five locals from River Road had gathered to watch the proceedings. June eased her into a wicker chair and patted her head before leaving.

Stillwood's gardens were peaking. The camellias were in full bloom; creamy ivory and pink petals were bursting from the dark green leaves and piling up on the sandy garden paths like vibrant carpets. Romany, Jacks, Desire, Lady Clare, Pearl Maxwell— Helena could name them all.

A bugler began to play "To the Color," and the crowd drew silent. It was forty degrees out, and Helena's toes were cold. She could feel the chill of the winter earth entering her body as she watched her mother dash across the yard, one hand holding up her generous skirt, the other clutching a green velvet pouch of silver.

For the first time, she was watching instead of participating, and the reenactment felt ridiculous to her, like a bad trip to the theater.

"You won't get everything," Mary-Grace yelled hysterically, as if her grandmother were yelling through her. Spit gathered at the corners of her mouth. "We've worked too hard, for too long."

Helena licked her chapped lips and felt nervous, as if she might laugh as Mary-Grace continued shouting at the Yankees.

"The house is burning!" her mother cried. "And the buffalo are loose!"

The old horses cantered onto the scene, the men waving smallpox flags. "You can't fool us no more," one yelled, half-heartedly.

Then, from the corner of her eye, Helena saw her daughter and Ase in the woods, traipsing up one of the many footpaths that snaked through the property. The boy had Skip by the hand, and they were running through the trees. Where was Marie? And Win? Why were the children alone? Nothing made sense, but this was not unusual in her world, where moments from the day were stitched together by naps in chairs and on beds.

Ase paused by one of the oaks. He began to pull down his trousers to relieve himself. Then Skip followed suit, pulling up her jumper and yanking her tights down to her knees, squatting like a peasant in the woods. A visible stream of urine poured from her body.

The crowd began to point and laugh. Mary-Grace stopped midsentence, assuming they were pointing at her. "What? *What?*" she kept saying, dumbfounded. She turned her head to look behind her. Skip, who'd not yet pulled up her tights, waved animatedly at her grandmother from the shadows of the trees behind the silo.

The bugler, perhaps wanting to help Mary-Grace save face, began playing "Taps." Percy waved everyone onto the path. "To the springhouse!" he said. The men on horses led the way down the path toward the river.

June, who'd been diligently chopping carrots and deviling eggs in the kitchen for the luncheon, stepped out onto the patio.

"What's wrong?" she asked Helena. "What in God's name are they rushing for? I'll never have lunch ready in time."

Mary-Grace stomped past both of them, cheeks flushed. "Those children have made a fool of me," she said, shaking. "And I will not stand for it. Do you hear me? I will *not* stand for it."

Helena laughed. She didn't care. She didn't care that her husband was missing or that he was probably locked in his study with his arms around Marie. She didn't care that her daughter was like a rabid fox, running around with the help's children, relieving herself in front of company. She didn't care that her mother was a fool obsessed with the past. She didn't care that her hair was brittle and her body was wasted. She didn't care. What a joy it was, not to care. What freedom!

12

In late February, Win called Helena's parents into his office. The space felt more his than any other room in the house. He was desperate for the tension to break. He felt he'd been dropped into someone else's life and was ready to reclaim his own.

The light was dying outside while June began making her evening sounds in the kitchen. Two oil lamps were lit on the heavy desk. The room smelled of tobacco, damp books, lemon polish. A taxidermy pheasant stared down at him from the shelves with gloomy eyes.

Mr. and Mrs. Glass came into the office together, side by side. To Win, they seemed like a pair of old geese, not in love, but dependent on each other. Percy, in his dinner jacket, smiled. Mary-Grace wore a morose expression, her newly graying hair pulled tightly back, and her mouth set in a small, straight line, as if bracing herself for a fight.

Win opened his mouth to speak, but Mary-Grace cut him off.

"If this is about Helena," she began, "I think we should enlist the help of the church. I know a minister who specializes in cases like hers."

"I've arranged for Helena to be transferred to a hospital," Win said, interrupting. The words came out fast. "It's on eighty acres of land, a few hours from here, a very pretty place . . ."

"A sanatorium!" Mary-Grace drew back, one hand to her heart. "I don't think she needs to go that far away. We can have her cared for in the privacy and comfort of her own home."

"She needs more help than we can give her here."

"What if we refuse?" Mary-Grace said, glaring at him. "Tell him we refuse, Percy." She looked to her husband for help, but he was quiet.

"I'd like you to accompany her there and remain in the area during her stay," Win said, careful to keep his voice firm. He placed both palms on the desk.

Mary-Grace seethed and turned again to her husband, but Percy nodded, almost as if the words had no effect. Lately he'd seemed to resign himself to his retirement, grooming his mustache, puttering around his old farm in a suit, smoking his pipe, firing guns at long-gone giant boars in the dark woods. He pulled his gold pocket watch from his pants out of habit, and turned it over in his hand, then put it back.

"You don't intend to . . . are you asking us to leave my father's land?" Mary-Grace asked. "You understand Stillwood is *my* family home? And all Helena has ever known? If she's going to get better, it's going to happen here. She loves this place, heart and soul, as I do. As we *all* do." Mary-Grace leaned forward.

"The paperwork has been signed," Win said, sinking back in his chair. "This was a difficult decision, but I fear for Helena's health. She's had no signs of improvement, and Dr. Harris is threatening to stop supplying her with the tonic. It's time. I don't want Skip to know her this way. I don't want this to be her memory of her mother, a woman who has given up on life. Plus," he added, "I'll make the trip worth your while."

"You're not doing this for *her,*" Mary-Grace said through gritted teeth.

"When do we depart?" Percy asked plainly.

"They'll come for her on Friday."

"*Come* for her?" Mary-Grace asked, horrified.

"It's a very dignified business," Win said. "They've assured me."

Silence fell upon the room. Win's stomach ached. He wanted this moment over.

"I understand this isn't easy for you," he began.

"You do *not* understand," Mary-Grace said, trembling. "First you dishonor our daughter, and take away the place in society she should have had. Then when the slightest whiff of trouble occurs, you turn to the arms of another woman and take this place for yourself. How *dare* you."

"Now, dear," Percy said, guiding his wife toward the door. "We shouldn't interfere in their business."

"This is robbery! How can you be so compliant?" Mary-Grace cried, jerking her shoulder away from Percy's hand. "So *agreeable?*"

"We have no recourse, Mary-Grace, aside from pistols,"

Percy said calmly, but loudly enough for Win to hear. "He's the one who has to sleep at night."

Win folded his shaking hands underneath his desk. He felt a twinge of pity as they walked slowly, even disbelievingly, out of his office. But mostly he felt relief.

He wanted to be free. Free to feel as though the house and farm were his. Free to make love to Marie in his bedroom and let her exclaim as she wished, because he loved the foreign words that escaped her lips. Free to buy her presents and peel her oranges. Lick juice from her fingers. Walk to the river and stare at the moon, holding hands.

I hope they never return, he found himself thinking in bed at night.

Dr. Harris and his assistant came on Friday morning to prepare Helena. She leaped from the covers, hair matted, sleep still in her eyes. Her white linen nightgown swung freely on her thin frame, and the length of her spine looked like knotted rope. Instinctively, she ran for the door, one pale arm outstretched. Dr. Harris held her down in the corner of the room. "My God," he said as she gritted her teeth and kicked. "How do you have any energy left?"

"Shhh, shhh," Mary-Grace clucked nearby, tears rolling down her face. "Don't fight, Darling. Don't fight."

Helena scratched Dr. Harris's hand when he reached for her wrist. Win could not believe that he was standing here in this house, with this thrashing woman who was his wife.

"She needs a sedative," Dr. Harris said, a note of desperation in his voice.

Win, jarred to reality, brought the doctor his black leather satchel.

He rested his hand on his wife's arm, and she shook it off.

"Don't you forget," she said, dry voiced, hate in her eyes, "this is *my* house, and that is my child."

He looked at her thin neck, the veins bulging in her throat. The raspiness in her voice was no longer pleasing; it haunted him.

Twenty minutes later, two large men in pressed, white uniforms escorted her into a waiting car.

In the hustle of Helena's departure, Mary-Grace lost hold of Skip, who climbed the library ladder to the top of the twelve-foot ceilings and screamed until Marie brought her down in her arms, both of them terrified, hearts pounding against the other's.

13

Helena woke up in the back of the car. The last dose of tonic was wearing off. She screamed so loudly that she threw up.

"I want my daughter," she cried, hitting the window with her fist. "I want my life back."

14

The morning after Helena was taken from Stillwood, Win woke up in bed beside Marie, something he'd wanted to do for a long time. He kissed her cheek, and she turned toward him, still sleeping. He rose, quietly, and then looked in on the children. Ase was spread out like a starfish on one bed, while Skip slept in a fetal position next to him, hugging her skinned knees, her blond hair fanned out across the white pillowcase. He left them there, wanting the children to sleep as long as possible.

He became aware of something like joy spreading through him. Relief. Freedom. There was no Helena, locked away in a dark bedroom or roaming the house at night. There was no Mary-Grace needling the servants, commanding them to prune the wilted camellias or reminding them how "Daddy liked things done." There was just this morning, with nothing on the calendar, and he would live the day on his terms.

Before they'd left town, Percy had pulled him aside. "In confidence," Percy said, stuffing his pipe, "I don't care for Stillwood as much as my wife does. You might find this superstitious, but I think this place is making me sick. What do you say we make a deal here—some extra money in the mail each month, and I'll keep her away from Stillwood and never say a word." Percy put the end of the pipe in his mouth and looked at Win with eyes that seemed older, yellowed.

"Perhaps a little place in Beaufort?" Percy added. His expression belied more clarity and intention than usual, and Win agreed, quickly.

Win walked into the gamekeeper's shed and slipped off his shoes in exchange for a pair of boots. The morning sky was lilac, and the grounds were humid, the tall trees shrouded in fog. He stood quietly for a long time, adjusting to the idea that Stillwood was finally his.

A neighbor was working his dogs across the river. Liver-spotted English setters were weaving among the horses, noses down, disappearing into the marsh grass. Suddenly ducks burst from the low ground, flushed by the dogs. They erupted from the grassy banks, wings flapping frantically as shots rang out, a cloud against the early sun. Their bodies dropped from the sky.

Win watched as the men took a small canoe out into the river and then paddled back to the banks, two dozen dead mallards with limp necks and shimmering feathers draped over their knees.

He walked back to the big house, leaving his muddy boots by the door. Marie was already in the kitchen, her auburn hair pinned haphazardly. A smile spread across her face as she saw him. She handed him a cup of coffee.

"Finally," she said.

He took a deep breath. "Finally," he said.

That night a violent storm came through, and with rain on the tin roof and the thunder booming across the river they made love as loudly as they wanted. Marie screamed, almost as if she was in pain, which he loved. Her body gleamed like porcelain when the lightning flashed, and they fell asleep in the damp sheets.

=

He walked into his office the next morning to find June Wheatley polishing the floors. "She's going to get better, you know," June said, eyeing him. She rose from her knees to stand.

"Helena's been this way before, back when she was heartsick in high school," June said. "The Lord has given her many gifts, and her dark moods are just the way he balances out her fortune and talent. That girl's got a will stronger than Sherman's army."

"That'll do, June," Win said, uneasy.

June wrung out her rag in a bucket. "Make no mistake, Mr. Spangler. Helena will rise."

Win cringed. The idea of Helena recovering filled him with apprehension that he quickly suppressed. He wanted that part of his life to be over.

"You've got obligations to honor, is what I'm saying," June said. She looked prim in her ankle-length skirt. He noticed her cheeks were flushed, as if she'd been drinking.

"Keep your thoughts to yourself," Win snapped. "Otherwise I'll have to ask you to leave."

June nodded, looking down at her shoes for a moment. Worn men's dress shoes.

"I'll let you finish your work," he said irritably. He left his office and went outside through the back door of the kitchen.

This whole damn place is loyal to Helena, he thought.

He stood on the front lawn where he could see a small steamship in the distance, puttering down the river, a handful of sightseers pressed to the rails. They came to look at the old plantations and their gardens. Some were ghostly and abandoned, others recently restored.

There were many marks of the Glass family life—over a hundred years of them—rice mills, springhouses, stables, and levees. There were odd outbuildings, scales, vials of specimens, threshing tools.

A visitor on a steamship could see the beautiful parts of Stillwood—the bright and vulgar flowers, the white facade of the house—and the ugly parts were mostly hidden. That was the ethos here on River Road, where people had somehow managed to be both cruel and sentimental.

15

Marie brushed the children's hair while a young portraitist organized his paints in the parlor. Ase's hair would not cooperate, his double cowlicks sending locks of white-blond hair skyward. Skip pulled out every accessory fastened in her curly hair, regardless of the time Marie spent placing it and convincing the girl that she'd look lovely.

"No," Skip said about the barrettes and pins, looking at each as if it was offensive. "I don't like it."

Marie knew she was indulging herself with the artist, but she and her siblings had been painted as children, and she wanted to capture the beauty of these years, and the bond between Skip and Ase.

The portraitist was now coaxing Skip out of the corner and back to the bench where he wanted the children to pose. "Please, little girl," he said.

She took off a shoe and threw it at him.

Skip, perhaps in response to her mother's absence, was beginning what Win referred to as her "unbroken horse" phase. She refused to wear tights and just yesterday had colored on the red toile nursery wallpaper in blue crayon.

Whenever she was obstinate, Marie found herself thinking of Helena, convinced she could see her rival's eyes shining back at her. But she loved Skip and worked hard to push these images from her thoughts.

"Skip," she said, kneeling to look the girl in the eyes, "this will only take a minute. Please do it for me."

Skip, in a moment of remorse, hugged her with sticky hands.

Ase and Skip eventually sat on the white bench as instructed, but shoes fell off and hair was pulled. He wiped his nose and pulled a dead cockroach from his pocket. Skip scowled.

"You may take creative liberties," Marie told the artist, who reassured her that no one was ever painted as they looked. "The truth tends to find its way out on the canvas," he said, paintbrush in mouth. "They're beautiful siblings."

When the portraitist presented the finished canvas a month later, Marie was amazed at the two blond children, heads tipped toward each other, faces softened, clutching each other's hands with fierce loyalty and affection. The truth had come out.

Ase and Skip had both lost parents, and endured turmoil in their young lives, but at least they had each other, she thought. They will *always* have each other.

She felt like a salesman, convincing herself and everyone else that they were a family, that this scenario was right, that the arrangement would bring them pleasure and stability. Didn't every family carry within it a tiny fissure of doubt that you had to sew back together at night so that the entire thing wouldn't rip wide open?

=

Marie and Win weren't social. They knew what their neighbors were probably saying, and they enjoyed their solitude, staying at home with brandy Win bought from behind the bait shop, and the radio.

Marie usually woke before everyone else, heading downstairs to the kitchen, fastening her linen apron. Win had given June mornings off so that they could preserve the feeling of being unwatched and sincere. Marie learned how to cook a few things, studying the books on the shelves, particularly *Mrs. Beeton's*

Hors d'Oeuvres and Savouries. She liked to give Win a chance to rest while she fixed soft-scrambled eggs and toast and listened for the children.

Skip often woke first and sang her favorite song: "*Alouette, gentille alouette*," a way of waking up Ase. Marie heard the strains of off-key singing at quarter past six. She sighed. If only Skip knew she was singing about plucking the feathers from a lark. Or maybe she did.

Ah well, Marie thought. It is good for a girl to have a little savagery in her.

Marie brought the sleepy-eyed children to the kitchen table and gave them paper and crayons to busy them while she cooked. She'd never pictured herself enjoying childcare, but she finally did. She liked the immediacy of it all, the way it took her away from her thoughts.

Skip drew circles and backward letters. Like all children, she was proud of her work, and when Win came down for coffee, she thrust the piece of paper in his face.

"What's this?" he said, kneeling beside her, looking at the circles she'd drawn.

"Mama," she said, suddenly solemn about her drawing.

He nodded, rose from the floor, and exchanged a look with Marie. She shrugged. Though it stung, it was natural for Skip to miss her mother.

She spooned a pile of eggs onto Ase's plate, and he dug in with a fork before she was through. He was the hungriest child she'd ever seen. His appetite was bottomless, and yet he was thin. Secretly she blamed herself for depriving him, forcing him to share her milk supply with Skip when he was a baby.

She served Skip, then placed the skillet in the sink. Win

walked toward the counter and put a hand around Marie's waist, and kissed her cheek. She ran her fingers through his hair affectionately and handed him his cup of coffee.

Years ago, she looked for different things in a man—wit, worldliness—but that was when she was a woman of means. She had different needs now, and needs quickly transformed themselves into desires.

After breakfast, the children took an old coverlet and slid down the grand staircase, screaming as they went, Ase biting his tongue. Marie blotted the blood with a handkerchief, then sent them out the back door. "Get outside," she said, "while the light is good."

At night, after Marie had kissed them and sung their favorite songs, Ase would wait for her to close the door, then sit up and call Skip to his bed. Marie knew the routine. She could hear Skip's footsteps as she ran over to Ase's bed, where the two children would talk and play until they fell asleep.

In the morning, the first one to wake would nudge the other. Skip would return to her bed, as if she'd been there all along. Marie let them believe in their ingenuity.

=

The nights were warm enough for Marie to wash the children outside as the sun set over the river.

Win sipped scotch and watched as Ase and Skip stood in the tin tub shivering while Marie wrung out a sponge. Skip's body was leaning out and already dark from the sun.

Ase started splashing Skip, and they began laughing about something only they could see, as if they had their own language.

Marie liked this time of day, when the sun dipped low. Her

mother had called dusk wolf-light, a time when things became wild again.

"The sea rises, the light changes, and yet," her mother would say when they walked outside to watch the sunset.

This sort of intimacy was lost years ago, before the arranged wedding and Marie's desperate, last-minute journey. Did her mother have regrets? She'd forced Marie to stay with an abusive husband instead of providing refuge when he threatened her life.

What was forgivable? Marie wondered. It seemed to her that adulthood was a series of mundane years punctuated by transgressions and apologies. If you didn't transgress, you died of boredom.

June cleaned the house daily and kept a quiet watch over Stillwood. She made Marie nervous. If Marie turned a picture of Helena or Mary-Grace facedown, June would right it. When Marie entered the kitchen, June left immediately.

After the children went to bed, Win and Marie would listen to orchestral productions, the news, stories about the flooded Mississippi, and the latest from Berlin.

They slept naked with the bedroom door locked. He once fell asleep with his cheek on the inside of her thigh. She knew he'd never had access to a woman this way, never known a woman's body like this. Sometimes he propositioned her several times a day—in the bedroom, the gamekeeper's cottage, his office. His desire flattered her, filled her with warmth, healed some of the wounds of the last few years.

"I never meant to live here," he told Marie one morning. "We could live anywhere."

"I don't want to spend my life running from one problem after the next," she said, taking the last sip of her coffee.

"What problems have you run from?" Win asked. He reached for her hand, holding it gently to the table.

"I left everything," she said, removing her hand from his grasp. "And that's all you need to know."

16

Win ceased to question his life with Marie. He knew happiness now: the European woman in his bed, the two children collecting frogs and fighting over the rocking horse like brother and sister, the sound of Marie's voice when she woke him in the morning and asked if he wanted coffee. He only thought of Helena when the camellias bloomed, when his eye caught sight of a pink blossom browning on the ground, or the marble statue reaching up for the sky. He rushed past the bushes in the fall; he did not want to smell the flowers she took such pride in. Her love of camellias made her a real woman instead of an invalid, and their heady, pungent scent evoked something like guilt within him. It reminded him of the life that he and Helena had briefly imagined together.

That morning he took the kids to the river to fish. He helped Ase bait the hook. He liked having a son. Ase was handsome— Marie said his eyes were the color of glacial ice—and Win took pride in him, buying him a small navy suit and tie for church services.

Skip, who hated baiting hooks and was already tangled in the fishing line, looked up at him and asked, "Where's Mama?"

She asked periodically, less so each month that passed.

"She's getting well again," he said. But he didn't want to believe it himself. He only had to picture Helena flailing on the floor. He went so far as to wish her confined for life in a vague pursuit of wellness, and eventually he came to believe in her absence as permanent fact. He even let Skip wander around in her mother's old, delicate pageant dresses, moth-eaten and fished from the closet. June rehung them in the evenings.

People left your life, he thought. His father, now Helena. You learned to move on. One day Skip would accept Marie as her mother, and the questions about Helena would stop.

The next afternoon, he arrived home from town and found a letter on his desk. He looked at the return address in disbelief. Helena had written from Wolcott Hospital. He slipped a finger underneath the lip of the ivory envelope, bracing himself for the full brunt of her fury.

But it was worse. It was a love letter. A heartfelt apology.

I look forward to returning to you healthy and ready to be the good wife and mother my family deserves. I miss the house and now that I've recovered I want to make the place feel like ours. Darling, you were so patient as I suffered.

The letters continued to come, one after the other, week after week. At first, he ignored them, placing them in his desk drawer like something poisonous to avoid.

He didn't mention the letters to Marie. They rarely spoke of Helena, and for this he was thankful. He still longed to know what had inspired Marie's journey across the sea, but she did not volunteer it, and eventually he accepted that they both had secrets. He dared not upset the happiness they'd found.

One evening, in a flash of guilt, he wrote a short reply: *I'm glad you're getting the help you need. We wish the best for you, and I am happy to pay for your continued treatment.*

The following week he went to town with hopes of working out the financing for a rare collection of Polynesian masks. He stopped for flowers, selecting a cluster of red tulips for Marie before heading home. But as he stepped from his car and looked at the house, the atmosphere was wrong, changed. Marie did not call out to greet him. The children were not shouting or racing through the house. He walked into the foyer to find a sharp-eyed Helena and Marie standing face-to-face.

He lost his breath and his insides felt frozen.

"Why is she still here?" Helena asked, turning to him, an incredulous look in her eyes.

Helena looked healthy and vigorous. She wore a cobalt-blue dress, one he couldn't recall seeing her in before. He realized that Marie's gingham dress was so worn its color hardly registered.

Why didn't I buy her a beautiful dress? he wondered. Why didn't we leave town?

Marie, mercifully, did not answer. Win ached watching her, backlit by the sun, posture proud, wiping her hands on her apron. He wanted to rest his hands on her hips and kiss her forehead, reassure her that they would figure this out. He wanted to hand her the flowers, but instead, he laid them on the table.

"I'll let you two get reacquainted," Marie said, moving briskly into the kitchen.

He longed to follow Marie, but something kept him rooted in place, perhaps a sense of decorum, or bewilderment. Fear, or an old promise. He shifted uncomfortably, cleared his throat to speak, but before he could, Helena rushed over and threw her arms around him. She leaned her head against his beating heart.

"I understand," she said, breathless. "I was gone for so long."

It felt for a moment that the walls had fallen away, the floorboards slipping beneath his feet. His wife was a stranger to him. Furthermore, he knew Helena was the type of woman who could only pretend to forgive.

She touched his shoulder, confusion on her face. "Aren't you glad to see me?"

"It's good to see you looking well," he said, opening his eyes, every word an effort. He did not warm to her touch, and instead felt his body become rigid.

"I suppose it's going to take time," she said, releasing him. He could see hurt in her green eyes. Perhaps anger as well.

"You know, Daddy had his indiscretions," she said, shaking her head. Her tone was measured. "And I'm willing to allow you yours, but not under this roof. Do you understand?"

He swallowed.

"Good. Let's move on," she said. "Where's Skip?"

He moved through the rest of the day without feeling. Skip did not want to be held by her mother and began to cry as Helena reached for her. Dinner was quiet. June served rabbit, and as she set Win's plate down she whispered, "You've got your hands full, sir."

He stared at his wife over the candlesticks. She was still attractive with her sea-green eyes, but her beauty did not move him. Even though he admired her fortitude and courage for attempting to reclaim her life, he did not feel any softness toward her, let alone love. Now he knew what it was. What it could be.

Helena insisted on putting Skip to bed. She reached out to stroke her daughter's blond hair, though Skip whimpered and inched away from her mother, planting herself against the wall. Win watched through the crack in the door. He ached for Skip; how could she remember anything good about her mother?

"You know me," Helena said, sitting on the corner of the bed. It was not a question. "You do. You *have* to. I'm your mother. I love you, and you love me."

Skip turned her face into the pillow. The room was getting dark now.

"Let me tell you the story of the white doe," Helena said, running her fingers along her daughter's back.

Helena began to softly tell the story of the first settlers of the Carolinas. When she got to the part about a jealous witch doctor turning Virginia Dare, the first child of the British colonies, into a white doe, Skip was asleep, her breathing slowed and steady.

"She lives here now," Helena said quietly. "In these woods. If you see her, protect her. She should never be hunted. Good night, my Skip."

As his wife perched on the edge of Skip's bed, Win walked down the hallway and fell across his bed with his clothes still on. He did not pull down the quilt, but simply lay on top of it, feeling as sad as he had ever felt.

Helena came to the door a few minutes later, holding a small oil lamp. "You're going to sleep?" she asked, the light warming up one side of her face.

"I need some time to adjust," he said gingerly.

She nodded and returned to her childhood bedroom, which June had made up for her.

Win woke in the middle of the night, realizing he could smell Marie on the sheets, her faint scent of honey.

Marie had moved back to her old tabby house on Indigo Run, quickly and without fanfare. He found her in the backyard with Ase the next morning. She stared off into the fields.

Ase ran to him and hugged him, cheerful and rigorous as always.

"Just give me a few weeks to figure this out," Win pleaded, grasping for Marie's arm. She pulled it away.

He'd never seen this look on her face, the wounded pride, the cold dignity.

"How could I have known?" he asked, hoarse. He looked up at the pines overhead. Any movement made him feel sick now. He needed stillness. He needed control.

She stared at him, biting her lip, trembling a little. "*I* knew," she said. "Somewhere inside of myself I knew she would come back. This place belongs to her."

They were quiet. Ase played with the duck decoy, unaware of the drama unfolding a few feet away. He hugged it to his chest, then drew it farther away from his body, spoke to it.

"Please give Skip a kiss for me," Marie said, straightening her shoulders.

"Don't say it like that. Like you're saying goodbye."

"Let me suffer this loss in peace," she said, turning from him. "Please."

=

On the foyer table, the tulips dried into pale, crimson husks. No one moved them for several days. The duck decoy was returned, left on the front porch in the rain; the wood split in the sun.

Marie and Ase disappeared from the tabby house for four days. Win made a private phone call to the police chief in town and explained that he wanted to know if she turned up. He needed to know where she was.

On the fifth night, he received word from a farmhand that she'd come back to the cottage. "No explanation, sir. Just back, with the boy."

Win, relieved to have what he thought might be a second chance, stood on her front stoop and lingered there for half an hour, but she shut the curtains. Even still, he was glad to have her close. It gave him time.

"Keep an eye out for her," he told his farmhands.

The following weekend Helena set up brown glass whiskey bottles on a fallen oak tree log behind the house. She took several paces, turned, and shot them each to shards, bottle after bottle, as if reminding them all what she was capable of.

17

Seeing her husband in love with Marie was like lagging behind a competitor during a pageant or the swim tournaments of her youth. Helena decided to train her eye on the goal and steadily make up ground.

Mary-Grace wrote from the rental house in Beaufort, which they'd kept throughout Helena's stay at Wolcott:

Your father insists we remain here so that you and Winston can become better acquainted again. Be calm but systematic in your approach. I've sent a dressmaker.

PS — your dear husband can pay the bill.

Helena sprayed her mother's gardenia-scented perfume and arranged to have her hair done twice a week. She turned Mary-Grace's bedroom into her dressing station and devised a plan to make herself so compelling Win could not resist reconciliation.

The following week, Helena stepped on top of a stool in the parlor room, sun hitting the butter-yellow walls. She let the stooped dressmaker with crooked teeth drape her in fabric, taking pins from her mouth to pierce the gowns in progress.

Skip watched from the corner of the room, playing with a wooden duck decoy. She darted around like an abused dog, interested in affection but never getting too close.

The next day, lingerie arrived from Paris in three pink boxes, smelling of lavender sachets. Skip pulled out a gown made of flimsy lace and put it over her head, dancing across the parlor.

"That's not for you," Helena laughed, gently removing the gown from Skip's hands.

The following morning, she brought a pen and paper to breakfast and, resting the tip of the pen in her mouth, asked Win, "What are your favorite meals?"

He looked at her almost sympathetically, his wavy hair slicked back with oil, combed in a new way he must have done for Marie.

"I want to know what you like to eat," Helena said, tilting her head. She could tell her efforts made him uncomfortable.

"But my dear," he said kindly, "you don't cook."

She laughed. "I have no intention of starting. But I can make sure you're delighted when you sit down to the table, can't I?"

It was the warmest moment they'd had since she returned, and Helena felt hopeful.

Skip joined them at the breakfast table, scattering the crumbs from her biscuit onto the place mat and floor. Some days she seemed anxious if Helena even stepped foot outside the house, as if worried she'd never return. But many evenings she wept when Helena put her down to sleep. "When is Marie coming back?" she cried once, lying in a heap at the bottom of the stairs.

"Do *not* ask that again," Helena said, standing over her, voice livid. She tried to hide the angry part of herself, for fear of scaring her daughter further away. She wanted her love. She needed it.

The next morning they sat down to country ham, eggs, and redeye gravy, which June set out on clean china. That night there was roasted chicken with buttermilk mashed potatoes and pecan pie with fresh whipped cream.

Helena smiled as Win ate, though she only picked at her food; she was eager to fit into her new dresses. "Do you like the menu?" she asked.

"It's rich," he said, patting his slim stomach.

"Indulge yourself," she said, throwing him a seductive glance. He turned away.

Helena wrote a letter to her mother and father and asked them to return. Two weeks later, her father wrote back, insisting that Beaufort was warmer and better for his health. "We'll be staying on indefinitely," he wrote.

She could see the lies she and Win were going to have to tell themselves to get to the other side of this ordeal. That there had been a miraculous recovery, and all were delighted to be reunited as a family. She wanted the lie so much more than she wanted the truth.

The next morning Helena found Skip at the dining room table writing a letter, her long blond hair uncombed. Helena wiped a crumb from her daughter's cheek. She wanted to brush Skip's hair and tidy her face, but knew it would cause a fight.

"Who's this for?" Helena asked, smiling and lifting up Skip's paper to get a closer look. She was careful to show attention and interest.

"Marie," Skip said, a daring look in her eyes.

Helena's breath caught in her throat.

Skip looked up and must have seen what was coming. She leaped from the chair and ran to the library, bare feet pounding loudly on the wooden floors.

Helena followed her. Every breath she took in was oxygen for the fire.

The library was dim. She could hear the sound of Skip moving but couldn't find her. Suddenly a bit of movement caught her eye, and she saw her daughter at the top of the library ladder.

"Get down from there this minute," she said, but Skip just stared at her, crouching on a rung near the top shelf of books, a mixture of fear and resentment on her face. "Sally-Anne, don't make me come up there."

Skip was frozen, breathing fast. She looked like a small, hunted animal. "No," she said.

"I said get *down*!"

Helena, exasperated, reached up and began pulling at Skip's legs until her daughter fell into her arms. As soon as they reached the floor, Helena turned Skip around and spanked her. But her hand struck something hard and she pulled back in pain, staring at her palm in disbelief.

Skip had slipped a book into her underwear to protect herself.

Helena reached for the book and threw it against the wall.

"Go to your room," she said, suddenly too tired to fight for the love she wanted from her husband and daughter. She could see it had receded further than she expected. What work it would take to get it back, she thought, sinking to the floor of the library. What faith.

She felt a pang and knew what it was—the desire for the tonic. For numbness. For escape.

18

Which mother was the real mother?

Skip drew them both. They both left a hole. They both hurt to think about.

She was lonely without Ase in the house. She flopped onto the bed, wishing he were there.

They liked to play Animal Hospital. When you played Animal Hospital, you brought all the broken animals you could find to the nursery windowsill.

She collected seven-legged spiders and a newly fledged robin with a broken wing. Its orangey beak looked too big for its body, and it opened and closed the mouth at her. Open, close. Open, close.

When Skip woke up in the morning, the robin was dead. Crying, she dumped it outside behind the kitchen. June found her standing there with the dead bird and asked her if she needed a whipping. She said no, she never did think she really needed a whipping, but thank you.

Sometimes you're too tender, and sometimes you're too

tough. That's what Marie had said the week before she left. The week before her mama came back from the dead, or wherever she had been.

Ase had come running back onto the property one day, and they sat in the springhouse with the lizards racing all over the walls and sang songs because when you sang in the springhouse, your notes bounced from one thick wall to the other, and you sounded good even if you sounded bad.

June came in with a broom and chased him off. "You don't live here anymore. Get back to your own house, where you belong."

Ase left, crying and wiping his nose. His eyes turned extra blue when he cried, like the water Marie grew up with, water so blue it could hurt your eyes.

Too tough.

19

When spring came again, Helena instructed June to rehang the portrait of Lindley Glass in the crimson hallway, as well as the oil portraits of her ancestors that Win had replaced with landscapes in her absence. He watched them go up with resignation. That was the thing about this old house, he thought. It had residual order, a persistent way of being that was bigger than any one person.

"Doesn't it just feel right," June said, looking up at the paintings, one hand on her hip. "Having things as they've always been."

He snorted and left the room. June could complain with the best of them, but when it came to Helena, she had a blind spot. Maybe that blind spot was love.

At night he lay in bed with his arms crossed over his body, and though he was still, his mind was erratic. What was he going to do? Was he going to do *anything*? What was the *right* thing? Would Marie leave again? And regardless of the course of action he decided on during the wretched night, he woke up, went to breakfast with his wife and daughter, and remained in the flow of his life, as if it were a strong current he could not escape.

Helena had set the box with the wedding pistol inside on the top of his desk, a silent reminder of his vow. He locked the gun away without acknowledging it.

One clear May morning they went for a family walk in the old, fallow rice fields. He lagged behind, letting mother and daughter reconnect, watching the two traipse through the green grass together, blond hair catching the sun, the same swing in their arms as they moved. Pale moths, stirred to life, fluttered upward as they walked. Helena picked wild violets and tucked one behind Skip's ear. His wife and daughter were beautiful to look at, yet he felt separate from them.

"I always thought this was the most magical piece of land in the world," Helena said, reaching for Skip's hand as they walked. "I've never wanted to live anywhere else. And I've never wanted anyone else to own this land under our feet, this bend in the river."

Skip was chewing her nails, and Helena swatted her hand from her mouth. "Of course," she continued, "you don't yet know what an enormous gift it is to be born on a place like this, to call it yours. But one day you will."

Skip offered a half smile. Win saw his daughter working hard to be polite, and he appreciated her instincts. It was as though they both realized they were living in a precarious situation, that at any moment the footholds might give, and their family would slip again into darkness.

Overhead there was a sudden trail of panicked birdsong, then an eagle passing through on his way to the river to hunt. They all paused to watch.

"People don't think of passing down their land through their daughters," Helena went on. "But my mother did it, and now I've come back and done it, and you will, too. Girls understand what home means in a way men don't."

Win knew she intended for him to hear the comment.

"It's what made me want to get well again. Saving this farm for you. A woman with money of her own is a strong woman, you know."

"My legs are tired," Skip said, stumbling.

"Don't forget how strong you are," Helena said, tweaking her daughter's chin. "Do you hear me?"

"Yes ma'am." Skip tried to do a handstand, legs kicking toward the blue sky. She fell to the ground in a heap, then sprang up and returned to her mother's side.

"I've got so much more to tell you," Helena said, "now that you're so grown-up. I've got to tell you about my daddy taking us looking for the last Carolina parakeets. And one day we'll talk about the people that live in the big swamp. You can see their fires rising from the trees, deep in the swamp with the biggest alligators and snakes. They string their hammocks up between the trees and hunt wild boar. Some of them were born in that swamp and have never known anything different."

"Why would they want to live there?" Skip asked.

Helena was quiet for a moment and looked up into the sky, then back at her daughter as if she'd been jarred from a daydream.

Win felt uncomfortable, as if he could sense reality closing in on them there in the grass. Everything they were not willing to say or name about the cruelty of life was waiting in the wings, and their complicity in it, everything he wanted to keep his daughter from knowing—he saw then how it could rush in at any moment. Whenever Win felt guilt stirring in his mind, his thoughts followed a familiar pattern: *I wasn't born yet. It wasn't my fault. It's the way things were. It's the way things are. There's nothing I can do.* There was a long pause as the three of them stood in the damp field, slapping bugs on their arms.

You had to learn to tamp it down, all the horrible things inside you. All the horrible things your ancestors had done. All the horrible things you wanted.

20

Skip knelt at the open nursery window in her flimsy lilac nightgown to listen to what was happening on Indigo Run. With her parents gone, the days had become fascinating: there were gnats in the Vaseline, June entertained her friend Nolan over catfish stew in the kitchen at night, flowers browned in the vases. Things Skip had seen and heard for years seemed suddenly new. To her, the people on Indigo Run possessed mysterious lives, like fish in winter.

Her mother told her the dirt road was named for people who stole scraps of indigo and ran them to black market ships, where the lane met a deep spot in the river.

Front doors on the lane were still painted a rich indigo blue every few years, but the last coat was blistered and fading in the bright sun. Cottage ceilings got the haint blue, too. June said that the blue paint looked like water, and ghosts wouldn't cross it. "Keeps the hag away," she said.

June didn't mind what Skip did as long as she came when the old dinner bell was rung, a bell June claimed had been salvaged from a pirate shipwreck. She tended to exaggerate when Skip's parents were out of earshot.

"Tell me a story about those Indigo Runners," Skip said that morning, halfway through a banana, staring up at June's plain expression. She had a good storytelling face. You couldn't always tell when she was lying.

"True as it can be, and could happen again. People like your family start taking too much, and the Indigo Runners take it back."

"You make up your stories."

"You have to put lipstick on the pig," June said, leaning down in her face, all coffee breath and bad teeth. "Because the pig is *everywhere*."

June's friend was still there. Nolan drank coffee with June in the kitchen and held her hand when he thought no one was looking. He had one blind eye because a thermometer had shattered in his hand when he was a child and the mercury got in. It was a fascinating eye to look at, sort of white. Skip knew she would never run with a thermometer, ever.

"Good morning, Sally," Nolan said, smiling at her over his cup of coffee.

"Morning," Skip said, trying not to get caught looking at his eye. Then she turned to June. "How do I get a storytelling face like you have?"

"Pshh," June said, taking a sip of her coffee. "I don't have a storytelling face."

"Some people get one by playing a lot of cards," Nolan said, glancing at June, raising his eyebrows at Skip until she laughed.

"I *don't* play cards," June said, looking serious. "And he's *not* here drinking coffee."

"I know, I know. Is the icebox broken?"

"Go on," June said firmly, swatting her on the backside. "Get yourself some fresh air, and stay out of the chigger weed."

After grabbing a slice of peach bread, Skip walked River Road toward Indigo Run, wanting to see Ase and Marie. She knew they lived on the lane; she saw them sometimes, walking back from an errand. She'd wave frantically from the back seat of the car, but they didn't look at her. "Settle down," her father would say, embarrassed for reasons she didn't understand.

But she *had* to see them. She missed her brother, especially at night when her room felt empty and quiet, and her mother's bedtime stories took on an alarming life in her imagination. Her mother felt unknowable, and there was something hurt and wild in her green eyes.

Skip missed sleeping in the tiny twin bed with Ase, the security of being smashed up against the wall so they could fit, his heel digging into her leg. The thought of Ase's company made her feel brave and less alone. The only child in the house now, she paid attention to everyone else's affairs, listened to adult conversations, and tried to make sense of the world. But she missed her earlier family.

The men of Indigo Run worked for the Glass family sunup to sundown, and most of the women, too. Some worked in cotton and tobacco while the others leased fields and grew their own crops. The white sharecroppers lived on the north end of the lane, and the Black farmhands kept their houses on the southern end. The front lawns were of swept dirt, dotted with chickens and sleeping dogs.

Mim's house was in the middle. She made sure everybody got fed, especially the old ladies and children. God bless Mim, June always said. When her parents died of the flu, Mim had taken her in first, before Mary-Grace put her to work.

"Mary-Grace acts like she's all saintly and charitable," Skip heard June say of her grandmother. "She just wanted a maid. That's all there is to the so-called rescue. But I ain't got nothing better for now, and I can't leave Helena. She's like a sister to me."

Skip walked as close as she could without turning down the lane, bringing the toe of her shoe right to the place where it branched off from River Road. Today she could hear the whine of a rusty water pump being primed.

She saw a young girl, five or six years old, standing in the front yard of an unpainted shack. The girl was beating a tin bowl like a drum and singing "Jesus Loves Me" with abandon. The house listed to one side, and its windows were thrust open, a single curtain blowing through to the outside. A tomato plant grew out of a broken barrel by the front steps. The girl's stringy sun-bleached hair fell over her shoulders and covered her bare, flat chest. "Hey!" she called out to Skip, one hand cupped around her mouth.

Skip turned and ran home. She knew Helena wouldn't stand for her getting any closer to this girl, even if she was the only girl her age in sight.

"Why can't I play with the other kids?" she'd asked before.

"Because their daddies curse, their mommies don't have teeth, and the children have lice," Helena would say as if she were handing down the word of God. Her mother was like that—opinionated.

The next morning Nolan was there again in the kitchen when she woke up.

"Morning, Skip," he said, nodding at her.

"We're having some more problems with the icebox," June said solemnly, handing Skip another slice of peach bread and ushering her outside into the warm morning air. The mosquitoes were already biting.

Unable to fight her curiosity, Skip turned toward Indigo Run again. She walked the lane for a while, pausing to watch Mim snap shrimp heads off and throw the bodies into a tub of ice. "Go on," the woman said, shooing her away.

Skip stopped at the next house on the block. She knocked on the door, and a boy hollered, "Come in already." She stepped into the house and found Marie and Ase in the hot kitchen of their cottage. Flies hung in the thick air. Marie's belly was swollen, and she sat in a wooden chair with broken caning, resting a cup of water on her stomach, her long hair piled on top of her head. Skip's mouth dropped open.

"Darling," Marie said, looking at Skip standing sheepishly in the doorway. "You aren't supposed to be here." The lines around her gray eyes seemed deeper when she smiled, but Skip liked that about her—the crinkling of her pretty face.

Skip looked around, taking in the clean but impoverished house, the lilting floor, the dark rooms. She stared at Marie's enormous belly, covered in a loose blue dress.

She began to cry and realized she'd been holding in her sadness for a long time. "Come," Marie said, beckoning her over. "Don't be worried. Come and hug me. I miss you."

Skip knew two women's bodies, her mother's and Marie's. They were different—her mother's was so warm that it was nearly impossible to lie next to her without sweating—but Marie's skin was nearly hairless and cool to the touch, and in that way, begged for closeness; you could press against one another without discomfort.

"I want you to come home," Skip said, wiping her nose. "Please."

"That's not going to happen," Marie said, drawing Skip near and kissing her forehead.

"I'm going to stay with you, then," she said, leaning into Marie's shoulder.

Ase, looking protective, moved closer, pulling Skip away from his mother. "Come play outside," he said. "Mama needs rest."

She instinctively wrapped him in a hug, nearly tackling him to the ground. He laughed. He was wearing a silver whistle and a pair of broken binoculars around his neck. It made him look like he had things to do, which she admired.

Skip followed him, and they kicked a ball around the sandy yard. Three girls with dirty faces and bandaged hands stood nearby, looking like they wanted to play. Skip kicked the ball to one, but she let it roll to a stop in front of her bare feet.

"Go on," Skip said, somewhat irritably. "Kick it back."

What was wrong with these girls?

"It's okay, Rebecca," Ase said, glaring at Skip. "She doesn't know anything."

"Why does *she* have to be here?" the oldest girl asked, scowling.

Skip felt embarrassed. It was a bad feeling, to be wrong and not know why.

"She's okay."

"I don't *want* her here," the youngest one said. She and her sisters went and lay down on their backs in the grass and looked up at the sky, joined by a mangy orange cat.

Ase came up to Skip and whispered, "They shuck oysters all day, and they're tired. Sixty cents a day, though. That's good money. I'd do it, but Mom won't let me. One day I'm going to get a boat and start fishing, and then we can move out of this ugly house."

"Don't move," Skip said, thinking about her fear of losing him for good.

He kicked the ball to her, and she kicked it back, feeling foolish. When she studied the girls, she could see the cuts on their hands.

Skip visited the cottage for the next two mornings while her parents were away. The oyster-shucking sisters warmed up to her a little and let her play with one of their feedsack dolls stuffed with cotton.

"You can hold it for a minute," the oldest one said, looking her up and down with exhausted blue eyes, "but you better give it back."

"I'd chase you home," Marie said upon seeing Skip again, "but I'm too tired. You should go. You know your mother doesn't want you here." She sat in her wooden chair looking uncomfortable, wearing the same blue dress, drinking water.

"She's in New York with Daddy," Skip said. "They're making up." Marie looked like somebody had kicked her in the shins. Skip felt bad for telling her, but the truth had sort of leaped out of her mouth like a frog.

"Hey," Ase said, pulling Skip outside. "There's buzzards circling. Someone must be cutting a deer." She looked up at the silhouettes of the large birds against the sun.

They ate peaches and threw rocks at imaginary villains in the thicket. She felt happier than she had in months. She felt at home.

On the last day of her parents' vacation, Ase discovered nits in Skip's hair. "Look," he said, showing her a couple in the palm of his hands. "They look like rice."

"Mama will kill me!" Skip said, gasping at the sight of the louse.

"We have to cut your hair," he said flatly, returning from the kitchen with a rusted pair of utility shears.

She sat cross-legged on the warm ground while he sawed into her hair with the dull blades.

"Hold still," he said. "God, your hair is tangly."

She liked the feeling of his hands in her hair, the sense of belonging she felt with Marie watching them through the window, shaking her head.

Skip knew without looking that it was the worst haircut she ever had in her life. Afterward, Ase covered her hair with old homemade mayonnaise fished from a cloudy jar. "It's the only way," he said as she gagged at the smell.

That night, when the dinner bell rang, and the sun glowed low in the sky, she walked past a circle of men with her newly shorn hair. They did not look her way, having just released two roosters into a ring, who collided into one another feetfirst, wings arched back, black feathers spread, spurs ripping into flesh. The birds called out into the dusk as they fought, neither to live.

21

Labor came in the night, ripping through her like a knife. Marie woke gasping, holding her belly with one hand, guiding herself out of bed gently. The room was dark. She was terrified to give birth here.

The tabby house was cold, and she felt as though she could smell decades of rain in the wooden floors and walls. She walked to the doorway of the second bedroom, so small it was nearly a closet. Ase was sleeping.

I'm sorry, she thought. I'm sorry for what I'm going to have to ask from you.

She'd thought about the burden on her son the first day she realized she might be pregnant with her second child, throwing up behind the bait shop after buying a loaf of bread on her way out of town. Her world contracted in that moment, options for escape falling away, the road forward narrowing.

She woke Ase. He opened his blue eyes. "What is it, Mama?" he asked. She knew he was sometimes disruptive at school and rough with his friends, but he always saved his best behavior for her. His respect. He made her fish sandwiches for dinner, hung the laundry out on the line, swept the front steps.

"I need you to run and get Mim."

Win had offered to keep Dr. Harris on call, but Marie didn't want a man delivering this child. She wanted a woman, preferably Mim, whom she knew roamed the countryside delivering babies and resetting bones, doling out fruit crates for use as cribs so babies wouldn't suffocate in a bed with siblings. According to locals, Mim didn't sleep more than one night a week. "When I sleep, women die," she said.

Marie wanted a woman who'd been through labor herself, who knew the hell of it. Mim didn't have a medical degree, but she had empathy, and decades of experience.

Ase jumped out of bed and was putting on pants in the dark, stumbling around, still drowsy. "I'll go as fast as I can."

"Thank you, *elskede*," Marie said, leaning her back against the wall. She gritted her teeth and uttered a low moan, wrapping her arms around herself.

"What's happening?" he cried, running to her side. He looked horrified.

She couldn't answer, but let the contraction roll through her. It was like hearing thunder in the distance, waiting for the clap of lightning. "It's completely normal," she said, straining to make her voice sound natural, trying to find her breath. "Now go on. Go find Mim."

She knew it was likely a fool's errand—Mim was often difficult to track down in the dead of night. Whose house was she inside? Whose bed was she leaning over? But Marie didn't want Ase to see what happened next.

Soon she was down on all fours, alone in that old house, inhaling the ancient dust from the floor as she panted through the pain.

Mim came by hours later in the dark, hurried and tired. She directed Ase to bed, poured herself a glass of water, cleaned up some of the blood, and settled in next to Marie, who lay quietly with the infant on the bed. Her presence was calming.

"It was a hard one," Mim said, a knowing look on her face as she lifted the sheet and looked at Marie's body.

"He was stuck." Marie began to cry, all of the fear and pain starting to break loose inside of her. "I did the best I could."

"Not enough air, not enough something," Mim said, blunt but kind. "It's the kind of thing that don't need words." She placed her hand on the baby's forehead, then Marie's.

Mim left her with a cup of blackberry tea. Marie slept in small doses with the infant on her chest.

——

The next day, Win was there at her front door, knocking, and when his knocks went unanswered, he stood by the back window, tapping on the glass. He'd been doing this for weeks, ever since one of his farmhands had reported her pregnancy. She'd hidden it for as long as she could.

Marie could feel him staring at her through the window, but she didn't turn toward him. She stayed as she was on the bed, back to the window, curled around the body of her son. The labor had been difficult; she'd pushed for too long and was worried now. Her second son seemed different than Ase.

"Marie," Win called out. "Let me see the baby."

His words were like an unwelcome breeze that passed over her warm, feverish body and kept moving. She ignored him.

This was her baby, no one else's. His mouth twisted as he attempted to latch to her breast. She had made him, carried him, brought him into this messy world alone, and she was determined to care for him the same way.

Wretched place, she thought, closing her eyes.

22

Skip knew she was outrunning something, something evil that lived on the grounds of Stillwood. She could sense it behind her in the lush hedgerow between the big house and Indigo Run, teeming with crickets at night, or when she turned her back to the river. She could taste it in the water and soup. She could feel it underneath the floorboards of Stillwood, in the rice fields, in the sandy soil underneath her fingernails. Whenever she felt the thing at her back, she ran fast, so fast that the tree trunks became a blur, and her legs ached.

Once this ancient, evil thing got hold of you, you were in trouble. It got into your blood and made you angry, like her father. Or it made you sleep all day, like her mother.

Skip knew she was brave until she wasn't. Brave until she had to go to sleep by herself in the old nursery, or retrieve a jar of strawberry preserves from the dirt cellar for June, fighting off the camel crickets that flung themselves into her hair. Brave until she had to bait a hook and then she looked into the shimmering, little minnow's eyes and it was all over.

Helena had cut camellias for the vases in the house, and bruised petals were falling onto the floorboards. Skip collected them into damp piles, attempting to delay going to bed and into the haunted nursery.

"Get on up to your room," June said, hurrying her up the stairs. Skip paused on the landing.

"I'm scared," Skip said. "It's dark up there. Can I sleep with you tonight?"

"Nonsense," June said, which Skip thought was unfair, because June was the most superstitious person she knew.

"But I don't *like* the night," Skip said. "The foxes scream, and the shadows move in my room. I know it's haunted here. I *know*."

"Night's the most natural thing in the world," June said, slapping Skip on the bottom. "Now get up there, wash behind your ears, and read a book if you have to. I've got things to do. Go on."

Skip did what she was told, but she kept the lights on in her bedroom, hoping no one would notice. She glanced over at the empty twin bed where Ase used to sleep, then propped herself up on a pillow, reading like she always did—partly out of boredom, partly out of fear. She often woke with books on her chest, a hardback cover open like a tent, spine up, pages bent.

If she stayed awake, she might slip away from the evil chasing her.

One of these days she was going to get a dog, something that would make her feel less alone up in this bedroom full of ghosts. All she had in the Animal Hospital tonight was a tailless lizard and a three-winged moth half-dead and thumping around on the windowsill. She wanted her brother.

Ase was so close, but she couldn't play with him. She could hear him laughing sometimes, playing stickball in the field with other kids from Indigo Run. She saw him walking to the bait shop. She didn't understand what had happened with Marie, why she and Ase had to live by themselves now. She knew, however, that it was a question no one in her house wanted to answer. Because she couldn't ask it, the question began to burn inside of her, and the ache for Ase became more insistent.

She was of two mothers, two families. One by blood and the

other from memory. One who was in her bones and another who was in her heart.

Her memories of Marie were fading, but she didn't want them to, so she tried to find her way back to them at night when she was alone. She conjured Marie's stories and songs. She tried to picture the favorite part of her life, when the house had been loud and full, her father had been happy, and Ase was her constant companion.

Hearing footsteps, she quickly tossed her book to the floor and pulled her covers to her shoulders while her mother settled into the rocking chair at the foot of her bed.

Her mama was the kind of person you had to prepare for. It was best to be still so you wouldn't get in trouble.

Helena wore a pink robe and silk slippers. Her hair hung loose around her shoulders and her face glistened with cold cream. "You know," she said, braiding her hair, "the Night Hag comes on nights like tonight, when people are stirring and planning, and their minds are not at ease."

Skip hid her head underneath her pillow, mostly to hide a grin. She was halfway afraid of her mother, but thrilled by her bedtime stories.

Helena continued, her chair creaking. "When the moon is big in the sky, she gets restless in that river of hers. She lies on the silt among the alligators and weeds, sleeping for weeks at a time."

"Have you seen her?" Skip asked, moving the pillow away from her face. She dreaded the answer, and loved it all the same.

"She visited my grandmother and my aunt, and she visited me as well," Helena said, her voice grave and knowing. "Some nights, Skip, when you're having a nightmare, unable to breathe, it's because she's been woken up by your worries. She walks on her scaly chicken legs from the dark river to the house, and leaps on top of your chest, and rides your body like an old horse. She can slip through a crack in the wall. No one sees her footprints, of course, because she sweeps them away with a broom. But you wake up paralyzed, unable to move. She's the one who stirs up the storms in spring and brings the hurricanes in fall."

Skip drew her covers into a knot and brought them to her chin. "Why? Why does she do it?"

"She's angry, of course," Helena said, speaking with utter conviction. "She was loved and left, and that drives women to madness, you know. Surely, you can offer her some forgiveness and understanding for the way she is?"

Skip shook her head. "I don't like her."

"Hush—we'll not speak ill of her." Helena put a finger to her lips and looked over her shoulder. "It's not wise." Helena gave her daughter a twisted little smile. "You aren't worried, are you? You won't stay up thinking? You'll go right to sleep like a good girl, my dear Sally-Anne."

"I will."

Helena rocked absentmindedly in the chair for a while and then rose.

"Good night, Mama."

"Good night, darling," she said, eyes trained on the world outside the bedroom window, the sloping lawn, and what lay just past.

23

Win sat on the veranda after dinner on New Year's Eve, staring at the moon's reflection on the black water. He'd come to know the loud silence of the river at night, when the workers returned from the nearby fields pulling their dusty mules. A ship blew its melancholy horn in the humid distance.

Some days he thought himself dutiful. Other days he knew he was a coward. Today was one of those days.

Helena surely knew about Marie and the baby. So why did he stay? Why did he feel so cornered?

He wanted some event, some person, to come and change the course of his life.

Be a man of action, his father always said. *Don't just let things happen to you.*

He left his glass of bourbon on the patio table and started walking toward Marie's house, determined to see her.

Surely, the children would be in bed by now. He knocked sharply, and when she answered, he held the door open with one hand.

"Please talk to me," he said, leaning into the door, which Marie was making a half-hearted effort to close.

"What could you possibly need at this hour?" she asked, looking tired. She was wearing a faded red robe. Her long hair was half pinned up, and her eyes were swollen. He couldn't remember how old she was.

"You." He put his arms around her. She was stiff at first, but then softened, as if giving in. Her body was familiar, cool. The embrace moved quickly into something urgent and sad.

The house was impossibly small, and every step caused a floorboard to whine. There were oranges in a bowl, fruit flies, an overturned coffee cup drying by the sink.

He took her to bed and slowly kissed her thin ankles, thighs, and neck. She kept her eyes closed, as if looking at him would be too much. He held her wrists, but not too tightly, his fingers slid-ing between hers when he was spent.

"I'm tired of trying to do the right thing," he whispered into her neck. "Whatever it is, I can't find it."

He breathed in the scent of her unwashed hair and choked back the urge to cry.

"I didn't handle things the way I should have," he said. "I want to make it right."

She didn't answer him.

He missed the freedom and catharsis of their earlier sex. There was no joy in the act tonight. It was almost conciliatory, resigned, a eulogy for something that once was.

They were so quiet and careful that he heard voices from the other cottages on Indigo Run. A couple fighting. Someone sing-ing a child to sleep.

"We could still be together," he said, but as soon as he said it she turned away from him. She was naked, wrapped in a white sheet, the last light of a long day landing on her cheekbones.

"It won't be perfect," he said, sitting up a little.

"It won't work," she said, cutting him off.

"Then why do you stay?" The question came out desperately, almost angrily. He felt if he could understand this one thing, he might have some peace.

"Shhh." She turned to face him with a warning in her eyes. "Because I have a house," she said, "and children who are used to this life. Because I'm avoiding more pain, for now. And where exactly would I go?"

He closed his eyes, the rush of familiar sadness coming over him. "You can't leave."

"Don't you think that if I had a better option, I would take it?" She was shaking with anger. He could feel it. He kissed her forehead and was surprised that she let him. He pulled her closer on the bed, wrapping himself around her, and they both fell asleep for what must have been a few hours.

Marie sat up, rubbed her eyes, and rose from the bed. Her hair was tangled and fell to the middle of her back. "I should check on Ukes," she said. "He might be awake."

"Can I see him?" Win asked.

"I'd rather you not," she said, her voice suddenly stern. "You should go now."

She went to the doorway and turned around. "I've learned it's best to have no expectations," she said, disappearing into the dark hallway.

Win was disoriented on his walk home, and thirsty. He stumbled along the road—it was too dark to take the path—and tried to collect his thoughts. He was anxious and unsettled.

He knew this strange boy was his punishment for the night on the sand dunes with Helena, his affair with Marie, for abandoning his father in Texas. It was punishment for something inside him, some sickness of the blood that had lived inside his grandfather, father, and this farm. It was so wretched and obvious he could almost name it, but when he began to think of it, it was like the sun, too bright—or like a case of yellow fever, the plague of his grandfather's sugar plantations, something that struck you from the inside out and colored your eyes, inhibited your vision.

He felt it in the stables, in the dark closet with the neglected whips and bits. He felt it in the fields.

There is no redemption, he thought.

He walked to the edge of the river, took off his clothes, and waded into the cold water. It was the time of night that an alligator might hunt, and he knew it.

Win lay on his back in a deadman's float, cold water rushing into his ears, staring blankly at the moon. His heartbeat slowed and he waited. For minutes, he waited, but nothing happened. If the Lord hadn't taken him when given the opportunity, then he was good enough. He'd made an offering of himself; now he could do as he wished. Didn't it work that way? Calmed, he swam to a place where he could stand and walked up the banks toward home, tasting the salt on his lips.

What had he ever gained by following the rules?

He would have her again.

The next morning he rose with a deep fear Marie had left in the night with Ase and the baby, and he took to paying an elderly neighbor, an old veteran with a long white beard, to watch for any signs of her departure.

"Check every morning and night," he said firmly. "I want to know everything. If she comes, if she goes, if anyone comes and goes. *Everything.*"

24

The real hell, Marie thought, was the water. The brown Ashley River was a dull contrast to the sapphire-blue sea she'd known in her Norwegian childhood, which was clear and gemlike, a joy to swim in. The water from the tap here tasted like the boiled eggs she made Ase for lunch. It was sulfuric and gritty, as if the silt from the tidal river came through the tap. Perhaps it did. She could hardly bear to drink it.

You have to, she thought. And you have to get out of here.

Whatever life she thought she would find on the other end of the trip across the ocean—this one here, on dusty, mite-ridden Indigo Run—was much worse. The drafty house, the mosquitoes, her hunger, her loneliness, the daily humiliation of being known as Win's mistress, the lack of options—it challenged her very sense of self.

Do not think of home, fine sheets, or good food, she thought. Don't dream of a better past. Just figure out the future.

Marie saw how privileged she'd been in her past life, how ignorant to real suffering. A cruel husband? A lost love? A mother who didn't understand? Please.

She'd heard that Mary-Grace was ill and would be coming home to Stillwood any week now. The woman nauseated her, how much she believed in her own superiority.

Well, Marie thought. I won't stay here and let the boys become part of this feudal system, rustling up a sad life on this dirt road in service of that family.

She got to the real work of escape, calculating the money she would need, and how she would get it. There was only one way, and it required perfect timing.

25

Helena, wearing a long nightgown and a fur coat, lingered in the doorway of Win's bedroom. She knew she was being foolish, nurturing this last bit of hope in her heart. But before she could give herself over completely to the darkness—which was waiting for her in a paraldehyde bottle hidden in the carved-out pages of a Bible—she wanted to try one last time. What if, despite everything, there was a chance he could see her again, actually *see* her?

She'd always wanted to be the kind of woman that a husband commissioned paintings and bought jewelry for. A legendary beauty. A woman of value.

"I bought a new mink," she said, turning to the side to reveal the shining, amber-colored fur. "Fox piping."

She'd shot some egrets off-season and sold them behind the bait shop, where Matthew shipped them to France for the millinery trade. She'd spent her hunting money on the mink and paraldehyde. Funny how fast money could go, and how it hurt more to lose it when it was your own.

"Mm-hmm." He was sitting up in bed, reading, his glasses on. He wore striped pajamas. She hated the sight of him, but hate hadn't dismantled lust, not yet.

She admired the definition of his chin, the day's whiskers showing. She wanted to touch him, especially now that he was a man and not the awkward boy of their first night together. She wanted to run the tip of her tongue along his jawline, feel his hands gripping her back.

Now that she was a woman, she had an appetite, but there was no one to satisfy it. No routes open to her, no one who felt safe. She was tired of satisfying herself in bed at night. But if she couldn't have something sensual, she'd settle for a transgression. She was *that* lonely.

"I've cut my hair," she said, slurring a little.

She'd had gin, for courage.

"It looks nice," he said.

"You're not *looking*."

"I'm sure it's fine." He flipped a page in his book. She knew he wasn't reading.

"Do you ever marvel at how years can go by and we stay the same?" Helena asked, inching closer. She was genuinely fascinated that each of them—as hardheaded as they were—remained locked in this way, miserable.

"I don't feel the same."

She walked toward him. "Can I get into bed with you?"

"You've been drinking," he said irritably. He took off his glasses, looked at her. The way his lip drew to one side showed his real feelings, she thought. His disgust.

She knew they hated each other, and yet this hate was a strange form of intimacy. It was a terrible thread that pulled their family together and bound them to one another. And no matter how much Marie had once distracted him, Helena felt she had an odd sort of primacy. Marie would always be the whore, the other woman. She, Helena, would be the Madonna, the mother, the woman wronged. That was power, wasn't it?

And he'd stayed. Only the Lord knew why, but he'd stayed.

"Why pretend that's the problem?" Helena said, stepping closer until she brushed up against his knee. "Why pretend anything?"

He stood up from the bed, towering over her. He grabbed her by the shoulders and threw her onto the bed. "Is this what you want?" he asked, anger in his eyes.

She didn't stop him, because in this moment it *was* what she wanted. It was the first time in years that he'd touched her. He opened the front of the mink coat. She dragged her nails down his back when he entered her. She slapped his face. He clutched her neck for a terrifying few seconds, leaving her gasping for air. When he collapsed on top of her, spent, she bit the smooth skin of his shoulder.

"God help us," he said, standing up, reaching for his robe. He glared at her, as if it was her fault, not just the night but the complicated life they shared. The house, the towering live oaks, the increasingly fallow fields, the people looking at them in town.

"I guess that whore of yours is too busy?" she asked, angry and unsatisfied. "You had some energy to spare?"

"You're unhinged," he said, cinching the tie on his robe.

"It's easier for you to think that," she said, sitting up. "Isn't it?"

"That's enough." He stood up from the bed, pushed her roughly out of the door, and slammed it.

She felt the urge to laugh, but as she stumbled backward into the hallway she realized she was crying.

Once inside her room, Helena shed her coat. It dropped to the floor like a dead animal. She climbed into bed slowly, too lazy to search for her pajamas. Unsatisfied, she moved her hand between her legs and brought herself to the edge, then to relief.

Afterward, she opened the Bible, removed the small brown bottle, and took a drink. Then another.

Surely, a shift was ahead, Helena thought. Some new chapter in her life as a woman. Something had to break open. Something had to change.

26

In early spring, Mary-Grace was driven by a private car to Stillwood to die, Percy by her side in the back seat.

Helena, riddled with nervous energy, had a bedroom made up for her mother in the parlor. June put linens on the bed while Helena kept watch. "Tuck that corner," she said. "You remember how she likes her pillows."

"Of course I remember."

Helena didn't know if it was her state of mind, but June seemed insolent. She was heavy-footed around the house, burning casseroles, and her cheeks were telltale pink more days than not.

Skip was spending most of her time in her room reading books. Her daughter was like a stranger she wanted to pull closer but couldn't.

The sound of the wheels in the driveway was terrible. Helena reached for an extra sip of tonic, then swished water around her mouth to remove the scent. Her mother would know. Her mother would see how poorly everything had gone in her absence.

Mary-Grace arrived weak and unable to stand on her own. Helena was overcome at the sight of her—limbs wasted away, a drooping eyelid, the glamorous sable-colored coiffeur replaced by a shock of short white hair. The nurse guided Mary-Grace inside the house. She closed her eyes and pressed her lips together, unable to speak. She let her fingertips graze the wall. She shook her head slowly.

"I'm sorry it's been so long," Helena said, rushing toward her. "I'm sorry we didn't get you here sooner."

Mary-Grace didn't respond. She indicated that she wanted to sit by the river, and a comfortable chair and quilt were set up on the banks. She and Helena sat together, looking out at the brown water and holding hands. The cordgrass moved in the wind. The tide drew back to reveal rich mud, jagged oyster mounds, the stumps of old trees.

"It has all slipped away," Mary-Grace whispered, her voice thin.

Helena knew she didn't just mean the house or her marriage or the farm. It was an entire era, a way of life. She could see it now. It was in the constant drip of the springhouse and the rusted spigot. It was the hush of a prayer meeting. The way the hams swung in the smokehouse, the taste of the brandy and bread and butter pickles. It was what was grown in the fields and who harvested it, the money in the account. It was bare feet caked with blood, backs split open. A hog with cholera, buried deep in the barnyard. It was a dress made of orangery and stitched by a woman with stiff fingers who couldn't read. It was showing up at church to be seen. It was the solemn parade of the Daughters of the Confederacy and the fathers and brothers they genuinely mourned, the sour notes of the bugle as men in fresh gray flannel uniforms re-created the Battle of Honey Hill.

Win kept his distance and claimed he had work to attend to in town. Percy sat in a chair nearby, smoking nervously, frail himself. When Mary-Grace dozed off, he approached his daughter. "I'll be going back to Beaufort when she passes," he said, looking around at the sky and the riverbank. "I don't belong here anymore."

Helena nodded and closed her eyes in the summer sun.

June came with ice chips and pound cake.

"Look at you three out here," June said softly. "As you always intended to be."

Dr. Harris came to administer morphine.

From her bed facing the river, Mary-Grace slept. The morning she died, she turned to face Helena. "Oh!" she said, closing her eyes. "I see it now. Yes, I see it."

What was it she saw? Helena felt something like jealousy, as if there might be relief and beauty on the other side of all this living.

Born, died.

27

That morning a vision of the Madonna appeared above a small shack by the beach, or was it a break in the clouds? A shot rang out. A dog howled, or was it a woman leaving home?

Marie moved quickly before sunrise, as she had done once many years ago.

The day before, when the Spangler family had been underneath the old oak, burying their matriarch, she had wandered the empty house, taking several pieces of silver and two pearl necklaces. Soon she and the boys would be on a train to Baltimore. Her two fatherless sons.

Did she feel shame? Some, but it was manageable.

Love, as usual, had taken too much.

Love, or its approximation. Its stand-in.

The herons and egrets chased fish in the shallows. The sun began to sink, and the bobcat came out to hunt.

28

Four days after Mary-Grace's death, Preacher Noble held a revival near the marina.

"I don't know why he suddenly needs to increase his flock,"

Helena said, irritable. She topped off her coffee, which she had to do often because the floral cup was small, and she needed a great deal of coffee in the morning to function. "Does he have any gambling debts that you know of?"

"He says it's our moral decrepitude."

Helena rolled her eyes. "That's nothing new."

"Preacher Noble says our decrepitude is worse than ever," June said, looking up. "Plus, everyone and their cousin will be there."

"Can we go?" Skip asked, suddenly animated. She was looking leggy these days, with a little sun on her cheeks, hair loose and well brushed. Lips scrubbed and pink. She had a damp circle of orange juice above her mouth, which Helena refrained from mentioning.

Helena knew Skip craved time off the property, anything that got them away from Stillwood and among people.

"I'm not terribly moved by the idea," Helena said, taking another sip of piping hot black coffee, one hand to her aching head. "But if it makes you happy," she said flatly, clanking her cup into the saucer.

That afternoon they got into the car together, June driving cautiously. She braked for shadows and light, for squirrels, and when someone spoke to her. Helena felt like she was going to vomit in the hot back seat.

"Pull over and let me take the damn wheel," she said. She didn't give a fig anymore about the appearance of having a driver, and she was tired of the lurching.

"Fine," June said, easing the Ford to the side of the road. She slid to the passenger's side, crossed her arms, and refused to say more.

"Stop with the hurt feelings!"

"Stop with the bad mouth, then."

Another two minutes and they arrived. Helena pulled into a crowded, grassy field.

The tent was standing room only, one section marked "white" and the other "colored," with rope separating worshippers, a central aisle between them. The ground was covered in sawdust. The pulpit stood on a temporary wooden stage, a rickety-looking platform on risers. Longleaf pines and palmettos closed in on the stage, the twisting brown river in the distance.

Helena held Skip's shoulders as they watched Sam Noble prepare to speak, already mopping his face with a handkerchief and swatting mosquitoes as the heat settled in.

He walked out from behind the podium and pulled off his tie.

"You effeminate Christians," he said, leering at the crowd. "You whiskey-soaked infidels! You members of this God-hating world of ours."

Helena drew in a sharp breath. She'd never heard him talk like this before.

Preacher Noble cupped his hands to his mouth. "I need to take you to the Lord's bath and hose you down. I need you to repent!

"If you think I am a kindly minister, in the employment of a certain family, then I say to you: you do not know me yet. *I* am a messenger of the Lord. Only *I* can show you how to steer your boat upon these shallow seas."

He paced from one end of the stage to the other, the audience rapt.

"You're asleep in your pews on Sunday," he said, shaking his head. "Wake up! And remember—you can get to the devil

261

quick. But the Lord takes time. I don't care for deathbed confessions, last-minute attempts. As far as I'm concerned, you'll die as you've lived, and from what I've seen around here, my friends, you are all going to die soon. I see your weak fishing yields, your empty nets. I see you sneaking into back doors, romancing another woman's husband, or another man's wife. Drinking wine and shine, shuddering in your addictions. I know what desire calls you to do, and I can tell you, *you will crawl out of this world naked and desperate for the Good Lord to forgive you."*

Helena was beginning to feel uncomfortable, as if his words were meant for her. Or her family.

"I can tell what sort of lives you women live; I see it in the lines on your face and in the downward turn of your mouths. The lipstick on your daughters. Get down on your knees! If you pray, we can tell. We can see it on your faces.

"And, men. The Bible says you choose between heaven and hell, so why do you wait? What about Jesus's love are you resisting? What is the paltry dollar you put in the offering plate? God wants the best that you have. He wants the blood in your body. You make promises to God when you are down-and-out, but when you are prosperous, you forget Him. The Lord doesn't fault you for your wealth," Sam said. *"So provide!"*

He threw down the wooden podium, and it splintered on the stage. The crowd gasped. There were a few shouts of "Amen!" and "Tell it!"

"The Lord will teach you how to live. He will teach you how to die. He will put a new song in your dirty mouth."

Sam stood on a chair and raised his fist. "Here on the Ashley River, we have a fight with the devil!"

"If you are a stranger to prayer, you are a stranger to God.

You are spiritually weak. The Lord is not deaf! If your prayers are not answered, it's because you're not right with Him.

"Would you even recognize exaltation if it slapped you in the face?" he cried from the stage. "Would you see the Lord's blessings in your blossoming cotton fields and your bulging nets?

"If it came down like a bolt of lightning? Are you ready for the rapture? Will you come to Him when he calls for you? I said will you *come* to him?"

"We will!" the crowd said.

Preacher Noble was frothing a little at the mouth. Helena was positive he was drunk, or worse.

"Will you let your love spring forth like a fountain?" he hollered.

"We will!" Skip joined in. Helena glared at her.

"Like Corinthians says, will you bestow all of your goods to feed the poor? If your enemies hunger, will you feed them? If they thirst, will you give them drink?"

"Yes!" Skip shouted along.

Helena gave her arm a pinch. "Pipe down," she said, realizing they were equally embarrassed of one another.

"Water cannot quench this love, floods cannot drown it," Sam said quietly, turning to the crowd on the left, one hand in the air. "We live in difficult times here, among hungry neighbors and tired hands. Among drink, infidelity, and distraction. And when you reach out to those who have not accepted the Savior into their hearts, this love will redeem them and catch fire within them, and if they have a soul to save, *you* will save it."

He faced the crowd at large now, raising his arm as if he were about to throw a baseball. He threw it down, as if he were beating something away. He repeated the motion.

"Just because you don't believe in hell, my friends—well, that won't extinguish its eternal flames. You want redemption, and so do I. You want eternal life, and so do I. Come to me now and profess your love of Jesus."

Skip made a motion to move toward him, but Helena jerked her back, mostly because fervor of any kind embarrassed her. It was unbecoming.

"But I accept Jesus as my Lord and Savior," Skip hissed.

"No need to make a performance out of it," Helena said, keeping a grip on her daughter's shoulder.

The people around them were weeping and holding hands as they sang "How Firm a Foundation." At the sound of the hymn, Helena was momentarily moved herself, but figured her grief over losing her mother had made her an easy target for emotion.

Skip was beginning to cry now, and Helena realized her daughter was falling into the collective mood, the crowd's emotions running through her. Their good intentions. Their hunger.

Helena led her daughter out of the tent as the offering plate was being passed.

"Why are we leaving?" Skip asked, blinking back tears.

"I give them two days," Helena said, shaking her head. "Two days before they get to drinking and beating their wives again. And what does anybody back there really have to give right now? Not a goddamned cent."

She pulled Skip by the hand to the car.

"We need to do more," Skip said, digging her heels into the muddy pasture.

"When you make your own money, you can do with it as you please," Helena said, yanking her by the arm.

The house was dark when they arrived, the gaslight left on by the front door.

"Run up to bed," Helena said. "I'm going to take a walk outside."

Helena stood among a patch of silvery, knotted driftwood on the riverbank.

Returning inside, Helena could see that Win was in his library with the door closed. She ran a hot bath, so hot that she recoiled upon touching the water with her foot but forced herself into the tub anyway. She took a drink of tonic and hid the empty bottle underneath a towel. She rubbed her skin red and raw in the scalding hot water. As if she were trying to take it off and get to what was underneath.

Something about that sermon. Something about the shame it stirred up within her. The changes in her face. Their fallow fields.

She heard heavy footsteps and waited for June to crack the door.

"What is it?" she asked from the bath. Her breasts were above the waterline, but she didn't care. June knew everything.

June stood in the doorway, nearly filling it up, biting her lip. Her familiar, frustrated affection.

"Just say it," Helena said, jutting her chin forward. Her movements were exaggerated, and her speech was beginning to slur. She flicked soapy water at June. Light caught the white flesh in the center of her stubborn part.

"There's a great deal of silver missing," June said slowly.

Helena shook her head in disbelief. "I'm sure it's just been misplaced."

"I've looked everywhere."

"We'll find it tomorrow," Helena said. She felt like her mouth wasn't cooperating. She was too tired to think about silver. She didn't want to think about anything at all.

"I'm scared you're going to hurt yourself," June said.

"And what if I did?" Helena asked, raising a soapy foot to the ridge of the tub. "My husband and daughter would be relieved." She sunk lower into the water. "You would be, too."

June covered her face with her hands. "Don't talk that way," she said. "Please. You know I love you."

"I'm tired," Helena said, eyes beginning to close. "Go away."

Someone pulled the drain.

"Lies, lies, lies," Helena mumbled. "All lies. Everyone lies. The Lord lied and our mamas lied and our daddies lied."

In her mind there was the sound of a far-off train. She imagined herself picking tiny seeds from wads of cotton, pulling them free. The light faded. She fell asleep in her childhood bedroom.

29

The old veteran with the off-white beard, stained by tobacco, was doubled over coughing on the front step. Helena and Skip were out at the revival, everybody crying, sweating in the name of Jesus.

"They're gone," the veteran said, wheezing.

"Can't be," Win said, numb with disbelief.

"The mother and the boys. The house is empty, chairs knocked over, linens gone."

"Did she leave a note?"

"No, sir."

"Nothing?"

"Nothing except a painting. Two little kids."

"Burn it," Win said, crushing his eyes shut. "I never want to see it again."

He fell to his knees as if physically hurt, as if the news about Marie's departure had crippled him. Like the day Helena returned, he found he couldn't breathe.

He watched the veteran limp off into the dark night.

He would never be the man he'd always intended to become.

30

For the final act of his revival, Preacher Sam Noble paced in front of the children who'd come to Swim for the Christ that Sunday morning. The kids wore black tank suits that either bagged at the stomach or clung to the buttocks. They stood shoulder to shoulder with their arms crossed, lips turning blue in the spring chill.

Skip stared out at the brown river, which was roughed up by wind into tiny whitecaps.

She thought of Ase and felt the sting of tears in her eyes. Where had he gone? She stood up a little straighter, tossed her braid over one shoulder.

Earlier that morning, before sunrise, a group of middle-aged men had taken a boat out and dropped the forty-pound statue of Jesus, carved of dark oak, into the river. Skip imagined it now, turned over on its side on the sandy bottom, minnows darting around the outstretched hands of the Savior.

Her teeth chattered as the wind moved over her bare skin. Win and Helena were seated with the other parents on the bleachers a few yards back.

"Today, boys, is a righteous day," Sam Noble began. Behind him, the trees, newly leafed out, rustled in the breeze.

Skip cleared her throat at the word *boys*.

Sam glanced at her and continued. "Today is a sort of resurrection. I charge you with showing us the strength of your commitment to Christ. The very *depths* of your love for Him. When the gunshot is fired, but not a second before, you will search for Him. The first one of you to bring him to the surface wins." He held his pointer finger up to the bleak sky.

Wins what? Skip thought.

The only thing she wanted was Ase. The possibility that she could hear him laughing on Indigo Run, nod at him from the back seat of her father's car, know that he was okay.

Maybe if she could get the Christ, things would be set right. Not just with Ase, but with her parents, and the darkness they were all running from.

There was a great deal of fidgeting and deep breathing down the line. Skip filled her lungs, expanding them. She stole one look at her father, sitting somberly next to Helena. When asked for advice on how to reach the Christ first, Helena had said, simply, "Decide you want it. And want it more than anyone else."

Skip then made the mistake of picturing the alligator who sunned on the sandy banks near Stillwood, and the black heads of moccasins that lifted from the water at dusk. You could see the venomous snakes, she reminded herself. They rose to the top to swim.

"Ready yourselves," Sam called out, raising a hand before turning his gun to the sky.

The shot rang out and Skip flew forward, churning out sand behind her, pushing to get ahead. The children grabbed one another for support as they clambered down the uneven riverbank to get to the water, which was unusually cool. Skip waded in and then plunged headfirst into a tangle of arms and legs, feeling strong and focused.

I can do this, she thought.

She swam farther out from the crowd to begin her search, plunging down into the clouded waters of the river and opening her eyes as wide as she could, her body electric with adrenaline. She could see rays of light penetrating the water, plant matter, the gleam of a minnow. She came up for air and plunged again, making wide motions with her arms and legs in hopes of bumping into the Christ. Everything she touched both excited and terrified her. She continued this cycle of sucking in air and returning to the sandy bottom of the river when suddenly she saw it, a dark shape, overturned just as she had pictured. She rose again for air and made what she knew would be her final plunge.

They won't believe it, she thought. They won't believe I've done it.

Her heart was pounding, and her lungs began to ache as she attempted to get her arms around the awkward shape of the statue, which was heavier than she had imagined. She embraced Christ from the front, wrapping her lean arms around his body. She had trouble staying at the bottom of the river and kicked mightily to keep herself there. Once she was certain she had a good grip, she pushed off from the bottom with her eyes crushed shut, craving air, waiting for the relief that was above, but just as she anticipated a large breath she felt herself pulled down.

Hands on her legs—why? *Who?*

She was running out of air and began to panic, but tightened her grip around the Christ. She didn't want to give it up, but it slipped from her arms, and she rose weakly to the top of the water, sputtering for air.

She staggered onto the shore. Her parents smiled weakly at her. She could tell they were disappointed.

She knew she'd left something old and essential at the bottom of the river, something neither she nor her family would ever get back.

31

1954

The alligator and her wallow.
    The egrets and their wasted nesting ground.
The chalky shell middens.
Your fingers, glowing.
The white doe, stuffed and moth-eaten in the dump.
The unmarked graves.

The river could be two colors at once, brown and blue. It could be black in the rain and lighten like glass in the sun. Skip knew the river all ways because it ran through her.

The wind was picking up. The storm was blowing in. The big one.

=

There was a moment when she thought she'd seen her brother one last time. She was at a piano concert on Folly Beach. People had gathered on the sandy lawn, seated on blankets, some on the dry grass. She'd found a place back from the crowd, only the dunes between herself and the ocean.

No announcements were made, but the knowing crowd drew silent. The woods were thick with crickets and cicadas. Skip slapped mosquitoes on her arm. She could hear the dull roar of the ocean waves crashing behind her.

She pretended to smoke, never good at inhaling. She ground the cigarette into the sand before it was halfway done.

The man—people said he would be a legend one day—began to play, and the people outside became very still. The first notes were slow and languorous. The pianist held his notes with dramatic pause. When the first number was done, Skip let out a long breath and wiped her eyes.

She saw a familiar figure leaning against a tree.

In that moment, with the light turning blue with the promise of evening, she could believe it was a sweet world and that she would find her place in it. She believed that she would slip out from underneath the weight of her parents and find her way back toward the boy. She believed that she and Ase would be close, the way they should have been. She believed in the unknown, the possible.

The next number started softly, too softly, the notes barely perceptible, but quickly rose into something both sad and spirited, and Skip felt for a moment as if her feelings had been fished from her body and hung out on a line for all to see. The music rose to an even higher frenzy, the pianist nearly banging on the keys, and then the notes trailed again to quiet, stretching in the hot air, returning to the mood of a melancholy walk. When she glanced back at the boy, he was gone.

===

The wind howled, rustling the ocean, lifting shingles on the roof.

Easy enough to strike a match and call it an act of God, Skip thought, and let the manor burn so that no one else could dare call it beautiful.

The insurers and preservationists would never be the wiser.

What was there to save here? Stillwood had been a monument to misery ever since the first brick of the foundation was laid. Her parents had stayed there, locked in the intimacy of their mutual hatred for decades.

Sometimes, looking out at the grounds, Skip could feel generations passing through her, different iterations of the farm, different men seated behind the oak desk in the library, different women burning their hair with hot irons in the bathroom upstairs, rubbing rouge into their cheeks. There were her dead grandparents and great-grandparents in the family cemetery. Lindley Glass watching them from his portrait in the hallway. Unknown bodies decomposing in unmarked graves. There was silver in the ground. Sacred mounds of oyster shells no one could explain. There were entire worlds colliding on this property, lives upon lives upon lives. Maybe, despite what her mother believed, this land was cursed and not blessed.

It would be her life's work to overthrow the stories, to weed them out of her mind until she could see clearly.

Her father had believed that the sins of their past, all of their pasts, would leap over her, and yet Skip could feel them pounding there in her heart and crawling underneath her skin. She knew that she carried the sins of her parents and grandparents around in her blood, something parasitic living there against her will. Their mistakes were inside of her, like the rings of a felled tree.

No matter how good she intended to be. No matter how much she wanted to be forgiven.

The Night Hag

Cousin of Eve, the hag was born not from a rib, but from a fish egg in a stream that cut through a verdant, coastal forest.

She emerged glistening. Her fresh skin could breathe the air. She lengthened into the shape of a woman.

When she came of age, she sat in a virgin cypress tree like a leopard, one leg dangling. She maintained a remarkable appetite for figs and fresh kills, all of which stained her lips deep crimson.

She was a well-kept secret; the forest held her that way, hidden in the vine-choked trees. But the men could feel her there—they could smell the mink oil she put in her thick, black hair. They began to imagine what she could give them. They lined up underneath her tree. They opened their mouths like foxes and waited for something delicious to drop, but she was chaste.

She laughed and looked but never planned to come down. The stories said she had to wait until she found true love. She would know it at once.

True love is the great salvation, the stories said. It will give direction to your life.

One day a man with brown eyes brought her the feather of a pheasant. He came every morning, bringing her cherries and figs, blossoms for her hair. Flattered, she let her guard down and grazed the man's mouth with the tip of her toe. She closed her eyes, readying herself for pleasure, but he pulled her down by the foot, laughing as he did it, leaping on top of her. And then he left.

She waited the next morning and the next hundred mornings for him to return with cherries and figs, but he did not. She could not climb back into the cypress tree. She did not know how to hunt. Her sadness became venom. She sat in the weeds, egrets nesting in her rich hair while the sun caught on their blinding white plumage.

=

The hag could see, now, the stories she had been fed. All of her learned incompetence. Her false innocence. When she smelled it on other women, her stomach turned.

Never believe the stories, she whispered to them.

Topless, she rode the white stag into town to the nearest tavern.

The hag wore a necklace of olive shells that fell between her breasts, and a strong perfume of musk from a deer she had killed. She rented a room over the bar where she tied war heroes and sea captains to the brass bed with bailing twine and exhausted them until she felt that some revenge had been taken, some balance restored.

I am not the girl you thought I was, she yelled into the throngs of men downstairs.

At night she lay on her bed of swan down and smoked a cigarette, satisfied until her thoughts turned again to the man who had pulled her from the cypress tree and left her alone underneath the hanging moss. Was there no peace? She ripped up fistfuls of grass with her bare hands and threw it into the air, drank vodka, gave herself a new haircut in case she ran into Him in town.

There was a brief interlude of righteous abstinence. The hag removed her skin, as if she were removing her armor. She wanted to reconnect with nature and became a vegetarian. She took a passing interest in midwifery, peering between women's legs as their babies crowned. Their innocence nauseated her. When the infants were girls, she whispered in the nursing mother's ear: How will we teach them to carry pain? How will we teach them to become *more* than the pain? To transform it?

She put her skin back on and pierced her ears with fishhooks, taught herself to sail, and took up residence in an old schooner named *La Faim* that she kept on the Ashley River.

Local men hunted the white stag and placed its rigid body in the bait shop, like a trophy. They stuffed the stag with cotton, doused its white coat in borax powder. Its mouth, just slightly parted, was full of half-smoked cigarettes and ash. Someone placed a red plastic flower behind its ear.

She thought: everything pure is eventually defiled.

A hundred years after she was abandoned beneath the cypress tree, the Night Hag grew her first scale. It formed on her right leg, followed by a second and a third. Vain, she scraped them from her body with a knife, bled, and watched them grow back like bark.

The hag drowned herself in the river but could not die, so she lived there, choking on the limp seaweed, wrapping it around her wrists, breath like spring onions and damp moss.

Nothing had dulled the memory of Him. Not other lovers, not time. She scared up storms when she remembered His face. Her greatest wish was to pierce her lover's chest with one hand and disembowel Him, and when she allowed herself to picture it, the winds rose, and the waves grew, gnawing at the shoreline, claiming houses and raking them into the sea.

And when she could not remember her lover's face, she stepped outside her skin, peeled it from herself and left it in a heap on the sand. Bare muscled with white teeth gleaming, she broke into houses and walked on her scaly legs up staircases and into the bedrooms. The crack in the floorboards, the whine of a shutter in the wind—it was her all along. Her restlessness.

The uglier she was, the more libidinous she became. She straddled men's chests and wrapped her legs around their sleeping bodies and squeezed the breath out of them with her thighs, bringing them to orgasm in their sleep, pulling hair from their heads, filling their minds with dark dreams. Those who had caused so much suffering deserved to suffer themselves.

The hag could no longer picture her lover's face—she had forgotten it entirely. To lose her suffering was to lose herself. So she called up the worst storm of her life. She let the winds howl, taking the ancient trees, ripping them up by the roots. She asked the sea to churn and swallow whatever was in its path, upending boats, crashing them into the shoreline. Taking roofs, drowning cattle. Cats mewed. Birds pointed flight toward the eye of the storm. Women gave birth as the pressure closed in, infants pealing from their bodies in hospitals, shacks, and caves in the swamp.

She let herself fall into a rage, rolling around in her old skin as if it were on fire. And then she decided to take it off for good, to walk around in the storm as she really was: blood, muscle, memory. She tucked honeysuckle behind her ear and flashed a pageant-worthy smile. Long ago she had filed her teeth to points.

She heard their stories. The men who thought she was nothing but a great destroyer of lives. But they did not know of her compassion. They did not know of the night she had come to the aid of the Catawba woman whose child was boiled alive by white settlers. The colonist's wife tied to a tree and raped by a soldier. The washerwoman whose daughter had been sold. The women who had been beaten and the women who beat themselves, drank themselves to death, traded their bodies. The hag had come to them and put them on her back and carried them on her scaly legs to the water to find peace or die.

You could fall to your knees and rake this earth with your fingers and hear it scream, she told them. The suffering here runs so deep.

Tired of compromise, the women in their afterlives clung to one another in the boughs of the last ancient trees, slept in the astral light, read books. Many of them had helped cause pain, and now they needed to heal it. Invisible, they rested until they were strong again. They walked between the burning crosses left on lawns and blew them out like candles.

She showed them how exhausting and beautiful rage could be. And how immortal.

Acknowledgments

To the communities that have supported my professional career for the last few years—thank you. At Bennington, specifically, Jill McCorkle, Amy Hempel, Sven Birkerts, Stuart Nadler, and Paige Bartels. At Middlebury, Antonia Losano, Dan Brayton, Rob Cohen, Jay Parini, and Jennifer Grotz. To the editors who gave these stories a home and some shine, particularly Adam Ross and Beth Staples, thank you.

To my outstanding agent, Julie Barer—thank you for helping me see the best path forward, even if it was a long one. To my wonderful editor, Kara Watson—thank you for your patience and belief in my work. To Nan Graham—thank you for the gift of time.

To the organizations like Conservation Law Foundation, BOMA Project, and 100 Miles—thank you for letting me engage in the good work you do and for keeping me close to the natural world. To my editor at the *Guardian*, Jessica Reed, thank you for allowing me to write and learn about nature in ways that informed my fiction as well.

To my wonderful friends—particularly Rebecca Schinsky, Erin Lyons, Heather Frechette, Henry Frechette, Taina Lyons, Jed Leslie, Alyson Beha, and Kathy Fairley—thank you for making me laugh and making space for authentic friendship.

To my Vermont family—Bo, Frasier, and Zephyr—thank you for giving life such purpose and meaning. Bo, thank you for always reading the stories with machines and animals in them, and keeping me honest. Frasier and Zephyr, thank you for the big love and conversation about stories, and for helping to fill the house with books, laughter, and interpretive dance.

To Mom, Dad, and Emily—thank you for the firm foundation of love, for the early southern adventures, and for four decades of support.

About the Author

Megan Mayhew Bergman is the author of *Birds of a Lesser Paradise*, *Almost Famous Women*, and *How Strange a Season*. Her short fiction has appeared in two volumes of *The Best American Short Stories* and on NPR's *Selected Shorts*. She has written columns on climate change and the natural world for *The Guardian* and *The Paris Review*. Her work has been featured in *The New York Times*, *The New Yorker*, *Tin House*, *Ploughshares*, *Oxford American*, *Orion*, and elsewhere. She has served as associate director of the Bennington College MFA program and director of the Robert Frost Stone House Museum. She currently teaches literature and environmental writing at Middlebury College, where she also serves as director of the Bread Loaf Environmental Writers' Conference. She lives on a small farm in Vermont.